SERVICE STATION

Angel

LISA J. SCHUSTER

outskirtspress
DENVER, COLORADO

Cover by Lisa J. Schuster

Outskirts Press, Inc.
http://www.outskirtspress.com

Paperback ISBN: 978-1-4787-2150-5

Outskirts Press and the "OP" logo are trademarks belonging to Outskirts Press, Inc.

PRINTED IN THE UNITED STATES OF AMERICA

This book is dedicated with appreciation
to Ernest Poisson. As a young girl, you inspired
me with your love for music and art. Most notably,
you showed me how to love Jesus. Your compassion
has enriched my life and I am forever grateful.

Love, Lisa

Acknowledgements

Words came easy telling the story in **Service Station Angel,** but I find it somewhat difficult for me to express my thankfulness fully to the many who have encouraged and supported me during the book writing and publishing process. Okay, I begin....

To my husband Jeff, daughter Savanna and son Grant: Thank you for believing in me and allowing me to tell my story. Completing this novel is a proud moment that I share and celebrate with you. Grant, thank you for helping Mom with the football scenes in the book; it was fun learning from you and sharing your joy in the sport.

To my mother, Cheryl Rozman: Thank you for allowing me to grow up in the small towns of Hubbell and Lake Linden, Michigan. Our family was fortunate to have friends and a community of people that cared for us. I think it is amusing that you always rented homes near a church so we had no excuse to be late or not attend. **Thank you to my stepfather, Richard Rozman,** for loving my mom and her five kids, while taking on responsibility for now a family of nine!

To my brothers and sisters- Linda, Scott, Darren, Kim, Jennifer and Laura: I laugh and I cry thinking about all we have grown through. I could write volumes of books, mostly comedic, with our family stories. -To my sister, Kim Yirsa- I am so grateful that while writing this book you listened to my excitement as the story unfolded, offered advice and took that walk with me down memory lane.

To my friend Paula Vallot: Thank you for the push to write a book in thirty days with NanoWriMo! It was an awesome challenge for the both of us and it ignited my passion for writing again.

To my friend Rachelle Nickell: You spiritually encouraged me to continue writing and sharing God's word, understanding my intention of reaching others for Jesus Christ.

To my book cover designer **Aprilily21** from www.99designs. com, you have made a beautiful and perfect book cover! You captured the essence of my story in color and design immediately. Love it!

To my editor, Aimee Heckel: What an amazing editing process we shared together! We not only finalized my first public work effortlessly, but we shared a love for scripture and witnessed how God worked mysteriously through us. He joined you and I in producing something for His glory, when we had many circumstances that could have derailed us (car accidents, floods and cancer.) Enormous gratitude and thanks to you!

To my Heavenly Father: I am in awe of how you formed me and I thank you for the life you have given me. You have granted me talents, made me unique and I am your daughter and servant. Father God, you stirred the words in my writing and helped me to express them. Words that have lingered in my head, heart and soul for two decades. I pray that you continue to be the writer of my soul so I can share utterances that draw others towards you.

Prologue

They say when you die, your life flashes before your eyes. But for Ernie Price, it was no flash. It was slow and soothing, memories rolling through his spirit like the creek near his old service station.

Everything was so simple in this small town, but it would never be the same. Not after this.

The final days of his life caressed his fading consciousness, carrying him deeper and deeper into a perfect peace.

"Look at those who are honest and good, for a wonderful future lies before those who love peace." - Psalm 37:37 (NLT)

Chapter 1

Ernie could hear the sharp whistle of the 8:00 a.m. train rumbling down the tracks. He hoped the man inside the station was clutching his coffee cup tightly, otherwise his crisp-pressed suit soon would be wearing Folgers.

The tiny gas station sat only twenty feet from the railroad tracks. Soon, the ground would be shaking under their feet. Ernie always smiled when he heard the familiar groan of the train, especially when he had new customers. It surprised them every time.

As usual, when Ernie heard the train's warning blow, he backed out from underneath the car he was working on. He gave the train conductor, Chuck, a hearty wave. And as soon as the train vanished into the trees, Ernie slipped back underneath the car. Out of the corner of his eye, he saw the gentleman walk out from the station. He was sipping his coffee. His suit was dry.

"I grabbed my coffee cup just in time from it falling off the table," the man said with a laugh.

Ernie let out a belly laugh and said, "I guess I should have warned you about the train coming by, but I wanted to get busy getting this tire on for you."

At just after 8:00 a.m., it was already a warm and muggy day in late July. The summer had been stifling, and today warned that another hot day was coming. Ernie would would rather have spent the day down at the dock fishing and swimming, but since he was the sole owner of the service station and did not have any staff, it was up to him to show up and be available to customers who might need him.

During this morning's drive into work in his old, faded red Ford truck, through the narrow streets of small town Hubbell, Michigan, Ernie had waved to friends out walking their dogs and neighbors retrieving their daily newspapers. He had also noticed that some stores still had their Fourth of July decorations bannered across their storefronts, still showing their country pride -- or their laziness of not moving past the holiday. It was not uncommon to still find Christmas lights wrapped in trees or hanging from rooftops all year long.

As soon as he pulled into the service station, Ernie had been met by the middle-aged man, who was pacing, rubbing his hand through his peppered, thin hair. He anxiously eyed the flat tire on the front passenger side of his silver Chevy Impala. Ernie parked, exited his truck and approached the man with a handshake.

The man warmly accepted his hand and said, "Sure glad you arrived early to work today, as I could really use your help. I got a sales meeting at 9 a.m., do you think you can fix it by then?"

"No worries. Come in the store and wait. I will get a pot of coffee going, too."

The man had gladly followed Ernie into the station. He took a seat on the wooden stool, rummaged through the stack of magazines and decided on a Reader's Digest. He thumbed through the pages to the Laughter is the Best Medicine section while he waited for the coffee to be done.

Soon, the bitter scent of coffee mixed with the ever-present odor of gasoline. Ernie went in the back room and returned with the tire for the man to inspect.

"That looks like it will be fine," said the man.

"I will get to fixing this -- and here's a mug to help yourself to the coffee when it stops dripping," Ernie said, flashing his gummed smile, handing the mug to the gentlemen.

Looking back, he should have warned the man about the train. And the coffee. But luckily, this time, it hadn't been necessary.

Ernie was not a strikingly handsome man. His dirty Detroit Tigers baseball cap always donned his bald head. His toothless grin and red cheeks showed a tender side, almost child-like. Always dressed in overalls, except for church, he always smelled of oil and gasoline. His hands were rough and dirty black, signs of a hardworking man. What he did not show in his looks or dress, he made up for in his big heart and gentle ways.

Now, Ernie tightened the last lug nut and was finished.

"All set to go. And you still have plenty of time to get to your meeting," he said. He looked at the dusty clock radio in the corner of the shop: 8:34.

"I can't thank you enough. I did not imagine my day turning around so quickly. I was lucky to find your shop open," the man said.

Ernie just smiled, as he was accustomed to hearing the same sentiments from many people. The man followed Ernie again inside the gas station, where Ernie rung up the bill on the antique cash register. It happily chimed as he shut the cash drawer.

"Do you have a map of the area that I may purchase?" the man said. "I am a salesman from Wisconsin, and the map I have shows Wisconsin and a small part of the Upper Peninsula of Michigan. I need a map with small towns and street names on it. You got one?"

Ernie grabbed a map from behind the cash register and said, "This will help you out so you don't get lost in our neck of the woods. Please keep it, no charge."

"I'm a paper-supply salesman with Kimberly-Clark," the man explained, carefully slipping the map into his back pocket. He pulled out another smaller piece of paper from his front shirt pocket and read through his list. "I need to make stops at Lake Linden-Hubbell High School. Then I'm off to Calumet High School, Suomi College and finally Michigan Tech University."

Ernie's eyebrows raised in interest.

The man continued, "I have a pretty full day ahead of me, and no time to get lost."

"Or a flat tire," Erie added.

"Right," the man agreed. "Thanks for your help."

The man paid the bill and gulped his last swig of coffee, before waving goodbye with a grateful smile.

Ernie picked up today's newspaper and took a seat in the small foyer. The small-town paper, The Daily Mining Gazette, didn't have a whole lot of news, other than an accident on the front page, an obituary column on the next page, the high school sports page (which had no write ups since it was summer), garage sale listings and area church news.

Ernie was scanning the church listings when a bell ding-donged outside. Another customer had arrived.

People regularly stopped by to get a full tank of gas, buy new tires or pump air into bicycle tires. Ernie's service station did not have the full amenities of other stations in the area. Tires, gas, air, pop and candy; it was pretty simple.

Whereas other nearby gas stations had started using self-serve pumps, Ernie kept his station full service, where he could meet and greet the customers and do the pumping of gas himself. He enjoyed giving this service to others. In a world that often seemed so fast-paced and self-centered, he liked the opportunity to let people relax while he pumped the gas and washed the windows. The customers appreciated it, too. It was almost a novelty, so Ernie's station attracted plenty of regulars. Even in a small town, his shop stayed busy -- and even with another gas station nearby that offered automatic gas pumps and more modern amenities.

Ernie approached the car and saw that it was his good friend Harry. Harry stretched out of the car, eagerly shook Ernie's hand and offered him some oatmeal chocolate chip cookies that his wife Greta had baked minutes earlier. Ernie gladly accepted the still-warm cookies, popping one in his mouth immediately, and he then ran them inside.

Harry and Ernie had been inseparable friends since high school and served for many years as members of St. Cecilia's Catholic Church. They both upheld leadership positions in the Knights of Columbus. They even opened their businesses next door to each other around twenty five years ago.

Ernie opened the service station, and Harry opened a barbershop. Harry often joked that Ernie got the better deal, as Harry always needed gas in his car, but Ernie, who was nearly bald, never needed a haircut. But Ernie would visit the barbershop anyway, for an occasional shave, the good old-fashioned way with a straight-edge blade, shaving cream and a hot towel applied to baby soft skin.

Harry and Ernie's fathers had been friends, as well, having worked together in the Ahmeek Mill in nearby Tamarack City, along highway M-26. The Ahmeek Mill was one of many stamp mills built to pulverize rock from the copper mines into fine sand. The workers would then mix the sand with water from Torch Lake to separate metal from waste sand.

Their fathers worked together until 1967, when a strike closed her doors completely. Mills and mines closed for good, and the railroads were no longer needed to transport the rich copper found deep within the earth. Many people moved on and out of the small towns of the Copper Country. In their wake: a bit of a ghost town. But many families did remain and they continue to tell the stories about the rich earth down below.

Over the years, small towns popped up. Thousands of people streamed in, many immigrants from Finland, Norway, Sweden, and

Canada. Today, the towns were dispersed sparingly with descendants, who chose to stay for the laid-back, simple, outdoorsy lifestyle. Remnants of abandoned mines and mills remain dilapidated, reminders of days gone by.

"Are you attending the Knights of Columbus meeting tonight?" Harry asked, leaning back onto the hood of his old white Pontiac.

"Sure thing. At 7, right?" Ernie asked, patting the side of Harry's car. He thought about washing his windshield, out of habit.

"Yep. I will swing home for a quick bite to eat and then will join you at the meeting."

Harry tipped his hat and said his goodbye as Ernie nodded warmly. Ernie resumed sweeping inside the service station until he heard the laughing of young kids nearby.

He looked outside to see the Muljo brothers, Scott and Darren, ages nine and eight years old, kicking dirt and chasing one another. The two boys liked to hang around the service station and often helped Ernie with pumping gas, washing windows, and filling air in tires. Ernie never minded kids hanging around if they would do some work. He liked to see kids work hard and have some purpose, rather than wandering around with nothing to do or looking for trouble. The boys didn't earn any money working for Ernie, instead they were paid with soda pop, candy bars and a good handshake for a job well done. Praise meant everything to these boys as their father was in and out of their lives. Ernie was loved and respected by the boys. A fatherly figure they much needed in their lives.

Besides, the boys' father wasn't around much after the divorce, leaving the mother to care for four children alone. Cheryl had remarried, but sadly, the marriage did not last long. Now she had five children to care for, alone again. Yes, Cheryl had it rough raising the kids, often relying on government assistance of food stamps, Medicaid and welfare checks. Extended family and friends would help out bringing by bags of groceries when needed or would slip a check under the door so her electricity or water wouldn't be turned off. Ernie had a heart for this family, many did. Cheryl's parents had grown up in Hubbell and Tamarack City, and they worked hard and attended the same Catholic church as Ernie. Small towns look after their own. So when Ernie saw the dust being kicked by these two boys, naturally he welcomed them back.

Ernie never had children of his own. Never married, either. He lived with his mother for a number of years, until she passed on two years earlier. The last two years had been difficult for Ernie. He missed the talks he had with his mother, remembering her delicious home-cooked meals, and the laughs they shared while watching "Hee Haw" and "The Lawrence Welk Show." But still he remained in the same home that his parents raised him. His father had died ten years earlier from a sudden stroke and Ernie would not leave his mothers side. When she passed, dying of dementia and congestive heart failure, the house seemed so small, empty and quiet.

Working at the station long hours, from sunrise to well after sunset, helped with the loneliness. Someone always seemed to be stopping by for help or just to chat. Ernie was needed. Within the borders of his service station, he was important, busy, purposeful and surrounded by familiar faces.

Returning home in the evening was sometimes unbearable. When he walked through the front door, the air was heavy and still. When his mom died, so did the house, in a way. Ernie was not a good bachelor. He never found the knack for cooking. TV dinners, Dinty Moore stew, and Hormel chili were often his idea of home-cooked meals. He did like to bake, however.

Every so often, someone would stop by the station with a dish of mulligan stew or chicken with dumplings or another dish to his liking. Or, to his delight, a *pasty*! Oh, the rich goodness of the pasty. Flaky, warm dough wrapped around bits of potato, onion, rutabaga and beef, delicious with a dollop of ketchup on top. Heavenly.

Every time Ernie ate a pasty, he thought back to his father telling him as a boy that the copper mine workers would take two piping hot pasties to work in the winter months, one for each coat pocket. Deep, dark and damp cold within the earth, their hard-working, chilled hands would reach into their coat pockets for warmth given off by the pasties. When lunchtime rolled around, they would find a place corner to sit, only illuminated by the glow of their kerosene lantern, and enjoy pasties with some steaming coffee from a thermos. Ernie said his dad never tired of the pasty routine for lunch, and Ernie never tired of eating a pasty either.

Although Ernie would enjoy the meal immensely, nothing replaced the fondness of sharing a meal with someone. Sitting at the same table together, saying grace, and having good hearty conversation made the meal immeasurably more appealing -- and his heart a whole lot lighter.

Sure, on occasion, Ernie got invited to dinner at someone's house, but mostly it was on holidays. And the next holiday wasn't until Thanksgiving. Seeing that it was only July, he didn't expect an invitation for months.

The Muljo brothers noticed Ernie peeking out from the foyer door, and they began kicking, laughing and rumbling their way across the parking lot toward him, as is the means of travel for all young boys.

"Hey, Ern!" Scott called, his dirty shoes puffing small clouds of dust with every step. "Can we help you today?"

"Sure thing, but before you can help me, did you do your chores at home?" Ernie asked, a smirk creeping onto his rosy cheeks.

Both boys looked sheepishly at each other, kicked the dirt again and Darren replied, "Aw, we better check with Mom. We kind of just hurried over here."

"We will go home and check with mom and be back soon, okay Ernie?" Scott, the older brother, excitedly repeated. Only a year apart,

Scott being nine and Darren eight, the boys looked like bookends: very similar in appearance. Darren, the younger boy, had slight auburn to his brother's chestnut hair. Both had the deepest blue eyes, and both struggled to keep their knee-high athletic socks from falling down their slender legs to the ankle. Ernie always laughed when the boys finally pulled their socks up, because they would have multiple rings of dirt around them. Ernie could only imagine how their bathtub looked after soaking away a long day of work and play. This made Ernie smile.

"We want to help pump air in the tires, and then maybe we can help you with the toys," chimed in Darren.

Ernie laughed at the boys' excitement. They were good kids with compassionate hearts. Always willing to help, sometimes even at the expense of not helping their mom first. (Of course, chores around the house never feel quite as fun as filling tires at someone else's station.) Ernie liked to teach the boys about responsibility, but also that honoring their mom should come first; after all, she needed their help certainly more than he did.

Ernie silently rehearsed his message for tonight's Knights of Columbus meeting: the start of collecting toys for the annual Christmas party. Though Christmas was months away and he was wiping sweat from his brow instead of bundling up for cold weather, it was already time for the Knights to start planning. Ernie's collection of toys were low at the moment, and he would enjoy getting more work done now, before the bustling months of November and December.

Throughout the year, Ernie collected toys, games, bikes, dolls and wagons and refurbished them, by painting and repairing them to like new. So new that the children could not tell the difference and were sure it came directly off of Santa's sleigh. He did all of the work in a cramped ten-by-ten-foot room in the service station. He liked to think of the room as a "franchise of Santa's workshop."

Spare bike parts, bags of doll limbs, beautiful doll hair and eyes, doll buggies and Red Flyer wagons filled the room. There, on the shelves, awaited various paints, glues and tools for working the most difficult and delicate of repair work. Ernie kept this room secret, but Scott and Darren were privy to the room's existence. Ernie invited them inside its mysterious quarters to help repair the toys, and they were hushed to secrecy.

Sadly, the boys often worked on the same toys they would later receive at the Christmas party. They tried to act surprised, but they knew the toys came from Ernie. Still, they kept the secret. They didn't want to ruin the surprise for the other needy and poor children in the community.

The Christmas party was organized to bless those who had so little and shed the light of Christ's love into the hearts of those who could not otherwise afford a toy or a hot meal at Christmas time. In that, Ernie's "franchise of Santa's workshop" was also his Christian ministry. The town's kids believed there really was a Santa Claus, and in a way, there was; he just went by a different name. And their parents believed God was looking out for them, not forgetting them in their time of need. Sure, the parents knew that Ernie had made the toys and organized the party, but they trusted that God had sent an angel in Ernie to do His work.

The boys hurried home to check on their chores, and they planned on returning later to help Ernie with odds and ends around the station. Ernie went back to puttering around the station, even finding time to sneak back into the workshop and paint a little on a donated wagon.

The red Radio Flyer wagon had a few dings and was in need of some paint. He picked up a hammer and began gently tapping on the inside of the wagon's metal, patiently smoothing out the dents. Then he picked up a paintbrush and swathed the wagon in one coat of primer and one coat of fire-engine red. That's when he heard the familiar pattering of small sneakers on the dirt path. Scott and Darren had returned.

The boys got straight to work. Scott snatched up an air hose and pressed it to a patron's tires, while Darren polished the window. He wavered on tiptoe, trying to reach the center of the windshield, but one circle in the very middle eluded his short little arms. Ernie swung Darren up onto one hip and leaned him in, to make the final squeaky wipe. No words needed be exchanged; they'd been following this routine for months. Soon, Darren would be tall enough, but until then, he had Ernie hoist him up to clean the windows.

On a hot day like today, Ernie was surprised that the boys wanted to spend the afternoon with him in the first place, rather than go swimming at the lake down the street. The temperature was well into the nineties and was so humid that your skin felt sticky with sweat; attracting dirt and flying gnats. Ernie would have liked to fling the "closed" sign on the door so he could take a dip in the refreshing lake. But that would not happen. He would be lucky to acquire a quick shower at the end of the day before his Knights of Columbus meeting.

At 6 p.m., Ernie cheerfully flung the "closed" sign on the door and locked up the service station. He ran across the street to Lewis's market to pick up a few items. What he wanted most was Paul's ham sandwich spread and some fresh French bread.

As Ernie pulled the store door open, the chimes rang loudly. A familiar hello shouted from the back of the store. It was Paul. He was probably busy in the meat and deli department.

Ernie yelled back, "Hey there, Paul. Got any fresh ham sandwich spread made?"

He walked down the aisle past the canned goods and pasta and found his friend leaning over what appeared to be a large side of beef. Paul looked up, his white apron now covered with blood.

"I wish I didn't have to see that," Ernie said, motioning to the blood smeared across his friend's clothes.

"I'm sorry, Ernie. Barbara must have slipped away from the counter to the restroom or upstairs to the apartment. I don't usually like doing this while customers are around but it needed to be cut before I have dinner and then head off to the Knights of Columbus meeting."

"It is fine. Just makes me remember my Pa cutting up deer he shot during hunting season to make venison steaks. I remember him telling me it was 'family steak,' because I told him I wouldn't eat venison. He even went so far as to wrap it in paper and cellophane and make it look like it came from a store!"

"Ha, ha. I have done the same thing with my two kids. He was a smart man," Paul laughed.

Paul removed his dirty apron and went to the sink to wash his hands. He returned looking more presentable, reached for a container and starting scooping ham sandwich spread into it for his friend.

Ernie didn't know what was in the delicious sandwich spread that Paul Lewis, the butcher and store owner made, but he knew that it was tasty and just what he was hungry for. The sandwich spread mystery was kind of like hot dogs: nobody wants to know how it is made; they just want to eat it.

"Gee, I sure love your ham sandwich spread. How do you make it?" Ernie asked.

"An old Lewis family secret," Paul teased.

"Please share the recipe with me. It is costing me a fortune buying it from you two to three times a week."

"Over my dead body!" Paul continued to tease, getting a rise of out Ernie.

Ernie didn't know quite what to say now and that surprised him because he was never at a loss for words. He just looked amused at his friend for a moment until Paul retorted and said, "Okay, I give in."

Paul starting fumbling through a recipe box on the counter and pulled out a recipe card and handed it to Ernie with a warning. "You keep this recipe to yourself. Do not give it to anybody, ya hear? You sharing the recipe could put me out of business. I make a ton of money on this sandwich spread!"

"Wow. I feel like I have been handed the keys to heaven! Thanks Paul," Ernie announced.

He looked at the recipe card in his hands and could tell that it had been written in a female's handwriting. In the upper corner it had the name Bea. Bea was Paul's mother. Must be her recipe.

"Now go on, Ernie, before I change my mind," Paul provoked.

Ernie quickly said, on the run, "Please put the sandwich spread, a loaf of french bread and a half gallon of whole milk on my tab, huh?" He grabbed the grocery items and ran toward the door.

"See you at the meeting in an hour, Ernie," Paul yelled out. He put a fresh apron on and went back to work cutting up the side of beef. Soon, his wife Barbara returned from their apartment upstairs with a aluminum-covered dinner plate and some extra clothes for Paul to change into before his meeting.

Ernie returned to his tiny blue house with white shutters at the top of the hill. He reached for the dilapidated handrail that needed replacement, walked up the two cement stairs and entered the heat of the living room.

"Whew!" he sighed, as he went to the window and threw it open.

He proceeded into the kitchen to open another window for a good cross breeze. Reaching into the refrigerator felt refreshing, and he stuck his head in there for a few extra moments, before grabbing the glass bottle of milk. Stacking four slices of Italian white bread on a plate, he took a knife and smeared the delicious sandwich spread across the bread. He licked the knife. His hunger took him by surprise, as he forgot to say grace first. He caught himself after a few ravenous bites.

"Bless us, O Lord and these, thy gifts, which we are about to receive, from thy bounty through Christ our Lord, Amen."

He sat in stillness, except for the curtain that brushed in the breeze. The quiet was almost deafening. He could faintly hear someone mowing their lawn, and he focused on the roaring motor a bit so he could be distracted from the loneliness he felt. He ate rather quickly and gulped down his milk. He took a quick shower, changed into clean overalls and headed to his Knights of Columbus meeting.

The Knights of Columbus meeting came to order at 7 p.m. sharp. Father Arnold led with prayer and then the gentlemen got down to business. First on discussion was the opening of adding more members to the organization in September. Next they talked about the upcoming pastry sale, with proceeds going to help the local food pantry. Lastly, they directed attention to Ernie and his workshop ministry of restoring toys.

Ernie nervously placed his hands on the podium.

"I've already repaired twenty-nine toys so far this year, but we need ninety-two to match the number of needy boys and girls signed up for the program," he said softly. He wasn't much for public speaking, but this cause was dear enough to him to push forward with talking.

"With the layoffs at the hospital and university in the past months, that number will probably increase this year's needs. I move in favor of starting to collect toys in the community now and assemble volunteers to assist with refurbishing the toys and planning the party," Ernie added.

All men agreed or nodded in favor. Bob Princeton, treasurer, spoke up.

"Ernie, as usual, you will be in charge of assembling the children's choir. We need a program for both the Christmas party and for Christmas Eve service. I will provide you with the approved budget" Bob said.

"Sure thing," Ernie exclaimed.

"We will assist you, too, Ernie with assembling a volunteer team to solicit and collect toys. Then we can plan some work days with you, maybe one or two Sundays a month to get the toys all cleaned up and restored," another member, George Clark, offered.

Father Arnold added, "The women's auxiliary committee will be of assistance for the Christmas party, as usual. I will contact Hilda Jacobs and Rose Montgomery to orchestrate the food and gift baskets."

Ernie grinned.

"I love how we have done this routine so many times that our planning is like a well oiled machine. Familiar and constant." Ernie gleefully said.

The gentlemen wrapped up their discussion and then sat around chit-chatting and talking business. Father Arnold then told a funny, yet clean, joke that kept the guys laughing until it was time to go.

Father Arnold began:

Two priests were going to the Bahamas on vacation and decided that they would make this a real vacation by not wearing anything that would identify them as clergy. They agreed to not do a baptism, wedding or funeral. As soon as the plane landed, they headed for a souvenir shop and bought some really outrageous shorts, shirts, sandals and sunglasses.

The next morning, they went to the beach, dressed in their "tourist" disguises and were sitting on beach chairs, enjoying a drink, the sunshine and the scenery, when a drop-dead gorgeous blonde in a bikini came walking straight toward them. They couldn't help but notice, and when she passed them, she smiled and said, "Good morning, Father. Good morning, Father." She nodded and addressed each of them individually, then walked on by. They were both stunned. How in the world did she recognize them as priests?

The next day, they went back to the souvenir store and bought even more outrageous outfits, including wide brimmed hats. Once again, they settled on the beach in their chairs to enjoy the sunshine.

After a while, the same gorgeous blonde, wearing a yellow polka dot bikini this time, came walking toward them again. She approached them, smiled and greeted them individually: "Good morning, Father. Good morning, Father." She nodded and started to walk away.

One of the priests couldn't stand it and said, "Just a minute, young lady. Yes, we are priests, and proud of it, but I have to ask, how in the world did you know?"

"Oh, Father, don't you recognize me?" she asked. "I'm Sister Martha!"

All shared a lengthy laugh. Harry couldn't pull it together and tears were falling from his eyes and he was rubbing his jaw from laughing so hard.

"That is a good one! I will have to share that joke with the guys at the barbershop!"

Bob threw his hankie at Harry and told him to clean himself up and to quit crying like a baby. They laughed again. All teasing aside, they loved Harry. He had the best sense of humor but he could not control the waterworks.

It had been a long day for Ernie, and he resorted to turning into bed early. He felt for the switch of the fan on his nightstand and began undressing for bed. The oscillating coolness felt good on his warm and tired body. He hung his overalls on the chair and tossed his T-shirt into the laundry hamper.

Walking into the bathroom, he turned on the cool water, grappled the bar of Irish Spring and made a lather to wash his face. When he finished brushing his teeth, he walked back across the linoleum floor to his bedroom, knelt down beside his bed, and gave thanks to Almighty God for another day given.

"Lord, we are Your people, the sheep of your flock.
Heal the sheep that are wounded, touch the sheep that are in pain.
Clean the sheep that are soiled, warm the lambs that are cold.
Help us to know Your love, through Jesus the shepherd, and through His Holy Spirit.

Help us to lift up that love and show it all over this land.
Help us to build love on justice and justice on love.
Help us to believe mightily, hope joyfully and love divinely.
Renew us that we may renew the face of this Earth. Amen."

Chapter 2

S aturday morning. While many people would enjoy a relaxing day of picnics, sunbathing at the beach, boating and camping, Ernie always worked on this day. In fact, Saturday was typically the busiest day of his week. Everyone seemed to save up their car repairs, questions and purchases for the weekend.

At 4:00 p.m., after a grueling day on his back underneath cars and on his feet behind the cash register, Ernie's black-with-grease covered hands flipped the sign on the front door to "closed," Soon he was home getting cleaned up, including the time-staking job of cleaning the grease from under his fingernails. Every Saturday evening, he looked forward to playing the guitar and leading a choir of about fifteen excited children. Music had always been a passion of Ernie's, and he delighted in seeing the kids take a liking to it, as well. Some children had such beautiful singing voices that they truly sounded like a choir of heavenly angels. Then there was the occasional child who sounded like a wounded cat. Ernie loved those voices just as much, with their innocence and honest inhibition. What was important was that the children were finding their own musical voices, however that sounded.

While singing, Ernie always reminded the children of the bible verse: *"Make a joyful noise unto the Lord. Serve the Lord with gladness; come before his presence with singing."* – Psalm 100: 1-2 (NIV).

With that said, who was Ernie to cover his ears if the joyful noise of a wounded cat was for the Lord and not for him? In peaceful moments throughout his busy workday, he would remember the song lineup for that evening and hum the songs while he worked. One song that especially spoke to his heart was called "All That I Am." This simple song always kept him mindful that he was God's creation, who was designed to walk on this Earth and use his given talents for God's glory. He had a lot to be thankful for, and he counted his many blessings. He had a thriving business, many friends in the church and community. He had his music and kids who wanted to spend time with him.

There were times of loneliness, though, when he wondered why he had never found someone to settle down with to have children. The white picket fence. The growing old together. If he dwelled on what he didn't have, it hurt doubly, because it also distracted him from all that he did have. And as God promised, it would always be enough. So Ernie rested in knowing that God was in control and knew perfectly the plan for his life. Loving and serving the Lord was a reward enough for everything that God had given him. It was Ernie's deepest honor and joy.

At 4:45 p.m., Ernie arrived at St. Cecilia's Catholic Church and set up his music stand and began tuning his guitar. He warmed up his fingers, strumming the light blue Fender MusicMaster guitar that he purchased in the 1960s. In a few minutes, the kids would come wandering in, ready to rehearse a song before the parishioners settled in the pews for mass.

Lisa and Linda Muljo were the first children to arrive. They were the older sisters to Scott and Darren, and because they lived hardly one-hundred feet from the church, they were always early. The girls liked coming in first because then they got the first choice of the dark blue polyester choir robe to wear. They did not want a robe that was too long or too short, ripped or one that needed to be laundered. You could say it was the fringe benefit of arriving early to church: first choice of the choir robe.

After their careful selection, they quickly slipped the robes over their heads and went and sat next to Mike and Mark Alcott, the two teenage boys who always assisted Ernie with the bass and drum. Handsome teenage boys, at that. Within minutes, the girls dissolved into the giggles. They covered their mouths to try to muffle their giddiness, but nothing concealed the ruddiness of their cheeks from blushing.

The boys shook their heads and shrugged at each other, trying to ignore the curious stares and whispering. Girls. They were so weird. The boys refocused on keeping busy doing what was expected of them.

Other kids joyfully came hustling in: Debbie, Teri, Renee, Sarah, Claire, Denise, Judy, Dawn, Shirley and Kathy. Each plucked a choir robe from the stack -- less carefully than the first two girls -- slid it on and took a seat near Ernie. But really, the other girls wished they were the ones sitting near dreamy Mike and Mark. Lisa and Linda just stuck out their tongues and raised their eyebrows in delight, in response to the other girls' jealous glances.

Ernie commanded the kids' attention. He said a quick prayer and starting playing the warm up song, "All That I Am." The song was a thorough warm-up song because it hit so many keys and had wonderful harmonies. The choir was able to practice the song twice before the parishioners began streaming through the heavy double doors of the the church. Body after body took a seat, usually was the same seat in the same pew, every week. Each family seemed to take ownership of their own pew. It felt like their home. Regular attendees knew not to sit in anyone else's pew, but darn the person who was new and did not know the protocol.

The children practiced great restraint to not talk to one another. Ernie had instructed them to sit quietly and use subtle charades or sign language if they urgently needed to communicate something, but not to speak a word until they heard the bells ringing in the bell tower, signaling that mass was about to begin. Kids started amusing themselves by playing the rock-paper-scissors game. Some girls braided each other's hair.

The air in the back room next to the altar grew stifling hot. The kids were all relieved when the awaited chime of the bell tower bells finally released them into the beautiful, open church.

They sang the opening song, "Holy God, We Praise Thy Name," with strong voices and brought the parishioners to their feet, joining in the familiar melody. This hymn was a traditional Catholic hymn that originated in the late 1700s, and had been translated into English in 1858. Typically, with a lengthy song like this with eight verses, the kids could handle singing only three.

Holy God, we praise thy name;
Lord of all, we bow before thee.
All on Earth thy scepter claim,
All in heaven above adore thee;
Infinite thy vast domain,
Everlasting is thy reign.

Hark! The loud celestial hymn,
Angel choirs above are raising,
Cherubim and seraphim,
In unceasing chorus praising;
Fill the heavens with sweet accord:
Holy, holy, holy, Lord.

After rehearsing this song, it seemed a different child always wanted to know who Cherubim and Seraphim were.

"Ernie, who are you talking about? Cher-r-r-rybum and

Sor-r-r-ybim?" little three-year-old Kimmy asked. Kimmy was tagging along with her older sisters, Lisa and Linda.

The older girls just laughed and repeated Kimmy's "Cherrybum" pronunciation, and Teri sat disgusted, knowing where the conversation would go next.

"Really? Do we need to go into *another* explanation of this?" she snarled, crossing her arms across her chest in a huff.

Ernie looked Teri in the eye and nodded sympathetically, then patiently explained to the others that Cherubim and Seraphim were winged creatures who appeared in scripture. They made their most memorable appearance in the books of Ezekiel, Isaiah, and Revelations. Although Cherubim and Seraphim were not specifically called angels, they were revealed to be living creatures or heavenly beings whose primary focus was to worship God at the throne.

The sound of the word "creature" made the children want a further explanation to ease their trembling minds.

"Oh, here we go again," Ernie smirked to himself. And the endless questions would start.

"Didn't you say before Ernie that a Cherubim looked like a four-winged creature?" little Shirley gulped.

Before Ernie could answer, smart Teri blurted out, "Yes, he did. And it has four faces, too! Imagine that!"

"And you better be a fast runner, or it will getcha!" Judy said, with wide eyes.

The kids stopped, silent, big-eyed, with mouths dropped open, waiting in anticipation for more information, afraid to move out of their seats as though an enormous Cherubim would devour them at any moment.

Ernie sat back in his chair and glanced at the wall clock. *This might take some time*, he thought.

"A Seraphim is a flying serpent, kind of like a snake, with six wings. Seraphims were creatures of fire," he said, looking into the faces of the young children, waiting for a response.

The kids gulped hard, still amazed at what they heard.

"Then why do we sing of such awful creatures?" asked Linda, shaking.

"Are they nice creatures to God?" Renee asked.

"Are you sure the devil didn't send those creatures to do bad things to good people?" asked Kathy.

Ernie tried not to laugh, but he stumbled as he tried to answer their thought-provoking questions. He tried to assure them that these creatures were from God, and were meant to serve and protect God and his kingdom, the Garden of Eden and the tabernacle. Ernie found it increasingly more difficult to explain so simplistically to the children, without evoking more fear or confusion.

Little Kimmy moved away from her sister Lisa's chair and now clung to Ernie's side.

"I'm scared, Ernie," she said, clutching his arm tightly.

Times like these, Ernie wished they didn't sing the familiar hymn, "Holy God We Praise Thy Name."

Finally, he said, "Hmm, you know what? If you have further questions, why not ask Father Arnold? He would be *thrilled* that you want to know more!"

Ernie knew that his quick response had gotten him off the hook for the moment, and he chuckled to himself knowing that Father Arnold would later be bombarded by children wanting answers about Cherubim and Seraphim.

Father Arnold wouldn't be surprised. He was familiar with Ernie's occasional devious sense of humor, and the pair had a great, playful, joking relationship. Father Arnold loved jokes, too, and he often pulled the wool over ol' Ernie's sometimes naive eyes. Beyond the robe, Father Arnold had a mischievous heart that he had never lost since childhood. Ernie liked to think of the scripture, "Do unto others, as they do unto you," and it applied perfectly in this situation. Ernie left church feeling satisfied that at least one choir kid would approach Father Arnold asking for answers to questions that Ernie had gladly deferred.

Father Arnold's best shenanigan to Ernie's recall was when he nearly burned the church down. Remembering the incident put a smirk on Ernie's face.

Two years earlier, Ernie had been trying to set up for a mass. He wanted to enter the back room to get some equipment and to put things in place before the choir kids arrived. He found the door locked and soon realized that he did not have a key.

Hmm, the door was seldom locked, he thought. More of a worry was that he could faintly smell smoke nearby. Puzzled, Ernie knew Father Arnold would not arrive for another twenty minutes, and he did not have the time to waste. With fear in his heart that the church was on fire, he ran outside and around the building, staggered up the flight of stairs and grabbed the rusty doorknob. With fear now in his throat, he rattled the door knob in his sweaty hand and gave the door a huge shove. The door flung open.

"Thank God!" he cried and rushed inside to a smoke-filled room.

The entire room was filled with gray smoke, and a choking smell overcame him, making him gag. Smoke burned his eyes and tears spilled down his cheeks. *No flames, just smoke. Where is the smoke coming from?*

His feet shuffled slowly as he tried to remember the layout of the dark room. *Where is that light switch?* His fingers reached forward and his feet shuffled until he had something in his grasp. His fingers soon felt soft fabric and he assumed he was touching clothing from the coat rack.

Still in the dark, he paused for a moment to think. He knew that smell. That awful smell. It was the same smell that priests assaulted the parishioners with on church holidays. The same smell that made him gag as an altar boy when he assisted with mass. *Foul, nasty.* It was that dang incense! Priests often burned palm tree leaves as a tradition during the mass and then waved the burnt offerings through the air, until their scent seeped high into the rafters of the church.

Ernie moved to the left of the coat rack and felt the hard surface of the door. One more reach to the left of the door and he felt the light switch. With a flick, the room was illuminated. His eyes danced around the room until they found the source of the smoke.

It was the priest's liturgical vessel smoking. And stinking. Luckily, the phrase, "Where there is smoke, there is fire," was erroneous. His heart slowed slightly and his panic subsided when he saw there were no flames. But all of this still did not explain what was really going on.

"Aw, what in the world?" Ernie mumbled out loud. His eyes blinked back the water accumulating, and he tried to suppress a choking sensation. To himself, he wondered why Father Arnold would leave the incense burning in a closed room. *How careless of him,* Ernie thought. *Is he losing his marbles?*

He carefully lifted up the scorching vessel with the sleeve of his choir gown and transported it at arm's length outside. Gasping and sputtering, Erne kicked open the door. Suddenly, a body jumped out from behind the wisteria bushes. It was Father Arnold. And he was laughing, in hysterics, actually. He clutched his stomach, unable to speak or stand straight up, as the laughter rocked his body. His hurled-over body finally stood up upright. He began flapping his robe like a overheated goose in a frenzy.

"Gotcha, Ernie!" Father Arnold hooted. "I know how fond you are of incense." The laughter overtook his speech again. "Nothing like keeping the smell contained in a small room for you to enjoy, huh?" More laughter. He continued flapping his robe, fanning himself for air, as he could hardly catch his breath.

He laughed again, this time falling to his hands and knees on the grass.

"Crazy old man! Get up or you will soil your gown" Ernie crowed while bending down to put the hot vessel on the stairs. "I thought the church was on fire when I entered the room. Oh, and that horrible incense smell! Can't you priests burn vanilla, cinnamon or roses? Anything else! Dang palm tree burning scent. So nasty."

Ernie pursed his lips, trying to control the laughter boiling in his chest. He didn't want Father Arnold to think that he had won this time.

"Yours is coming, Arnold," Ernie teased, wagging his finger as a promise to Father Arnold. "You know that, huh? Just you wait. Might have to substitute lemon juice instead of wine in your chalice at communion time!" Ernie warned, forcing his lips into an unbearable grin.

"Now I am in a dilemma. I have the choir kids coming in a few minutes. I cannot have the kids come into this smoky room. Do you have any suggestions on what I should do with the children?" Ernie asked, leaving Father Arnold to solve this precarious situation.

Father Arnold didn't flinch.

"Got that all planned out," he replied, not missing a beat. "Why don't you set up in the balcony and allow the kids to enjoy singing near the rafters? They usually only get to do that once a year, at Christmas time. They will consider it a special treat to get to do that today." He paused and winked. "Just say it was my thoughtful idea."

"Smoke rises, Arnold!" Ernie laughed. "However, I am sure the kids would delight in singing in the balcony, smoke and all. You are always coming out looking and smelling like a rose, aren't you?"

"And you, my friend, smell like burned palm tree," Father Arnold joyfully added, as he made an exit to the vestibule of the church.

Kids on the balcony? Oh boy. Ernie recalled another time when the children had the luxury of singing from the balcony. They were so energized, their voices were strong and crisp and their smiles stretched towards the rafters. Meanwhile, Ernie felt uneasy the entire time, like an octopus ready to snatch a child from falling over the railing. He would have to bribe them again with candy to be still and focused. This time he would give them the sweet butterscotch candy *after* mass was over.

Ernie could not stop thinking of Father Arnold's prank. While tuning his guitar and waiting for the children, he started reminiscing about times when he was a young lad. Harry, Arnold and Ernie were the best of friends, and they could always find some kind of mischief. Arnold came up with the wise ideas and snared Ernie and Harry into following along. Ernie and Harry got caught and were labeled "hooligans," while Arnold looked on innocently. Arnold still took any opportunity to pull a good one on old Ernie. Sure, Father Arnold teased Harry, too, but Ernie was more gullible and an easy target.

Pranks and all, Ernie felt fortunate to have two best friends from childhood. They all continued to live and work in the same small town, separated only when Ernie enlisted in the navy during World War II and Arnold consequently enrolled in seminary school. Harry stayed in Hubbell, got married to high school sweetheart Greta and then became the local barber. The small town, church, Knights of Columbus meetings and the occasional poker game kept the friends in steady company.

Chapter 3

Sunday is the day of rest, says the Lord. Ernie thought that to be an amusing statement, as he did not know what it was like to rest. He never stopped working with his hands or working with his mind. Resting caused him to think and worry about things he had no time for, so he chose to keep busy at any cost.

However, he did make a promise to the Lord that he would not work at the service station on Sundays. Therefore, in a way, he was keeping the commandment of keeping holy the Sabbath Day -- even though his Sundays were far from restful.

He figured there was no harm in doing a hobby or ministry work, and what he wanted to do most was fix toys. He had received a bag of toys from Harry at the Knights of Columbus meeting on Friday evening. Ernie had not looked through the donated items yet, but he anticipated the work and joy he had ahead of him.

Ernie wandered into the back shed and retrieved the overfilled potato sack. He gently pulled out each toy and observed it with a delicate eye. Ernie knew that with just a little work, the toys could be fixed back to new, and they would be loved and appreciated by many children. His fingers brushed something soft wedged deep within the sack. He slowly pulled them out, careful not to spill the rest of the contents. There were two teddy bears, one light brown and one black. Both bears needed a bit of sewing, some spot cleaning and new big red bow. He gave them a squeeze and smile, then placed them on the chair.

There was a Rock 'Em Sock 'Em Robots game that looked barely used, and a Lite-Brite game, whose many pieces needed organizing. The box needed glued, too. There was a Crissy doll that needed a bath, some styling of her auburn hair and a pretty new dress. The doll would make a wonderful gift for a little girl.

Ernie reached into the sack again. He quickly snapped back his hand.

"Ouch!" he cried.

He reached down slowly, peered into the bag and pulled out a pair of girls' ice skates. The sharp blades had nearly cut his finger, but he soon forgot about the pain when he saw how lovely the skates were. They were in excellent shape -- and definitely sharp enough. They only needed a little white shoe polish, new laces and maybe add a couple of fluffy, colorful yarn pom-poms, and they would delight any young girl's heart.

Ernie saw the work before him and was pleased that he could probably get all the work done this afternoon before choir rehearsal with the kids at six o'clock. He thanked God for his friend Harry's thoughtfulness and reminded himself that he needed to stop by the barbershop and thank Harry personally.

Ernie did not fix the toys or volunteer with the choir kids because he thought his good works would reward him in heaven. Rather, he did it because he was God's servant, and he was entrusted to fulfill the work in His kingdom and for God's glory, not *his* own. He often thought of the bible verse in Matthew 25:21:

"Well done, good and faithful servant! You have been faithful with a few things; I will put you in charge of many things. Come and share your master's happiness!"

The familiar sound of a grumbling tummy stopped Ernie from working the entire afternoon. He took a break and went to the freezer to see what he could cook for dinner. He found a Banquet meatloaf, potatoes and green beans TV dinner that sounded appetizing. He warmed the oven, set the timer and grabbed a Granny Smith apple to munch on.

After finishing the apple, he took a little nap while his dinner cooked for fifty minutes. He fluffed a pillow and placed it on the sofa where his weary head would lie. Soon, he was fast asleep, gathering energy before dinner and choir rehearsal.

Ernie awoke to the oven alarm timer going off, and he rubbed his eyes and rose to his feet. He grabbed the oven mitts and took his dinner out and placed it on the trivet on the table. He wandered to the refrigerator and poured himself a large glass of milk. He paused for a moment and thought that chocolate milk would be a great addition to his meal, proving that Ernie was still a kid at heart, or at least at stomach. He rummaged through the refrigerator and found the Hershey's chocolate syrup and gave a couple squirts of the delicious brown goodness into the milk. He stirred the milk and walked to the table to settle down for his meal. He gave one big stretch, a yawn and then bowed his head to give grace.

"Bless us, oh Lord and these thy gifts, which we are about to receive, from thy bounty through Christ our Lord. Amen," he humbly said.

He finished every morsel of the meatloaf dinner and drank the chocolate milk with gusto. He sat somewhat contently but felt the urge to top off the meal with something sweet. He knew just the thing.

He had two cookies left, and he salivated at the thought of Greta's homemade goodness. Greta was Harry's wife, and she easily made the best chocolate-oatmeal cookies on the planet. Obviously, with any cookies you eat, you need milk to wash them down. Eagerly, Ernie poured himself another glass of milk, no chocolate syrup in it this time because he wanted to taste the sweet milk chocolate in the cookies. He savored every bite of the cookies and then felt satisfied.

He cleaned up the kitchen quickly and sauntered upstairs to the bathroom to freshen up before going to choir rehearsal. Ernie enjoyed the rehearsals with the kids, as they sang beautiful songs that they would sing the following Saturday evening at mass -- but also because they would linger a little later into the evening, relax and sing some great country and crooner songs.

Many of the kids were used to listening to *that rock and roll music* on the radio or on records, but Ernie liked to introduce them to a different style of music that sometimes was forgotten by today's generation. He would play the guitar to music by Glen Campbell, Johnny Cash, Tammy Wynette, Eddy Arnold, Perry Como, Frank Sinatra and Dean Martin. Often he would play some old folk songs. The kids' favorite was "Red River Valley." Every Sunday night, he would play that song, and the children would pretend they were cowboys sitting around a campfire, lovesick about the true love that had gotten away. Just like the lyrics of the song.

Ernie wiped his brow from the trickle of sweat that was moving down his face. He could not get enough breeze blowing between the windows of his old pickup because the drive was a short distance at a 20 mph pace. He parked in front of the Catholic school where they held their rehearsals, and he strolled inside to set up. Mike and Mark soon followed to help Ernie with the amps and chairs. The kids slowly began wandering in, and they took a seat, the early birds racing to get the chairs closest to Mike and Mark.

Teri and Renee both raced for a chair near Mike. Teri got there first, knocking Renee completely on her behind. Some kids laughed at Renee and made her feel bad.

"No, no, no. Let's do a redo and try that again" Ernie interrupted.

Teri needed to apologize to Renee for knocking her on her bottom and those that laughed needed to apologize to Renee for being rude before they could start to rehearse. Ernie's correction of the incident was to assign both Teri and Renee to take a seat near him and leave the prime real estate chairs available for two other girls, who could take a seat nicely next to Mike without rudeness.

Teri and Renee apologized, gave a hug to one another and took their new seats next to Ernie. Soon they settled in, and were all smiles, as if no incident had ever happened. Ernie discussed the upcoming songs for Saturday evening mass and they practiced singing each song twice. The children learned no new songs this evening so practice went smoothly. Ernie assigned two solos for the song "Amazing Grace" to Denise and Lisa, as they had strong voices and could deliver the song beautifully.

Ernie then spent a few minutes in a prayer circle with the kids, and each child had the opportunity to request a prayer for something happening in their lives. Shirley prayed first, asking for prayers for her grandmother, who had been hospitalized from a diabetic seizure. Kathy went next, requesting that the group pray for her parents, who were discussing getting a divorce. Lisa prayed last, asking for God's strength to help her get over the grief of losing her dog, Lucky, who had been killed by a logging truck mishap yesterday.

Lisa's wide blue eyes pooled with tears and she had to remove her thick lensed eyeglasses to wipe the wetness from her eyes. From across the room she heard a noise that sounded like a trumpet blowing or maybe an elephant. She peered to see with limited visibility and saw Mark, a few seats over with his hands cupped tightly over his mouth. She quickly donned her eyeglasses and looked at Mark again; his shoulders moving up and down and the restless of his body in the chair. Mark could hold it no more. His laughter exploded in the room, which was a jarring contrast to the quietness of the prayer circle. He apologized for not keeping himself under control and then went on to explain.

"I am sorry, Lisa, for the loss of your dog, Lucky. I laughed because his name was Lucky and he, well, wasn't too *lucky* when he was hit by the truck. I am sorry. It must have been awful." Mark's face now showed that he meant it. The novelty of the name was lost on the tragedy.

"Yeah, it was awful. Lucky was his name and yes, he was not very lucky to be hit by a truck, a logging truck, no doubt," Lisa said, sitting upright with an extra burst of energy. "I will miss him. My mom said maybe in a couple of months we could get another dog, and the idea of that makes me feel better."

"Yeah, it is awful to lose a pet. I once lost a canary," said Sarah.

Judy quickly chimed in, "I lost a rabbit once."

"A cat and two fish," said Kathy sadly.

"Speaking of losing something, I lost a tooth, see?" said little Kimmy, brandishing a gap in her front bottom teeth. The kids all looked at Kimmy and rolled their eyes at her awkward contribution. Kimmy sat proudly, unaware of the other's snickers, but kept smiling, with her toothless grin.

Ernie stopped the kids from discussing every sad loss of any pet or lost tooth, broken body part or fever they had ever experienced. He knew from experience how kids could take a story and stretch it beyond imagination, and soon they would totally lose track of time and all focus of what they should be doing. Ernie spoke up.

"Dear Lord, we pray for all the pets that have passed on," he said, bowing his head into his clasped hands. "Please provide for their care in heaven and allow them the chance to meet with us again. Lord, please protect Shirley's grandmother from further illness, restore her to good health so that she can come home soon. Father, please embrace a family and a husband and wife who need healing. We pray for Kathy's parents as they discuss divorce and pray that their marriage can be restored. Amen."

Ernie announced that he would be staying another half hour for any kids who wanted to sing more songs. A handful of kids would stay, the usuals; Lisa, Linda, Denise, Sarah, Judy and sometimes little Kimmy. They sang and danced to their favorites, like the "Red River

Valley" folk song, "Folsom Prison" by Johnny Cash, "Baby Blue" by George Baker, "Come Fly With Me" by Frank Sinatra and Dean Martin's, "That's Amore!"

When the last song hit their lips, the children jumped out of their chairs to dance and reenact the lyrics as they interpreted them. They pretended to be a big Italian family at a restaurant eating pizza pie, rolling noodles on forks and pulling noodles out of their mouths and noses.

"When the moon hits your eye like a big pizza pie,
That's amore'..."

The half hour would fly quickly and soon it was time to pack up and go home. The night would wrap up by someone quickly shouting, "Good night, sleep tight and don't let the bedbugs bite." Then the kids would laugh and pinch one another as if she were a bedbug.

"You are dismissed, kiddos. Go directly home. No mischief, no dilly-dallying. Capisce?" Ernie announced.

"Capisce, Ernie," the kids echoed back, folding up their metal chairs and placing them back in the cart.

Ernie, Mike and Mark packed up their guitars, amplifiers and microphones and said their goodbyes with a hug or handshake. Ernie drove home feeling pleased about tonight's rehearsal and the time he spent with the kids singing afterward. It had been a great night, as many other nights in his eighteen years of volunteering had been.

Ernie had seen many children grow up to become responsible adults, who went on to have successful careers and raise loving families. Some entered the military and a few went on to performing arts or ministry careers in voice, orchestra or theater. He received letters now and then from former students updating him on what has been happening in their lives, and they often sent pictures of their family and home. Each letter would fill Ernie with joyful emotion, as he recalled the fond memories and how he had touched another's life for good, and for God.

Chapter 4

The days turned into weeks, and Ernie watched the changing of the seasons. The muggy, humid days were now replaced by crisp, cold air. The green leaves transformed into crimson, orange, rust and yellow and then dropped from their branches.

Fall was Ernie's favorite time of year. There was nothing quite like taking a picturesque drive along the Lake Superior shore, up to the farthest northern spot in Upper Michigan, a town called Copper Harbor. When in Copper Harbor, Ernie never missed the winding road to the top of Brockway Mountain, the highest scenic roadway between the Rockies and the Alleghenies. Overlooking Lake Superior with iron ore boats in the distance and the majesty of God's colorful palette, Erne thought the drive up Brockway Mountain was the closest glimpse into heaven he could ever get on Earth.

This fall, just like every year, Ernie parked his truck at his favorite lookout point toward the end of the road. He got out of his truck to embrace the rich, natural beauty. The air smelled clean and new, brisk on his cheeks, as if trying to awaken all of his senses. He felt his breath catch in his chest as the perfection overwhelmed him. How awesome is our God, he thought, how incredibly awesome.

After a bite to eat and some souvenir shopping, the return ride took Ernie through the town of Eagle Harbor. Along the lakeshore, he watched tourists dip their toes in the sand and frigid water one last time before the flurries of winter would come. Nearby, children dug in the sand, hoping to unearth an agate, some greenstones, quartz, or unique driftwood. The children knew that beneath that wet sand, there was always a treasure to be found.

Ernie was no different. He parked his car near the beach and meandered to a small opening on the shore where the water was calling him. He rolled up his overalls, took off his socks and boots, and waded through the icy water. Every few seconds, the chill bit too deeply; he jumped out to warm his tootsies in the sand. And moments later, he sloshed back into the water for another thrill. He felt like a child, giggling with delight. He played a game, timing himself to see how long he could actually stay in the water before he could take it no more. *Fourteen seconds.*

As the sun started to set, revealing it's colors of orange, red, and purple, Ernie gathered his blanket and his empty orange soda bottle. He looked over his shoulder for one last glimpse of the idyllic water and setting sun and whispered, "I'll be back after our long winter, my friend."

———— ◦((◦))◦ ————

Fall was also the season of apple-picking. Ernie enjoyed picking apples, making applesauce, and making delicious apple pies. He was not an experienced cook, but he made the town's best apple pie, due to his watchful eyes and helpful hands as a child, watching his mother bake pies. Local ladies marveled at how delicate and flaky his crust was and would bug him for the secret.

His reply: "Use lard ladies, not butter." And soon, they were able to make pie crust as good as Ernie's.

Besides making apple pies, he enjoyed Friday night football games played by the local high schoolers. Many of the kids he knew, including Mike and Mark, played for the team. He enjoyed every moment of showing the kids his support.

This Friday night's game should be a close one, as the Lake Linden-Hubbell Lakes were playing the Wakefield Warriors, and both had the same 7-0 record. As Ernie drove to the football field that evening, he saw swarms of people lined up at the ticket booth. Ernie found a parking spot one block away and strolled to the ticket line. He joined the crowd and could palpate the energy around them. Soon Ernie was laughing and cheering with the others.

As Ernie approached the ticket booth line, he spotted Harry and Father Arnold. They had already waited in line and secured Ernie's ticket. He felt fortunate that he didn't have to brave the crowded line. He shook his friends' hands, they exchanged hellos, and Father Arnold gave Ernie his ticket.

Seating was limited, but they were able to find three seats together near the 30-yard line. Besides, when you go to a game with a priest, it is like the parting of the Red Sea. People will either move over or give up their seats for a man in collar.

"Father Arnold, over here. Father Arnold!" yelled Clara Thomas, who stood up waving her blue and gold flag.

Father Arnold noticed Clara in the stands and gave her a hearty wave.

"Father Arnold, we have a couple of seats over here if you want them."

"Sure, how could I refuse?" Father Arnold answered, turning to Harry and Ernie with a wide smile on his face and a wink of his eye. Harry and Ernie just chuckled because of the familiarity of opportunities opening up for them whenever they were with Father Arnold. Clara Thomas sat down with a proud look on her face too, as if she was guaranteed a fast ride pass to heaven for her good service.

The gentlemen sat down and made small talk with Clara and the fans around them, then Harry waved down a concessions attendant.

Ernie ordered a Nesbitt's orange-flavored pop, and Father Arnold shared a bag of caramel popcorn with Harry. Ernie wished he could eat the caramel popcorn, but due to the limit of not having teeth on top and only a few on bottom, caramel popcorn was not a wise choice.

Before each game would start, all would stand for the singing of the national anthem. Ernie peered toward center field and saw a small brunette girl approach the microphone. She faced the stands and introduced herself as Debbie Pascoe, a student at Lake Linden-Hubbell High School. Ernie was delighted that Debbie had been chosen to sing tonight, as she was a member of the choir that Ernie led at St. Cecilia's church. Ernie was confident that she would belt out an outstanding anthem.

The band began playing the "Star Spangled Banner," Debbie opened her mouth to sing, and her giant voice filled the clouds -- so full that the stars must have twinkled and danced. Ernie smiled, proud of her astonishing presentation and a tear fell, too. The song was always a sentimental one for Ernie.

He recalled his time served in the Navy, fighting for freedom during World War II, and how proud he was to be a citizen of this great land, the United States of America. How lucky he was to afford the freedom of sitting under the stars at a high school football game, when others were living under the stars with no home or protection. Other people were cold, hungry, and forgotten, while Ernie stood toasty warm in his down jacket, with a tummy full of burps from drinking his Nesbitt orange pop too quickly. He often felt guilty about having so much when others in the world had so little. He had a comfortable and secure life, food, water, a home, freedom, and the right to worship God without the risk of being killed for it.

Ernie often felt that when he had stood in line before the Lord to receive his spiritual gifts and talents, he must have stood in the line for compassion twice. He was taken by the need to help his fellow man, to ease his burdens, and witness to Jesus Christ's love whenever possible.

He exemplified the Bible verse from Psalms 82:3-4: *"Defend the poor and fatherless; Do justice to the afflicted and the needy; Deliver the poor and the needy; Free them out the hand of the wicked."*

By halftime, the hometown Lakes team had a slight lead at 10-7. So far it was a clean game with the referees, without any slighted or questionable calls. The energy of the fans was exhilarating, thanks to the cheerleaders with their chants and dance routine. People mingled, hustled for more food to eat, and talked about the possibility of playoffs.

One minute into the second half of the game, the opposing team, the Wakefield Warriors, had advanced to the Lakes' 30-yard line and were within field goal range. On the fourth down, they kicked a field goal to tie up the game. The score was then tied at 10-10.

The score remained tied for what seemed like forever. The faces of everyone in the stands grimaced red with tension. Every attempt by the offense seemed to end in an interception or some kind of turnover. With three minutes to go in the game, the Lakes now had control of the ball at the 48-yard line of the opposing team. On the fourth down, the Lakes' quarterback, Mark, threw the ball 30 yards. Mike caught it and ran in for a touchdown.

The fans went crazy -- arms flailing and voices screaming -- as they thought they had taken the lead. To their dismay, the referee threw down a flag and said, "False start, number 56, offense."

A false start penalty against the Lakes for a player moving over the line before the ball snap. Instead of a touchdown, the Lakes were back up 5 yards, and the crowd sat down in disappointment.

"Oh, Judas Priest! I can't believe that just happened!" Father Arnold huffed in a heated temper.

"Watch your language, Father! You aren't watching this game from the comforts of your own living room," Ernie reminded him, knowing that Judas Priest represented Jesus Christ in a non-derogatory manner.

The opposing team now had control of the ball at the Lakes' 28-yard line. The Wakefield Warriors tried running the ball, but stood no chance against the Lakes' defense.

"C'mon, Lakes. Defense!" Father Arnold yelled.

"Hold'em!" Harry added.

It was now fourth down, and the Wakefield Warriors would have to settle for a field goal. The kicker lined up and the fans hushed into a piercing silence. The world stood still. The kicker lined up the ball. Thud! His cleat cleared the ball across the field, but it was low and the Lakes' lineman blocked it. The Lakes fans launched to their feet with roars of cheering. Their team had the ball once again.

With mere seconds to go on the clock, the game would now go into overtime and another entire quarter of play. The fans could no longer sit in the stands, but rose to their feet for play after play. Both teams had high hopes that they would run the ball in for a touchdown and they would be the talk of the town by pulling off a sensational win.

But each team's optimism was shattered when their plays were unsuccessful. *Pass-run-fumble. Pass-incomplete-sack.* One turnover after another. Neither team had much luck when they had control of the ball. Frustration and nervous tension plaqued the fans, but the cheerleaders cheered on: "Go, fight, win! Go, fight, win!"

Now the Lakes had the ball again. Quarterback Mark threw the ball to a open slotback, but he failed to convert a first down on this recent third-down play. The Lakes had one last try, as this was the fourth down. Would the quarterback pass or punt? Looked like he is going for the first down.

"What a nail-biter!" Ernie whispered to Harry.

"I have had to pee for the past ten minutes, but I cannot get myself to leave. I hope I don't have an accident," Harry said aloud, and the people in front of him turned around and laughed at his boisterous honesty.

The Lakes lined up with three wide receivers, one tight end and one running back at the opposing team's 40-yard line. Mark, the quarterback, threw the ball laterally to his brother Mike, the wide receiver, still behind the line of scrimmage. Instead of running down field, Mike threw the ball laterally across the field to the tight end, Steve Wilkes. As the defense had now shifted back and forth once, Steve then threw the ball across the field to Mark. He ran the ball forward, zigzagging around defenders until he crossed the goal line.

Touchdown!

The play was amazingly breathtaking, and it put the Lakes ahead to win the game.

The fans rushed the field in excitement to congratulate their team on a unforgettable game and a promising 8-0 record. The write-up up in the local newspaper tomorrow would be a good one. Fans slowly moved out of the field and the three gentlemen-two pals and a priest- said their goodbyes and headed home, as well.

What an awesome night, Ernie thought as he slowly drove home, still buzzing from the excitement. *Thank you, Lord, that I can enjoy good times with good friends.*

⎯⎯◦《◎》◦⎯⎯

The next morning, Ernie arrived as always, to the service station at 8 a.m. The local newspaper was sitting at the doorstep. He quickly picked it up so he could read the article of last night's high school football game. On the front page in large letters read:

Bootlegger's Liquor Store robbery on Friday night

Ernie was both surprised and curious about this article, as no crime usually happened around this neck of the woods. He decided he was more interested in reading about the write up of the football game first, and then would go back to reading about the robbery. He turned to page four, the sports section, when he heard the ding-dong bell outside the service station. Someone needed assistance. He greeted the young mother, filled the woman's gas tank, washed the windows and gave a goofy smile and wave to the kids who were watching him through the back rear window. A good start to his day.

He went inside, picked up the newspaper again and turned immediately to page six. His eyes focused on the headline: **Lakes team takes another win**. The story highlighted the play-by-plays and had great pictures to support it. One picture showed the ecstatic fans. To his surprise, he saw his face, as well as Harry's and Father Arnold's staring back at him.

He laughed. Once again, sitting with Father Arnold had its advantages. The photographer had captured a priest and two good friends high-fiving each other with grins that could surely sell a story on its own! He would have to cut the picture out after he read the other leading story about the robbery. He turned back to the front page and read:

Police are looking for a man who stole money from a Dollar Bay business, according to Lt. Sheriff Bob Sheeves. On Friday night at approximately 8:15 p.m., officers say a man went into the Bootlegger Liquor Store, located in Dollar Bay, Michigan. The suspect walked to the counter and purchased a pack of gum with a $20 bill. While the clerk was counting his change, the suspect pulled out a gun and reached into the register. The suspect ran from the store with $656 from the cash register. The clerk, though shaken, was not hurt in the incident. The suspect is described to be about six foot tall, approximately 170 pounds, and possibly 20s to 30s in age. He was wearing a blue ski mask and ran east on foot to a back alley and could not be apprehended by the clerk who had chased after him. Anyone with information about the incident can call the Torch Lake Police Department at 296-4300.

Ernie no sooner finished the article when another car pulled up. Ernie recognized the jovial faces to be Mark and Mike. They immediately launched into the talk of the day: the outstanding football game. The boys were all grins. They discussed the incredible lateral play and how risky it had been to perform it on a fourth down. The boys said they had practiced that play in the past few days and had been ready to use it for a time just like this. Little did they know it would actually work. The boys wrapped up their talk about football and went on to talk about the other incredible talk around town, the liquor store robbery.

"Did you read the article in the paper about the robbery in Dollar Bay?" Ernie asked, as he wiped the dust off the window of Mike's car.

"Yeah, Bootlegger's Liquor Store on Highway M-26," Mike added.

"Hard to believe the clerk had the nerve to chase after him. Too bad he didn't catch the guy," Mark interjected.

"Let's just hope it is an isolated incident. We don't need any trouble around here," warned Ernie, and they all agreed.

Mike walked over to the trunk of the blue Chevy Impala and opened it with his key. He reached inside the trunk and pulled out a heavy black garbage bag and placed it at Ernie's feet.

"Here are some toys that Mom wanted us to drop off for you for the Christmas party," Mark said. "Some good stuff, too: a football, two baseballs, two child's baseball gloves and some old sports jerseys of ours. Some little boy would love this stuff. Maybe you can think of someone who would enjoy it."

"That is great! Many thanks to your momma, boys." Ernie loosened the knot and peered into the bag. He saw the items that the Mark described and they appeared in fantastic shape for two overzealous athletes.

"I can think of two brothers who would be overjoyed to receive these as gifts for Christmas," Ernie beamed.

Scott and Darren Muljo came immediately to mind. Two brothers' sports equipment passed down to two other brothers, who would hopefully get the same thrill of using them.

At 4:00 p.m., Ernie closed up the service station, as he needed to clean up and get to church for Saturday evening mass at 5:30 p.m. The children did a terrific job with the songs for the congregation, and Ernie was especially proud of Denise and Lisa with their "Amazing Grace" solos. Their sweet, angelic voices brought tears to many eyes, as they shared the uplifting melody for the soul. Ernie enjoyed the gospel message at mass from Luke 10:25-37 (NIV):

Just then a religion scholar stood up with a question to test Jesus. "Teacher, what do I need to do to get eternal life?"

He answered, "What's written in God's Law? How do you interpret it?"

He said, "That you love the Lord your God with all your passion and prayer and muscle and intelligence — and that you love your neighbor as well as you do yourself."

"Good answer!" said Jesus. "Do it and you'll live."

Looking for a loophole, he asked, "And just how would you define 'neighbor?'"

Jesus answered by telling a story. "There was once a man traveling from Jerusalem to Jericho. On the way he was attacked by robbers. They took his clothes, beat him up, and went off leaving him half-dead. Luckily, a priest was on his way down the same road, but when he saw him he angled across to the other side. Then a Levite religious man showed up; he also avoided the injured man.

A Samaritan traveling the road came on him. When he saw the man's condition, his heart went out to him. He gave him first aid, disinfecting and bandaging his wounds. Then he lifted him onto his donkey, led him to an inn, and made him comfortable. In the morning he took out two silver coins and gave them to the innkeeper, saying, "Take good care of him. If it costs any more, put it on my bill — I'll pay you on my way back."

"What do you think? Which of the three became a neighbor to the man attacked by robbers?"

"The one who treated him kindly," the religion scholar responded.

Jesus said, "Go and do the same."

While packing up the equipment into his truck, Ernie couldn't get the gospel message out of his head. He liked how Jesus expounded on love, the definition of and the meaning of love -- and how he taught that love takes action and is more than just a feeling. First, you are called to love God with everything in your being. Then you are asked to love your neighbor as yourself. Jesus did not define "neighbor," but rather used a story to make the point discernible. The robber beat and stole from a man and abandoned him for dead. The priest and Levite both caused further harm by not responding to the man in need alongside the road.

Ernie pondered more, taking in the moral of the parable. He soon made the connection that sometimes doing nothing can be just as bad as doing something harmful. The choice to do nothing is a choice not to love. The priest and the Levite were not demonstrating decent kindness to another and absolutely not showing authentic love.

The Samaritan, however, with his compassionate heart, assisted the man, bandaged his wounds, got him off the desolate road, gave him money and promised to return and check on him. Jesus was like the Samaritan, as he was willing to touch the unclean. He would also touch the lost, sick, outcasted and needy. And Jesus knew what it was like to be shunned; he was cast off by lawyers, priests, Pharisees and Sadducees who were not neighborly to him.

Isn't it amazing how merciful Jesus' love is, that he is accepting of anyone, even those who despised him? Ernie pondered. *And Jesus only asks that we show the same love and mercy to others.*

Ernie tried each day to find opportunities to reach out to

someone in need. He even prayed that God would present ways each day where he could step out and display his faith and love in action.

⸺◈⸺

At nearly 7:00 p.m., Ernie hurried to his truck, mindful of how hungry he had become, as his stomach gave out a loud roar. He drove to nearby Lewis' Market to buy a few groceries before the store closed for the evening. He had a hankering for kielbasa sausage, potatoes, and sauerkraut; topping the meal off with some of his homemade applesauce he had canned a month earlier. Nothing too difficult to cook and it would satisfy his ferocious appetite.

He walked into the market rehearsing in his mind the grocery list that he didn't care to put on paper. *Let's see. Kielbasa, a half gallon of whole milk, a dozen eggs, wheat bread.* And of course, his beloved ham sandwich spread. He walked through the quiet store and did not see another customer or a clerk, for that matter. He strolled back to the deli to get the kielbasa and sandwich spread and waited at the counter for a minute, hoping to get some service. Ernie, never appearing an anxious man, crooked his neck and wondered where Paul was. He called out Paul's name and rang the bell that was on the counter. Still, Paul did not show or call out.

"Perhaps he is taking out the trash," Ernie sufficed. He didn't dwell on it, and turned his shopping cart around to continue his shopping.

Bang! The nearby storage area back door suddenly flew open. Boxes fell from the ceiling to the floor. Ernie shuttered, raising his arms to cover his head. Then he gasped. A masked man was stumbling over the pile of boxes about twenty feet away. Ernie stood frozen, hoping not to be seen. The masked man rounded the meat counter. His wide eyes were the only thing Ernie could see, darting

— 46 —

back and forth behind the holes cut into the long blue ski mask. The eyes behind the mask then locked eyes with a frightened Ernie. Suddenly in Ernie's line of vision was the hole of a smokey black pistol.

"Get on the ground, now!" the angry man demanded, his voice loud but quivering.

Ernie backed away from his cart and slowly lowered his body to the ground. He studied the man. His face was concealed by the dark blue ski mask. Ernie noticed the blue and green checkered flannel shirt, faded blue jeans and the Adidas running shoes on his feet. The man seemed to be an ordinary height and weight. Ernie couldn't gather anything else about the man -- or what he was going to do with Ernie.

"Please, spare my life and let me go," Ernie desperately stammered, lowering his head after a quick glance into the eyes of the man now in charge.

The man did not flinch or lower his pistol.

"Please just lower your gun and walk out that door," Ernie again pleaded.

The masked man did not answer but appeared more agitated. Ernie's nerves trembled in time with his hands, poised in prayer, as he knelt before the perpetrator.

The gunman's movements seemed livid, unpredictable, jittery -- ready to make a rash decision in a flash of an impulse. Ernie felt a sudden flush of excitement rush through his chest. He tried to be calm and concentrate on his breathing, as he listened to the man talk nonsense. Through the man's mumbles and moans, Ernie could not understand what he was saying, but the man appeared tormented in his thoughts. Was he mentally ill or on drugs? Ernie did not know but he prayed. *Lord, be with me. Lord, be with him.*

Suddenly, a thundering racket boomed from the back room, startling both Ernie and the masked man. A stumbling, bloody Paul lunged toward the masked man, waving the large meat hook through the air, just missing the left side of the intruder's head.

"Ahhhh!" shrieked Paul, with physical strength and effort far beyond what his wounded body had in him. A valiant try. Paul's decision to try and save Ernie's life may have cost him his own. The masked man turned toward Paul.

"Stupid fool!" he shouted.

Without hesitation, he aimed the pistol at Paul and flicked the trigger. A circle of blood tore through the shirt of his upper abdomen. Paul's body, once so full of vitality, flew lifelessly backward into the boxes strewn across the floor.

Before Ernie had time to let out a whimper or scream, the man turned the gun on Ernie and shot him twice. Blackness. Ernie fell hard against the cold floor. He felt warm, sticky blood ooze near the center of his chest and through his overalls. He could not move, for the pain, for the shock, and for fear of more danger. His thoughts weaved in and out of consciousness. Breathe, he reminded himself. He then heard the bell on the cash register ring open and the front door slammed closed.

"God save me," he whispered.

Stillness.

Shirley Rivers wanted to make a pineapple upside-down cake for her husband, Dave, for his special birthday dinner. It was his favorite. Leave it to her to forget to do the shopping until this late hour of the day. She left home in hope that Lewis' Market would still be open and she could make the cake tonight. She rushed over, thinking the store closed at 7 p.m. She looked at her watch; it was now 7:10 pm.

Oh darn, she thought.

She walked up to the front door to read the sign: "Open until 8 p.m. on Saturdays." She sighed with relief and entered the store, while pulling her shopping list from her disheveled purse. She meandered down the third aisle, which had the baking goods, while she tried to read her shopping list.

A motionless body stretched out on the floor ten feet in front of her. She squinted, unsure of what she was seeing. She removed her reading glasses that she had put on to read her grocery list. She peered again down the narrow aisle.

How can this be? Has someone fainted?

Quite shaken, she moved toward the body with hesitation and then came to the realization that this person was desperately in need of help. Red blood pooled on the floor and the body was not moving. She knelt down quickly and grabbed the limp wrist to feel for a pulse. She felt a weak heartbeat.

"Ernie! Ernie!" she yelled, recognizing the kind man who ran the service station across the street was now the man now lying on the cold floor.

She faintly saw his chest rise and fall. She tilted her head to the side and lowered it just above Ernie's face so she could feel his breath on her cheek. Very little air was being released with his exhale.

She raced to find a telephone behind the deli counter and stumbled upon the boxes scattered all over the floor. Throwing boxes aside, she saw the partially hidden body of Paul. He did not look well. His face was ashy gray and his shirt was saturated in blood. He was not awake.

"Oh, dear God," she said and quickly went to his aid. Something was terrifyingly wrong here, and it was more than just the service station owner's emergency. *Two bodies lay lifeless.* She could feel a fearful sweat rise to the surface of her skin, but she kept moving mechanically. She had to get help.

She saw Paul's shallow breathing but had difficulty finding his radial pulse. She checked the pulse on his neck and it was very faint. Her second and third fingers felt only a slight, slowing thud in his carotid artery. She noticed again his graying color and knew he was not getting oxygen or blood. Paul was near death. She stepped gingerly over his body and grabbed the rotary phone on the wall, quickly dialing 0 for an emergency.

The operator calmly answered, "What is your emergency?"

"Please help me!" Shirley shrieked.

"Stay calm, ma'am," the operator replied. "Are you the person in need of help?"

Shirley stood feet away from Paul with her back against the wall for support so she wouldn't collapse, and blurted out, "No, not me. I am at Lewis' Market on Duncan Avenue in the town of Hubbell. There are two men here that have gunshots! There is a lot of blood and I don't know if they are going to make it! Please send help right away!" She grabbed a tissue from the sleeve of her sweater and wiped her seeping eyes. She was thankful that she had taken her nurses aide training a few years ago and could realize the serious of the situation and the immediate need for help. Labored breathing, slow pulse, blood and unconsciousness were serious conditions for concern.

The operator confirmed the location and reassured Shirley that help was on the way.

"Ma'am, are you sure you are alone in the building, besides the two wounded men?" the operator warned.

Shirley felt a sudden leap in her chest. She could have gone into sheer panic but somehow she felt certain that she was safe.

"I didn't even think that the intruder could still be here. But I do believe that I am alone. All is so quiet here. I am fine."

Shirley hung up the phone and reassessed the situation, kneeling by Paul and taking his pulse again. She still could not feel a pulse. This time, she felt nothing. Her fingers wildly pressed on his arteries of his neck and wrist, but she got no response. She remembered Ernie had a stronger pulse when she had checked, so she decided to stay and treat Paul. She placed her hands on his chest and began compressions to try and start up his heart, each thrust pushing an agonizing wail from her lips.

"Dear Lord, I don't know what to do! Help me!" she cried.

She continued dedicated compressions, hoping for a miracle and a restart of his heart, until she heard the police call out and enter the building. They secured the building and found it clear for entry by the paramedics. The paramedics rushed to the back of the store, where they saw the two badly wounded men on the floor.

Shirley crumpled to the floor in tears when she saw the paramedics round the corner of the aisle. "Help them, please!"

Two paramedics went to Paul's side and two others ran to Ernie. The paramedics assessed the needs of the men. After a thorough inspection for blood loss, breathing and heart rate, they quickly determined that Paul was unconscious, weak from extensive blood loss. The paramedics donned the blood pressure cuff on Paul's arm, pumped the bulb, and waited while the numbers rose and fell. His blood pressure was 60/30, very low and barely alive.

Next, the paramedics took Paul's heart rate in his wrist and found it was increased at a rate of 144 beats per minute; the normal range is 60 to 80 beats. His heart was pumping too hard to try and push blood that was not there. Paul's breathing was shallow, so they placed an oxygen mask over his nose and mouth. They started an IV to help replace the fluid and blood loss, otherwise he could suffer shock from loss of blood volume. CPR compressions and breaths began, and then momentarily stopped so Paul could be lifted onto a long spine board, in case his spine had been injured and to prevent paralysis. Paramedics then transferred him to a gurney.

The paramedics worked quickly, with voices loud and direct, with no expression on their faces. This worried Shirley, who stood in the doorway holding the door open as the gurney rushed by her and rolled to the waiting ambulance. Paul was the first to leave by ambulance, and his situation looked grim. Shirley struggled to keep her sadness from overtaking her and instead moved toward Ernie to check on his condition.

The paramedic who was working on Ernie was greatly concerned that a bullet had pierced Ernie's lung, based on his labored breathing. He worked swiftly, inserting an endotracheal tube down Ernie's throat to help open his airway and restore his breathing. Another paramedic quickly cleaned Ernie's wounds and then called the ambulance dispatcher, updating her on both Paul and Ernie's conditions. The paramedic explained that Paul was en route and that the second patient would be leaving in a few minutes.

The paramedics lifted Ernie onto a long spine board and then onto the gurney and sped him to the waiting ambulance. Both ambulances now raced on the same dark country road within five minutes of one another, in hopes that the medical team waiting at the hospital could restore life to their critically injured bodies.

The police continued to circle the crime scene, taking pictures, taping off areas and dusting for evidence. Shirley waited patiently, though distraught, rubbing her hands over and over, for she knew the police would soon speak with her. She was a possible witness to the crime, and the police would have questions. All she wanted to do was run far away from this horror scene.

"Your name, please?" the one officer asked, looking intently at Shirley.

"Shirley Rivers."

"Please spell your last name."

"R-I-V-E-R-S."

"Address and phone please?'

She answered the policeman slowly, so he could write down the details. As she spoke, she tried to slow her rain and emotions, bracing for the questions to come, the ones that would not be so easy.

"Please tell me clearly every detail you can remember and the time of this event."

Shirley swallowed hard and began.

"I came into the store at 7:10 p.m. I remember the time because I looked at my watch and thought the store may have closed at 7 p.m., and to my surprise the store hours on the door read 8 p.m. I was glad they were still open because I wanted to pick up some ingredients to bake my husband a birthday cake," she responded straightforwardly, giving the facts, but still visibly shaken.

The officer continued to listen to Shirley's statement as she gave explicit details. She couldn't forget a thing, even if she wanted to.

"I walked down the baked goods aisle and saw a man on the ground. I immediately saw a some blood on the floor and I couldn't believe my eyes. I went over to him and recognized the man to be Ernie Price, a gentlemen who owns the service station across the street."

"Did you see anyone else in the store or hear anything?"

"No. I did not hear anything but Ernie's struggle to breathe. I didn't see anyone else until I got up to go to the phone, near the deli, and that is when I saw the owner, Paul Lewis, on the floor partially covered by some boxes."

Shirley bit her fingernails as she waited for the officer to write down her statement. She glanced down the aisle and Ernie's blood was still visible on the linoleum tile. She felt sick to her stomach and shuffled her stance. Had she been minutes earlier, she too could have been one of the dying bodies on the gurneys. But then again, she thought, if she did not walk into the store when she had, the men could have died on the cold floor.

The officer finished his statements and said that Shirley could go home. Shirley felt relief but there was one last thing she needed to do.

Shirley knelt quietly nearby, and out of the way of the police. She prayed reverently for two men who needed God's tender mercy now more than ever.

"He who dwells in the shelter of the Most High will rest in the shadow of the Almighty. I will say of the Lord, 'He is my refuge and my fortress, my God, in whom I trust.' Surely he will save you from the fowler's snare and from the deadly pestilence. He will cover you with his feathers, and under his wings you will find refuge; his faithfulness will be your shield and rampart. You will not fear the terror of night, nor the arrow that flies by day, nor the pestilence that stalks in the darkness. Psalm 91: 1-6 (NIV).

"Dear Lord, be with your children, Paul and Ernie, and surround them with your angels. Give them your love and protection. Amen."

Shirley rose to her feet and left the market to drive home to her husband, Dave. He must be so worried. What a story she would tell him tonight.

⸻ ◈ ⸻

Ernie could faintly hear the siren of the ambulance and the voices of the paramedics as they tried to resuscitate him.

"How is the bleeding?" one paramedic asked the other.

"His bleeding appears under control but who knows what type of internal injuries he has. But he does appear in better shape than the guy in the other ambulance," he declared. Ernie heard another voice respond, as if Ernie were not there. But he heard.

Ernie lay helpless on the gurney, unable to move or speak, as the two paramedics worked desperately to save his life. They worked without hesitation and kept talking to Ernie intermittently, leaning down close to him, speaking firmly as if to stir a response.

"Mr. Price, we are two minutes from the hospital. You hang in there. Be strong," the first paramedic encouraged, hoping that Ernie could hear his words beyond his trance. They patted Ernie's hand and shook the gurney, anything to alert him.

Ernie could sense the pressure of the tube in his left wrist, and the gentle tugs of the paramedics as they continuously monitored his vitals. His eyes were heavy and he was unable to open them. This was probably a good thing as Ernie was afraid of the flurry of activity he might see. Try as he might, Ernie could not respond to the paramedics requests. He wanted too but was incapable of doing so. His eyes were heavy and unable to open, but his ears were alert and took in the commotion around him. His mind was strong and he aware of his surroundings. His thoughts flashed back to the masked gunmen who paced incessantly before being startled; turning the gun on Paul and then Ernie. *But why? Why did this happen?*

Suddenly, he felt an explosion in his chest, a pain so pure and full that the sensation ripped his consciousness away from his body, unexpectedly extracted his soul away from his life and thrust him into an uncertain realm that only few experience. Ernie was gone. Gone from what he understood as life on Earth, at least. He could feel his body shake and he grimaced. Yet, it was not his body anymore, just a mere vessel without self control. The shaking subsided as he rose above it all into a lightness. The tranquility was indescribable.

The space around him appeared to close in on him, except for a halo of light that pulled him into what appeared to be a passageway or tunnel. The light was magnificently bright, growing brighter the further he traveled through this passage. He had no concept of how fast he was going, or why this was happening, or where he was going. And oddly, he did not care.

The tunnel ride, with its turns and bright lights was the best carnival ride Ernie could ever be on. He smiled and delighted in each twist and turn, anticipating the next. But the ride soon slowed down and came to a stop. He was still smiling and content even though he did not know where he was.

Ernie no longer felt enclosed. He gradually drifted into an area ablaze in numerous colors; as vibrant as a rainbow and radiant as jewels. This place seemed to glisten like snow on a sunny day or raindrops on reflective glass. It was the most beautiful place he had ever seen.

He tried to step forward into this incredible place. His feet did not step, but rather he *flew* forward with no effort of his body whatsoever. What he heard could only be described like the fluttering of feathers of birds at a park. He looked about and did not see any birds but heard soft voices, giggling, and the cooing came closer.

He felt a hand on his shoulder and he turned to see the loveliest face that he could ever remember. He thought his eyes were deceiving him. Standing before him was his mother in a beautiful cream-colored lace dress. She looked young, vibrant, healthy and oh so happy! Her blue eyes sparkled like the azure ocean.

"Mother! Oh, Mother! I have missed you," Ernie exclaimed.

He reached for his mother but could not feel her touch. Rather, his hands swept through her image, like he was trying to grab for a ray of light. Ernie reached for her again. Though he was standing only an arm's length away, he could not reach her. But in irony, when she reached forward to hug him, he felt the warmest embrace, and it was just like he remembered. Loving, protecting, welcoming.

Walking up behind his mother was a tall, handsome young man, smoking a cigar and wearing a gray flannel fedora. The woodsy fragrance of the tobacco infused the air with it's mellow scent. It was a smell he fondly remembered.

Ernie focused his eyes again. Yes. It was his father. He, too, looked marvelous, young and had so much vitality. He walked with a skip in his step and appeared to be dancing, as he made his way toward Ernie. Gone was the bad limp his father had walked with for years. Gone was the slim rosewood cane that was always near his side due to his rheumatoid arthritis.

"Son. We have waited for this time!" his father said, holding his son in his arms, while patting his back three times like he had always done.

Ernie was overtaken with excitement and disbelief. Standing before him were his mother and father! He felt overwhelming love and happiness, but he could not shed a tear. He felt the pressure in his eyes to cry but not one tear drop fell. How odd, he thought. Tears fell naturally when he usually thought of his parents and how much he missed them. It had been nearly fifteen years since he heard his father's deep baritone voice and two years since he had seen his mother's sweet smile. Ernie looked quizzically at them both and tried to make sense of where he was and how this could possibly be happening. In order to see his parents, this had to either be a dream -- or he had to be dead.

Was this heaven -- this beautiful place before him? Or was this the most detailed, unimaginable and unattainable dream he had ever dreamed? If it was a dream, he never wanted to wake from it. No. He for certain believed this was heaven. Because a dream could not possibly look or feel this glorious!

"Son, you have been in an accident," his mother said gently. She hesitated before continuing. She reached over to touch his hand, anticipating his shock and disbelief. "You are indeed... dying. And you are on the edge of heaven. As much as we want to welcome you to heaven and share this wonderful place with you forever, we have been appointed to ask if you are ready for your life on earth to be over?"

"I am dying? *Dying*. But I feel no pain!" Ernie stated numbly, surprised by his thoughts and his words.

"There is no pain in heaven, son," his mother answered. "God wipes away all tears from your eyes. There will be no more death, sorrow or crying here. God's kingdom is glorious that's true, but better yet is that we get to see, feel, touch and talk to our Father God any time we wish."

"When will I see God?" Ernie gasped with glee. "I have imagined this moment my whole life."

"We were sent by our Lord to greet you and to explain to you that your journey here may be short. God has allowed this glimpse of heaven to you so that you might witness to others that there is, indeed, a heaven," his mother explained. "Our time is also to give you hope, knowing someday you will return."

"Return? But I just got here! I don't understand."

His father chimed in, "God knows how much you have missed us and how difficult it has been since your mother has passed. The years without us has left you lonely. Our time together, though short, is meant to comfort you."

"It has been difficult living day to day without your company. The little house is still too big for me," Ernie muttered.

"And you may return to that 'little house' for years before you come back here to the 'big house.' Heaven that is," his mother smiled.

Ernie thought for a moment and asked his pensive questions. "If I go home, who will take care of me? Will I be able to recover from the injuries of this accident? Can my life be as full as it once was?"

"Sure, you will experience pain upon your return to Earth, as you will need to rehabilitate yourself following your accident. You will recover in a short time and you will be stronger in body and in character. God's plans for you are incomplete and there are many good and godly things awaiting you on earth. Leaving that life now will leave a hole in the lives of many who need you," his father beamed.

"We are privy to what is in store for you, son, and we promise, you won't want to miss a moment of it. Our God is so good in taking care of the details," his mother added.

"But the decision to stay or go is yours. Either way, it is a win for your mother and I," his father said.

Ernie pondered their words and his feelings were stirring. It was hard to choose life. Death was so easy, in comparison to returning to a place of toil, pain and uncertainty. A place separate from the vision and hand of God, anytime. And his parents. This sensation of bliss in their presence warmed and tickled his spirit. To return to Earth and step away from this place would hurt more than anything physical. The mere idea felt like it was ripping his soul in half. All his life he had strived just to bring himself closer to God, and that perfect union was now just one choice away.

But earth was also a place of growth, he reminded himself. People needed him back there. Who? He wondered. And what -- what exactly did God have lined up for him? What experiences lie ahead that would stretch his mind, ignite his soul and build his character? He didn't want to leave, but deep in the core of his being, he sensed God's calling for him -- still calling. He was not done doing God's work. Not just yet.

"I do love my life, but I don't want to leave just yet," Ernie finally said out loud. "Please, let's walk and share these special moments together before I must go."

Ernie felt his mother and father take his hand and move him forward. Each step was like walking on a cloud of fluffy marshmallows.

Ahead in the distance he saw a huge structure that was shiny and gold. The closer he got, the more he could make out the details. It was an enormous gate with high arches and ornate detail. Large iridescent pearls decorated the gate in amazing opulence. The gate was open. He saw people pass through it, and he heard roars of laughter and applause.

"At the gate, we will need to leave you," his father said. "Once you pass this gate, there is no turning back, and you will remain in heaven forever."

Ernie steps ceased and he squeezed his parents hands, before he released them slowly. He fidgeted nervously as if he was again a young lad with something bad to tell his parents. He didn't wanted to disappoint them.

"As much as I would love to stay and meet my Maker face to face, I trust that he has unfinished work with me," Ernie said. "I love my life on Earth. I have a job, friends, my volunteer work --"

"It is apparent that you are loved very much and your absence would be felt and missed by many," his mother added.

Suddenly, Ernie thought about his mother's own passing into heaven.

"Mother, on the day that you died, did you question if you should return to earth or stay in heaven?" Ernie asked.

"I did not question it at all."

The answer surprised Ernie.

"Why not? Didn't you miss your life and feel bad about leaving your life or leaving me?"

"Of course I felt the apron strings stretch wanting to be back in my home and to continue to be your mother. But you were a grown man. Besides, I was sure that God would take care of you."

"What does being a grown man have to do with anything? I loved living with you and was especially fond of caring for you once father passed away."

"But caring for me left you a bachelor."

Ouch. Even in heaven his mother could have a "Mother Knows Best" moment. Her words stung, as he knew they were partially true.

"Mama, that is not true," Ernie said, trying to be convincing.

"Honey, besides your work, church and caring for me, it left little time to find love."

"Mama! That's hogwash! How do you *find* love anyway?" he retorted. "I figure if it is to happen, God will make it happen. It just hasn't happened with me. Not everyone settles down and gets married."

Ernie's father piped in and said, "You can find love in the strangest of places. I met your mother when my horse got lost and wandered into her backyard while she washing clothes on the washboard outside. The horse ran blazing saddles through her clothesline of freshly dried clothes! Your mother dropped her washboard and helped me chase down the horse. Days later, we fell in love."

His mother bellowed, "I got a horse and husband. Not a bad deal." They all broke out in joyous laughter.

"I find this all to be so strange. I am in heaven talking with my mother and father about falling in love. Shouldn't we be talking about more interesting things on our limited time? Or fun, fascinating questions about the Bible- like, where did Noah park the ark? Where are the lost tribes of Israel? Who is the Beloved Disciple?"

"Or what came first, the chicken or the egg?" added his father, and they all rumbled again with laughter.

"You have such an incredible heart, son," whispered his mother. "You have so much love to give. Don't be afraid to share it. May you experience every day with an optimism to find all of its treasures, including the love of a lady you can share your life with."

Ernie smiled politely but wasn't buying it. Love, that is.

Their laughter faded and the walk got quieter, as they drew closer to the gate, each knowing that this moment was not infinite and would soon be over.

His father spoke up. "We are at the gate now, son. I apologize for the haste, but we need your official decision."

"I am certain about my decision, that I will leave you both at this gate and return to Earth. I know we'll be together someday, but not now," Ernie said.

His parents cheered, which was not the emotion Ernie had expected.

"Next time we meet, and on that glorious day, it will be for eternity. Now go back home and continue to work on your crown of life. The crown you will receive when you come back to heaven for good will be magnificent," his mother said, beaming.

The three became distracted by a loud cheer, and Ernie turned and looked to his right. He thought he recognized a familiar face. This man was wearing a long, white flowing gown and he was moving rather quickly towards the gate. A loud voice amplified the area and announced, "Please welcome, Paul Anthony Lewis."

Ernie was startled by the name. At first, he smiled, picking up on the excited energy and recognizing his friend's wide grin. But then he realized what it meant. He wanted to yell out, "No!" He was unable to express his true emotion as he realized that Paul, too, was dying, and he may not be returning to the same place Ernie was.

"Paul! Paul!" Ernie loudly yelled.

Paul stopped and looked over his left shoulder to see Ernie a few feet behind him. Paul waved happily and leaned over to two people, presumably to be his loved ones, said a few words, and then rushed over to Ernie. Paul threw his arms around Ernie's shoulders and gave him a big bear hug.

"Ernie! Meeting at the pearly gates! Is this place amazing or what? Do you start your new life in paradise today?" Paul asked.

"I am awestruck by it all, and I don't know what to say."

"This is the place we have prepared for our entire lives, and the best is beyond this gate; at least that is what my father and sister told me." Paul pointed to the direction of the gate where his father and sister, Janie, were standing.

"You remember my father, John, don't you, Ernie? And this is Janie. Do you remember her, Ernie?"

Ernie recognized Paul's father. He had passed away just two years ago of a sudden stroke. Ernie felt a pit in his stomach when he looked at Janie. He thought of her often and struggled with a decision he had made long ago that he wasn't proud of. Janie did not deserve to be treated that way.

Ernie and Paul had been young boys. Ernie was nine and Paul was seven when Janie had been found facedown in the lake during a church event down by the water. The little three-year-old had wandered away without anyone noticing, probably chasing butterflies or jumping toads. It was Paul and Ernie who had found her lifeless body unresponsive when they pulled her from the lake fifteen minutes later. She was already dead.

The sweet little girl who only wanted to play ball with Paul, Ernie and the older boys that day, was told to "find something else to do." Paul did not want to play with his younger tagalong sister. Besides, it was a special occasion that young Paul could play ball with Ernie and the older teenage boys. He admired them so much and wanted to be a big boy like them that day. So Janie had found something else to do on her own, and that day haunted Paul and Ernie every day of the rest of their lives. They felt tremendous guilt over sending her away.

The little blonde girl in pigtails now stood before Ernie. He looked down at her, trembling, but she smiled. She grabbed his shaking hand and said, "Ernie, don't be sad that you didn't let me play ball. God told me to come down to the lake. He wanted me to see the angels."

Again, Ernie could not cry. But he wanted to. He picked up Janie in his arms and held her close, rocking her and whispered, "I am so sorry Janie."

She just giggled. "You are so silly, Ernie!"

Ernie felt the guilt of a lifetime banish from his soul as he placed beautiful Janie back on her feet.

"So are you coming, Ernie?" Paul insisted and took Ernie's hand, trying to lead him toward the enormous gate. Ernie squeezed Paul's hand and pulled back.

"I will be back here someday, but for today, it is just a visit and a glimpse of how wonderful it will be when I do return," he said.

"I understand. It is not your time. But for me, it's today. God's plan for my life is finished. It was written since my birth, and this now is now my eternal home," Paul said.

Ernie was surprised by the news and quickly said, "But you are younger than I, Paul. You have a family to go back to."

Ernie's parents laughed.

"Son, God does not keep track of when He should take an old person or a young person to heaven. No balance sheets or tallies. We welcome people of all ages, races, shapes and sizes. God welcomes everyone who chooses to follow Him and live their life according to His plan. Even children dance in heaven's streets."

"I dance in the streets everyday and paint and play harps and work in the garden and --" Janie exclaimed, almost out of breath.

Ernie's thoughts went back to Paul's family who, in Paul's absence, would be devastated. "What about Barbara. And the kids?"

Paul paused for a moment remembering his beautiful wife, son and daughter. "God always provided for us when we were all together as a family and he will continue to provide for Barbara and the kids in my truancy. Please tell her and the kids how much I adore and love them and that we had a beautiful life together. I will be watching with anticipation from above to see how their lives unfold. Please watch after them for me," Paul said. "Goodbye, Ernie. I love you, brother."

He turned away and walked toward his loved ones, eager to see everything that awaited him on the other side of the ornate gate..

Ernie murmured his name again. "Paul! Paul! Goodbye. I love you, friend. Goodbye Mr. Lewis, goodbye Janie."

Paul did not turn his head toward Ernie again; rather he grabbed the hands of his father and sister, and they walked cheerfully through the gold and pearl gate. Well, actually, Janie skipped.

Ernie's parents laid their hands on Ernie's shoulders to comfort him.

"It was his time, son. Paul fulfilled God's purpose and plan and he is now home in heaven," Ernie's father replied.

"There will be tears of sadness on Earth in Paul's departure, but those who love Christ will come to understand the joy that awaits Paul and everyone who believes in Him," assured his mother.

Ernie questioned, "And Janie believed in God? She was so young. Did she fulfill her purpose?"

Ernie's mother continued, "She did. Her soul was pure and shined with love for our God, even at the tender age of three. Her time on Earth was a gift from God but only for a short time. That was always God's plan."

Ernie's father cleared his throat and began the dismissal process.

"It is time to go now. As we walk through the gate, you will return to earth and your life as you know it. I love you, son," said his father, embracing Ernie.

"I love you so much," his mother said, stroking Ernie's face with the most jubilant smile of love on her face.

They all held hands and walked to the gate. There was no sadness, just contentment and understanding.

Ernie smiled back with his arms outstretched, taking it all in. Angels fluttered about, some giggling and some singing. He touched the engraved golden gate with its pearls the size of baseballs. He reached for the gate handle to lead his parents back inside, when suddenly the light became dimmer and dimmer. The jewels adorning the gate began to lose their lustre.

His body felt strange and heavy. A dizzy feeling came over him, and he began moving quickly away from the gate by a force not his own. He saw his parents in the distance waving. Angels were no longer giggling or singing. Instead, he heard voices yelling and machines beeping. Then a final buzzing sound vibrated through the machine. Someone spoke.

"Flatline. Time of death: 7:55 p.m."

The room was still, except for the doctor who removed his surgical mask. He threw the mask to the floor and started heading for the door. A nurse unplugged the machine. Another nurse just stared. This was her first day as a registered nurse, fresh out of school. This was the first person she had witnessed pass away.

Suddenly, Ernie gasped for air, choking on the tube that was inserted into his throat. He felt his body thrash upward, and he was restrained by two firm hands on his shoulders. He opened his eyes slightly and could see many faces of people he did not know hovering over him. They started yelling.

"Mr. Price, Mr. Price! Can you hear us? Wake up, Mr. Price!"

One nurse shouted out, "He is coming back! Doctor! Wait!"

Another nurse plugged in the machine and waited for signals of his heart activity. "Yes! His heart is beating again."

"Praise God!" the new nurse cried out.

The faces of the medical staff went from discouragement to delight. They were witnessing a true miracle.

"Get him hooked up to the ventilator quickly. Call the operating room immediately. His lung is probably swimming in blood. He needs surgery now if there is any chance for his survival beyond this moment," the doctor ordered, not ready to smile just yet. "He has a chance."

Chapter 5

Ernie winced at the glaring, bright light. Finally his eyes adjusted. He managed to focus his eyes on a nurse who hovered above him. Her eyes were wide and teary, but the smile on her face told him it wasn't sadness. The whole room bubbled with excitement.

"Mr. Price. Mr. Price, please squeeze my hand if you hear my voice."

Ernie stared at the pretty redheaded nurse and comprehended her request. His nimble fingers reached for the comfort of her grip, and he managed to squeeze he gloved hand lightly. His eyes continued to blink slowly, gazed over with confusion. She knew she would not have much time to provide comfort and reassurance before he dozed off again.

"That is great, Mr. Price. Mr. Price, you are in the hospital, and we are taking very good care of you. We need to do an operation to help you with your breathing. Do we have your consent?" the nurse inquired.

He could feel the touch of the doctor and other nurses working on him. The blood pressure cuff squeezed his arm again and the doctor kept checking his reflexes in his feet and hands for blood flow and sensation response. The pain in his chest increased. He winced, arching his back, as a gasp hissed from his lips.

"Try not to move, Mr. Price. We need you to remain still. Mr.

Price, do we have your consent for surgery? Please squeeze my hand for your answer to be yes."

Ernie again touched the gloved hand and squeezed it as tightly as he could. He remained still, listening, waiting to respond to any additional requests.

"Schedule the operating room stat. We need to get this bullet out of his lung immediately. Call the anesthesiologist to get his surgery IV started," the doctor ordered.

As his chest throbbed again, Ernie's thoughts flashed to a smokey black pistol pointed at him. Be still, he reminded himself. He now understood the reason for his excruciating pain, his struggle with every inhale and the seriousness of his condition. *Be still and know I am God.* He then drifted back to sleep.

The surgery team assembled and began the grueling operation twenty minutes later. They knew the difficulties of this surgery. Would his heart give up, trying to work despite his lungs filling with blood and not air? Could they sustain his blood volume after he had lost heavy amounts of blood?

Beyond the surgery ward, friends started assembling in a nearby waiting room. They waited nervously, yet patiently. Some were on bended knees and others clutched each other's hands in a prayer group, as they awaited any news about Paul or Ernie.

Harry, Greta and Father Arnold sped down the long hallway toward Barbara Lewis, who was crouched over in a loveseat with her hands covering her eyes. Her long blonde hair fell around her face and added a shield to hide her from the blackened run of her mascara. Sobs were heard the closer they became.

"Barbara, dear," Father Arnold murmured.

Barbara heard the familiar voice and stood, shaking, but eager to feel the embrace of someone who cared. She took an unsteady step toward Father Arnold. She fell into his outstretched arms and sobbed uncontrollably again his chest. Greta stroked her Barbara's golden hair and Harry stood nearby with his head downward, tears falling to the floor.

Suddenly, the door to the operating room swung open. Everyone in the waiting room froze, whipping their heads around to see who it as. A tall, slender, middle-aged doctor walked out to meet them. His expression was unreadable and was not immediate hope for the waiting bunch. Was the news about Ernie or Paul?

"Barbara Lewis?" the doctor asked. Still, no waver in his voice gave away whether this would be the hardest moment of her life, or the most relieving one. Time seemed to move in slow motion for her, and she could barely utter a response from her lips.

Barbara turned to the doctor and shuddered. "Yes, I am Barbara Lewis." She took a step toward the doctor, and his gaze dropped downward.

The doctor pushed his wire-rimmed silver glasses higher up onto his nose, when he finally raised his glance to meet Barbara's anxious eyes. He spoke.

"Your husband came in with two severe gunshots to the abdomen, and one bullet severed a major artery. The emergency surgery was very difficult, and he lost a lot of blood prior to arrival to the hospital. I am sorry --"

Before he could finish the sentence, Barbara felt her knees begin to buckle. Father Arnold grabbed her elbow to hold her upright, as the doctor continued, his voice growing softer with sorrow.

"Our surgery to save his life was unsuccessful."

Barbara opened her mouth but could not make a word or even a sound.

"We could not save his life," the doctor repeated. "I am so very sorry."

Every muscle in her face and neck felt so tense, that she felt they might burst. Her beloved Paul was gone. She felt the unbearable weight of her world crashing down onto her shoulders.

Harry rushed to help Father Arnold, before she completely collapsed to the floor. They carefully lowered her to a nearby loveseat. Harry held Barbara and she dug her face into his strong shoulder. Harry felt the wetness of her tears soak through his shirt onto his skin.

The doctor remained in their presence for a few moments. His eyes watered beneath his eyeglasses and he began to sniffle. He could never explain the difficulty of bearing this kind of unforeseen news that would change so many lives in an instant.

He paused, knowing that what needed to be said next was the most difficult to say.

"Mrs. Lewis, when you are ready we can take you back so you can say your goodbye to your husband. We also have staff who can assist you with funeral planning," he said solemnly. He walked over to her and placed his hand on her shoulder. "Again, my deepest condolences."

He turned and walked away.

Barbara felt panic in her throat and her legs shook. She, as well as the others, were all completely unprepared for this. Barbara sat on the loveseat with her knees tucked tightly against her chest, rocking and crying inconsolable tears. The love of her life was gone.

She had spent every day since she was sixteen with Paul by her side. Every morning she heard his voice and felt his kiss on her lips, and every night before bed, his arms cradled her to sleep. *This cannot be real! If it is, how could life go on without him?*

How could she break the news to their two young children, Randy and Rachel? She thought she might be sick. She leaned over, clutching her stomach tightly. The children adored their father, and at the tender ages of ten and eight, how could they deal with their father's absence? *They are too young to deal with this! I cannot deal with this!* Barbara worried if her faith was enough to sustain her through her sorrow. *Lord, I need you! Help me!*

Greta and Father Arnold tried to comfort her. They allowed her time to talk and cry and yell; let all her emotions come out. And they prayed.

Ten minutes later, Harry returned from the cafeteria with a cup of ice water and a box of tissues. Barbara sipped the water and it soothed her aching throat. She reached for Father Arnold's hand. He took her trembling hand into his sweaty palm.

"I can't even pray right now. I know prayers are needed at this moment but my words would only be a jumbled, emotional mess. Father Arnold, could you you please pray?"

Father Arnold nodded his head yes and reached his other hand to Greta who at his left. The prayer circle formed, hand in hand, with all the shaken in the room. They bowed their heads.

"Father, the cares of this world have overcome us with sadness, at the loss of our brother, Paul, who is a husband to Barbara, father to Randy and Rachel and friend to us all. Help us to never doubt You or Your loving care for us in our time of need. Help us not be fearful or anxious and to grant us peace and understanding in the days ahead. We pray your protection over our friend Ernie who is fighting for his life. Give him strength to hold on."

Father Arnold then recited Psalm 23:

The Lord is my Shepherd, I shall not want.
He makes me lie down in green pastures,
He leads me beside quiet waters, he restores my soul.
He guides me in paths of righteousness for His name's sake.
Even though I walk through the valley of the shadow of death,
I will fear no evil, for You are with me;
Your rod and Your staff, they comfort me.
You prepare a table before me in the presence of my enemies.
You anoint my head with oil; my cup overflows.
Surely goodness and love will follow me all the days of my life,
and I will dwell in the house of the Lord forever.
Amen.

After the prayer, Barbara staggered over to the receptionist in the waiting room and said the most difficult words she thought she could ever say.

"I would like to say goodbye to my husband, Paul Lewis." And she wept.

"Yes," the woman answered.

The unit clerk stood up and gingerly took Barbara by the arm. They slowly walked down the never ending hallway, followed closely by Father Arnold, who would administer the last sacrament rites. Harry grabbed Greta's hands, and they continued to pray for Barbara at this incomprehensible time. They prayed for Ernie, too. They had not received any word of his condition yet.

Father Arnold stood by the door with his head lowered as Barbara walked into the quiet room, trying to surmount courage beyond what she thought she was capable. She saw a large hanging light above a bed in the center of the room. Her eyes followed the white sheet from the bottom to the top until she was face-to-face with her beloved Paul.

How serene he looked at rest, she thought. There was no trauma to his face, and he looked as though he were merely sleeping. Barbara knew that below the clean sheet was a gruesome sight of blood and bullet wounds. She tried to erase that last thought out of her mind and tried to concentrate more on how he was now at rest with his Savior, Christ the Lord. She knew his home on Earth was temporary and his home in heaven was eternal. Yet her heart still struggled, because she wanted him here to continue to live out their lives together, to be the wonderful husband and father who loved her and the children with his entire being.

She walked toward Paul and rested her hand in his. His lifeless hand was still warm to the touch. Her fingers squeezed his hand, and she could feel the wedding ring that graced his left ring finger. Her finger repeatedly circled his wedding ring. Til death do us part. No, she was still his. Always would be.

Her heart flooded with the memory of the day they had bought their wedding bands. Paul wanted a gold band with two small diamonds side by side, because they would be side by side, forever. Barbara liked the two diamonds for another reason. She always wanted two children and the diamonds represented the love of their union and hope for a family. The rings also symbolized unbroken love and commitment. She vowed to honor him all the days of her life. She had never imagined on that happy wedding day that death too early would rob her of a lifetime of tomorrows. *Do we ever know what the days have in store for us?* She wondered. *Only God knows.*

Barbara recalled the Bible verse from Romans 8:38-39: *And I am convinced that nothing can ever separate us from his love.*

Or Paul's love, she added silently to herself.

Death can't, and life can't. The angels can't, and the demons can't. Our fears for today, our worries about tomorrow, and even the powers of hell can't keep God's love away. Romans 8:38 (NLT)

"Nothing in all creation will ever be able to separate me from the love of my husband, Paul." This time, she spoke the words out loud. They seemed to hang in the air, searching for something to grasp onto, searching for Paul's response.

Tears flooded down her face as she leaned in to kiss the lips of her husband for the last time. Their lips touched, and a tear fell peacefully between their joined lips.

Barbara breathed, "I love you always and forever."

She held Paul close one last time, her head nuzzled gently under his chin. His Aqua Velva after-shave lingered, and she deeply inhaled the fresh smell, feeling it travel to the depths of her lungs and filling her body. She had watched Paul splash the after-shave cologne on his shaven face this morning, while she leaned over the sink brushing her teeth. This everyday routine would forever change. She cringed inside.

She reached for Paul's left hand and slowly removed the wedding ring from his left finger. She held the ring tightly in her hand and turned toward Father Arnold. She motioned for him to come forward. He moved to her side and stood peering down at Paul, his friend, who was covered to his neck with a white sheet.

Paul's emotionless face was hard for Father Arnold to accept and his eyes welled with tears. Paul had always been a happy, gregarious man with a zest for life, warm smile and a jolly laugh. Arnold was comforted knowing that the man before him was now a spiritual body soaring with the angels, living a happy, eternal existence. His natural body, like he was witnessing now, would remain on Earth, an empty vessel that had fulfilled it's earthly purpose.

Father Arnold began to administer the Anointing of the Sick sacrament, otherwise known as, the last rites. He took the bottle of holy oil and touched Paul's forehead and made the sign of the cross. He spoke.

"'Through this holy anointing, may the Lord in his love and mercy help you, Paul, with the grace of the Holy Spirit."

Father Arnold then anointed Paul's hands, making the sign of the cross with the holy oil, saying, "May the Lord who frees you from sin save you and raise you up. Amen."

Father Arnold then nodded to Barbara and turned toward the door. Barbara looked again at Paul, and she could not resist touching his face one last time.

"For whatever reason, God wanted you in heaven now, my love. I may not ever understand why. So, I ask God right now to pour his peace over me. When I am fearful of my future, let me remember that it is God who has given us a number of days to walk this Earth. And even though you have left my side, Paul, God will never leave my side. When I am overwhelmed and don't know where to turn, I will trust in Him and he will make my path straight. And someday that path will lead me back to you, my love. I love you. Goodbye."

When Barbara and Father Arnold reached the others in the waiting room, they were met by another doctor, who finally had an update on Ernie's condition. Apprehension filled their hearts and rattled their minds. *Would there be good news this time?*

"Ernie arrived at the hospital with two gunshot wounds to the chest. The injury lodged a bullet in the lower left lobe of his left lung. He is in surgery now to examine the extent of his injury and hopefully we can repair the lung. He is in critical condition at this time and it is uncertain if he will be able to survive the injuries he received," the doctor cautioned.

A hush fell among the friends, as the grave danger of another friend possibly dying became frighteningly eminent.

They huddled in prayer, lifting up their friend Ernie and asking for God's protection of his life, and for the surgeon and team working on his fragile body.

"Father Arnold, could you please drive me home? I am exhausted and need to rest before the children wake up. Will someone keep me informed of Ernie's condition in the morning?" Barbara asked, after the prayers faded off.

Greta spoke up, "I will call you in the morning, Barbara. Please try to find some rest. Let me know how I can be of help tomorrow."

"Thank you so much, Greta. Thank you all." Barbara looked gratefully into the eyes of Harry, Greta and Father Arnold, people who had loved her and Paul through the years. "Your support now and in the days to come is so appreciated."

Father Arnold guided her down the long hallway and out the door into the cold, dark night.

On the drive home, Barbara kept thinking of her children, Randy and Rachel. They were surely asleep at this late hour, while her own parents grieved quietly and waited up for Barbara to return home. She decided she would wait and let the children sleep peacefully tonight, before delivering the alarming news: that their daddy was no longer coming home. The news would change their lives forever. *Be with me, Lord.*

Harry and Greta agreed to remain at the hospital until the doctor could give an update on Ernie's condition. They made more phone calls and the prayer chain grew. The prayer group prayed for the days ahead, for the Lewis family following the untimely death of Paul and for the successful outcome of Ernie's operation. They prayed for the perpetrator who committed the crime and prayed for their small town to recover from such a heinous act.

———————⟫•⟪———————

News about the shooting was circulating around town that late evening. The townspeople heard there had been a robbery at Lewis' Market and that two men were shot. People speculated that Paul was probably one of the victims, as he owned the store and worked countless hours there. Ernie's red Ford truck was parked in front of the market, so many believed Ernie was the other victim. Numerous police cars were parked near the market with their beacon lights orbiting in the dark night sky Crime scene tape marked off the entrance into the market and the shades were pulled down in the windows. The sign in the window still read "open."

Soon the news would be confirmed; indeed, Paul had been killed in the robbery and Ernie's life was hanging on by a thread. People wondered if the burglary tonight was connected to the liquor store robbery the night before. Why would someone harm two people in attempts to get a couple hundred dollars from a cash register? Why?

The entire town would share the pain and grief. This close-knit town of family and friends shared each other's joys and sorrows, lifting each other up when someone stumbled, and cheering from below when someone soared. They would need to all pull together so sorrow would not overcome them.

——————

Hours passed away. Harry and Greta managed to rest a little on the couches in the waiting room. Everyone else had left and gone home. Dozing in and out of slumber and restlessness, they prayed when there was a wakeful moment. Still no word about Ernie. Had someone forgot to update them? Did the hospital staff not realize that they were waiting for news?

Greta decided to find a nurse who could possibly learn anything to ease their worried minds. The nurse returned shortly to Harry and Greta in the waiting room.

"The surgery is complete and they are almost ready to move him to recovery," she said.

"Recovery? So, he will be fine?" Harry asked.

The nurse gave a reassuring smile, "He is in critical condition and will be in intensive care and carefully watched for days. He had his lower left lobe of his lung removed and has a chest tube inserted into his lung cavity to help remove fluid and to keep his lung functioning properly. If he is strong and does not develop an infection, he will heal in a few weeks and can recover," the nurse instructed.

Greta spoke, saying, "Thank you for the news. Will we be able to see him later today? Just to be at his side or hold his hand?"

"Are you family?" asked the nurse.

"Well, we are his closest friends, as he has no immediate family. No parents, a sister in another state, and no wife or children," Harry explained.

"I will see that your names are added as authorized visitors," she said, smiling.

Harry and Greta hugged each other when they realized that their friend could survive this horrible ordeal. Yet, they felt heaviness in their hearts, too, as they knew another friend lay lifeless just down the long hallway.

⚫

Barbara lay alone in bed clutching Paul's pillow close to her chest. She could smell his Aqua Velva cologne again, and she hoped that scent would never fade away. Tears fell softly onto the pillow, and she prayed that God would give her some rest before she braved the dawn of a new day without her beloved Paul.

"Mommy! Momma!" Rachel yelled from her room. Her shrieks jerked Barbara from her bed. She sprang to her feet and ran to Rachel's bedroom.

"What is it honey?" she asked her frightened daughter, holding her tight.

"I had a bad dream, Mommy!" she cried.

"Oh, honey. I am right here. It is okay." Barbara embraced Rachel with a hold that not only comforted the young girl but was an anchor for Barbara in the moment. Barbara felt, too, that she had had a bad dream. But sadly, she was living it.

"Mommy, can I sleep with you and Daddy?" the alarmed girl asked.

Her question stung Barbara, and she gasped to catch her breath. She cleared her throat and replied, "Come sleep with Mommy."

She lifted the little girl in her arms, carried her to her bedroom and rested her in the spot where Paul used to lay. She pulled the blankets up to her tiny chin and kissed her on the forehead.

Rachel soon patted the bed and asked, "Mommy, where is daddy?"

Sting. Sting like one thousand bees stinging her heart. Barbara was not going to break the news to her daughter at this moment. Instead, she held her close and told her, "Shhhh. Shhhh. Everything is going to be all right. No more questions. Sleep now."

The two fell soundly asleep, as God provided them the rest they needed before the worries of the new day.

Chapter 6

Barbara opened her eyes and looked around the familiar room. For a moment, she thought she overslept and would be late for work at the market. Then reality set in. She would not be going to work today. She would not be rushing with Paul in the bathroom, him shaving and her brushing her teeth. This day was a new day of a life which she was unfamiliar.

I need to plan his funeral, she thought.

Rachel had moved from the bed and was downstairs playing with her brother, Randy. They were laughing at the cartoons. Bugs Bunny. Barbara glanced at the clock: 8:05 a.m. Normally on Sunday mornings, the family would join for breakfast at the kitchen table and then attend church. Barbara and the kids would not be at church today. She wasn't ready to be in the public eye, just yet.

Her mother, father, and sister would be by at 8:30 to help her make funeral arrangements. She tried to pull herself together, putting a bathrobe over her T-shirt and underwear. She washed her face and brushed her hair into a ponytail. She walked downstairs to find the kids eating bowls of cereal at the kitchen table.

"Hi Mommy," Rachel said, cheerful as sunshine.

"Hello, my sweeties," Barbara said, as she leaned over and kissed them both on their foreheads. She pulled out a chair and sat with them at the table. She blinked hard to try to stop her eyes from tearing up.

She rose quickly, trying to regain her composure, and wandered over to make a pot of coffee. As the coffee began to brew, she went back to the table with the children. Their laughter continued as Bugs Bunny was hiding in his hole in the ground, trying to outsmart Elmer Fudd. She wanted to get caught up in the laughter, too, the way they used on the weekends.

"Randy, Rachel," Barbara paused. "How much do you know about heaven?"

"Huh?" Randy asked, his eyes focused on the television.

"Randy and Rachel, please look at me," Barbara repeated, trying to get their attention.

The two children didn't understand why, but there was something in their mother's voice, something different. Both sets of eyes looked back at their mother, while they continued to eat their Cheerios.

"What do you know about heaven?" Barbara asked again.

Rachel spoke first, smiling. "Heaven is beautiful. It is where people who love God go to live after they die here."

Barbara was pleased, relieved too, then responded, "Yes, that is true. What about you Randy? What do you know about heaven?"

"Rachel is right. It is beautiful, beyond what we could ever imagine. I know our time here on Earth is short compared to living in heaven. In heaven there is no end of time. It goes on for a gazillion years! And the cool thing is that you get to live there with God and everyone who loved him."

"Yes, that is a good answer, too," Barbara said. "I am glad you both know of God and heaven because there is something I need to tell you both. Before I say anymore, I want you both to know that we will be strong through this as a family. God will be with us and we need to trust him, okay?"

Both kids nodded and were eager to hear more.

She continued, "Last night while Daddy was working at the store --" She had to stop to slow her pounding heart. *Breathe.* She continued, "There was a robbery --"

Randy, two years old than his sister, knew that this was not good. His face immediately went pale, and his eyes opened wide with alarm.

"Your daddy was hurt really bad by a robber who had a gun. Your daddy is in heaven now."

"No!" Randy screamed. "No! No! This is *not* happening. Not my daddy!"

Randy rose to his feet in a huff and threw his wooden chair over on its side. He sprinted to the couch and hurled his body into it, punching the cushions. With each punch, he wished he could change reality. If he could only hit hard enough. His small fists pummeled the pillows as screams roared from his throat.

"No, God, no!"

Rachel sat frozen in place, her tiny face red and crumpled into the deepest sadness, a face no parent ever wanted to see. Tears streamed ceaselessly down her rosy cheeks, as if they were in a race.

Barbara grabbed Rachel by the hand and pulled her out of the chair. They rushed over to Randy on the couch. With one arm, Barbara stroked Rachel's damp blonde hair and tried to comfort her. She leaned in toward Randy, placing her other hand on his back. She could feel his panicked breathing and racing heart, and she understood, because she was scared, too. But right now, it was not her turn. Right now, she had to be a rock. A strong shelter and refuge.

"The truth is hard. I am so sorry. I am in pain, too," she whispered. "But I want you both to know that Daddy loved you so very much. It is okay to get mad or to cry. I have those same feelings."

"I am mad! Why did he have to die?" Randy screamed.

Barbara choked back burning tears. She could not answer.

Little Rachel answered instead. "I think Jesus needed another angel in heaven, and he wanted our daddy."

Barbara looked into Rachel's innocent eyes and saw strength in her that could only come by God's penetrating love.

"I think you are right, Rachel. Daddy loved the Lord, and I am sure he took Daddy home to be with him," Barbara said.

"I know that is true, Mom. But why does it hurt so bad?" Randy asked, wiping tears from his dismal face.

"Baby, there are things that we will not ever understand on this side of heaven. But one day, we will see daddy again, and we have God's promise on that." She pulled her kids into her chest tightly. Randy's tense shoulders relaxed and he melted against her. They wrapped their arms around each other in a tight, warm ball, sharing tears, until they were startled by the doorbell ringing.

"That must be Grandma and Grandpa Allen and Aunt Kathy," Barbara said, wiping her tears with the arm of her bathrobe She took a deep breath and rose up to answer the door.

As the door swung open, her sister Kathy fell into her arms. Weeping, Kathy held Barbara and rocked her slowly side to side.

"I am so sorry, Barbie. I am here to help you with anything," Kathy said and entered the grieving home, whose air was heavy with loss.

Barbara hugged her parents, not wanting to let go. They were heartbroken knowing that their daughter was in pain. They wished they could strip away her misery and accept it for themselves.

The kids sluggishly moved to the front door and fell into the open arms waiting for them. Maybe they were tired or could it be shock? Barbara felt a gush of reality release when her family arrived. They were not here for a friendly visit, a chat over a cup of coffee or to care for the children. They were here as support and to help plan her husband's funeral. *It cannot be.* They would carry her, Rachel and Randy, so they could brave the next few unbearable days.

"I put coffee on, so please help yourself. I need to go and take a shower before I go and meet Father Arnold to make funeral plans. I am meeting him at 10:30. Daddy, can you join me in making the funeral plans? I really need your support right now. I don't think I can do this alone." Barbara asked, suddenly running a to-do list through her brain. It was easier to focus on the list than on her emotions.

"Absolutely, honey. I am here for you," her father said, hugging Barbara.

Barbara ascended the stairs to the master bedroom and stood for a moment near the bed. She lay down on the bed and again clutched Paul's pillow to her chest.

She whispered out loud, "Dear God, help me. I miss him so much already. I am lonely, afraid and unsure of my life without him. My identity was in Paul. I was Paul's wife and Paul's assistant at the store. What am I without him? Sure, I am still Randy and Rachel's mom but how good of a mom will I be with this void in my life? Please remove this doubt and fill my heart with hope. I am so very afraid. Help me!" She buried her face in Paul's pillow and sobbed, the anguished noises clawing their way out from deep in her gut.

Then Barbara summoned whatever strength she could muster to walk to the bathroom and start the shower. One step at a time, she needed to pull herself together. Hopefully the shower could refresh her and clear her head a little.

<hr />

Today was Sunday morning and many parishioners of St. Cecilia's Catholic Church would be going to mass at 9 a.m. Many had already heard the news of the shooting and others would find out the shocking news for the first time at church. One member of their parish had perished and another was hospitalized and critical.

The parishioners rose to their feet for the opening hymn, "Thank God, From Whom All Blessings Flow." The sweet hymn lacked the vigor of Sunday's past, and many could not sing because of the shattering news. Father Arnold, visibly shaken with sadness, addressed the friends and family of the church. It was a time of deep reflection and a time to mourn.

Something like this had never rocked their community or church before, and Father Arnold felt that the best way to handle it was to speak openly about how they could support the Lewis family and Ernie. Many volunteers raised their hands to be of assistance to the Lewis family for prayer, funeral arrangements, food hospitality, help with the children, and more. Many offered to pray for Ernie and make hospital visits. One man who had been out of work recently, offered to work at the service station so Ernie wouldn't lose the business while he was recovering.

Members of the church vowed to use whatever gifts or talents they had to be of assistance to the Lewis family and to Ernie Price. The love and support initiated from within this family of believers was amazing. Despite the circumstances, Father Arnold found joy in his heart, witnessing the love and support initiated from within the family of believers. He felt proud of his church family who was pulling together and extending God's merciful love.

Yes, God's love was shining radiantly in the hearts of the people in this church, and they knew they could make it through the upcoming difficult days by leaning on and into one another for strength.

Ernie's eyes slowly opened to find a nurse at his side taking his vital signs.

She smiled when she saw he was awake and said, "Good afternoon, Mr. Price. You are in the intensive care unit of Portage Lake Hospital, and you are doing fine. My name is Nurse Beverly, and I will be looking after you today. I am adjusting your pain medicine right now and when you are feeling up to it, we can bring you some clear liquids, maybe some chicken broth. Just pull this cord here to buzz me if you need assistance." She placed the long cord in Ernie's hand.

Ernie nodded. He tried to talk, but no words came out.

"You had visitors just a moment ago, and they went to get some lunch. They will be back in just a little bit. Harry and Greta were there names," she said.

Ernie managed a smile and found comfort in knowing that his friends were here. He was not sure what had happened or the condition that he was in. He figured when he could finally speak, he would get the answers that he needed to rest his mind.

Ernie could see a large "Get well soon" banner on the window that looked into the nursing station. He smiled again at its sentiment.

He rested his eyes until he heard the hushed voices of some people entering the room. He cracked his eyes just a little and saw Harry and Greta at his side. They each took one of Ernie's hands and spoke quietly to him.

"Ernie, it is Greta and Harry. We are here for you," Greta said.

Ernie managed a smile and squeezed their hands.

"Ernie, you are strong and did great in your surgery," Harry said, reassuringly.

Ernie nodded.

"The whole town is praying for you, Ernie," Greta encouraged.

Ernie squeezed Greta's hand again and then grimaced. He was desperately trying to say something. He moaned and then mouthed out the word: "Paul."

Harry and Greta looked stunned at one another and hesitated.

Both were unsure if sharing the news with Ernie was too soon for him to handle. Would he suffer a setback with the heartbreaking news? Yet they did not want to frustrate Ernie by not answering his question either. Finally, Harry quietly answered Ernie.

"It is with sadness that Paul is no longer with us. But there is joy that he rests in heaven now," Harry affirmed.

Ernie swallowed hard and his lip quivered. A tear slid down the side of his face. Greta squeezed his hand, and Ernie squeezed back, as he comprehended the loss of their dear friend. Harry took out his Bible and turned to 2 Corinthians 4:16-18 (NLT) and began to read:

"That is why we never give up. For our present troubles are small and won't last very long. Yet they produce for us a glory that vastly outweighs them and will last forever! So we don't look at the troubles we can see now; rather, we fix our gaze on things that cannot be seen. For the things we see now will soon be gone, but the things we cannot see will last forever."

Barbara and her father met with Father Arnold to go over details of Paul's funeral. They wanted to make it a beautiful time to remember the incredible man that he had been. They also met with the funeral director and discussed whether Paul would be shown in a casket or be cremated. That was a difficult decision for Barbara to make, because she thought of her kids and how they would handle seeing their dead father lying in a casket or in an urn filled with ashes.

She could remembered two funerals she had attended as a small girl that were memorials in nature, with no casket. There were pictures on a table, flowers, and trinkets that were important to the deceased. But no body. Barbara had difficulty connecting that the person was really *gone* and no longer with her because she didn't see a body and did not have a chance to say goodbye. And for that same reason, she decided that having a showing of Paul in a casket -- so that her children could have closure and acceptance of their father's passing.

She picked out a deep red mahogany casket with a cream lining. A pewter cross adored the top of the casket with the words "Beloved Husband and Father" inscribed on it. Father Arnold would make arrangements that Paul's burial would be in the plot alongside his already deceased father and sister, John and Janie Lewis.

Barbara was relieved when the funeral arrangements were complete. She nuzzled into her daddy's embrace and felt that familiar rush of energy exit her body. Another reality checkpoint was done. *I am still holding on. I feel you near God. Thank you.*

Barbara picked up the phone from the funeral director's desk and called her mom who was at home with the children.

"The funeral is set for Wednesday at 10 a.m. at St. Cecilia's Catholic Church. The cemetery plot is paid for. We need to be at the funeral home on Tuesday night at 6 p.m. for a showing and --"

Barbara's mother cut her words off and interrupted, "Honey, just come home. I want you to rest. It has been a tiring and emotional day for you. Please, come home. I have made mulligan stew and fresh bread. Come have a bite to eat."

She was right. It was the most difficult, tiring, heart-wrenching day she had ever experienced. She decided, that after her mother's dinner or whatever she could manage to keep down, she would spend time with Rachel and Randy and then go to bed early.

Barbara was exhausted by night's end but thanked the Lord that she could even make it through a day like today. As she climbed into the empty bed, she grabbed his pillow and moaned out a few big sighs to stop the tears that wanted to burst out. She pressed her face into the pillow and wanted to pound her fists into the bed.

Somewhere between denial and anger, her emotions were erratic. *Lord, this is only my second night without him. Help me through this!*

Barbara heard the small faint voice say, *I am here.*

—————————◦《◎》◦—————————

Hometown high school quarterback, Mark Alcott, reached down on the cold driveway and retrieved the late Sunday morning newspaper. He quickly walked back inside to get out of the frigid air. He threw the newspaper down on the table and poured himself a glass of orange juice. Pulling up a chair, he sat down and removed the brown paper cover off the newspaper inside. Smack on the front page was a huge headline that read:

ANOTHER SMALL TOWN ROBBERY: One life taken and another in critical condition

"Oh my. What? Another robbery?" he said aloud in disbelief. He hurriedly read on.

A second robbery happened over the weekend, rocking the town of Hubbell on Saturday evening.

Lt. Sheriff Bob Sheeves, from the Torch Lake Police Department, reports that at approximately 7:10 p.m., a gunman entered the Lewis Market on Duncan Avenue and fatally shot the store owner, Paul Lewis, 38 years old, from the town of Hubbell.

The gunman, allegedly alarmed by a shopper in the store, then shot Ernie Price, 53 years old, from Hubbell, according to police. Price remains hospitalized at Portage Lake Hospital in critical condition.

The unidentified gunman, who remains at large, appears to be a man in his early 20s, approximately 6 feet in height and 175 pounds. A witness who drove by notes seeing someone wearing a black or blue Arctic Cat ski mask. He escaped with $316 from the cash register.

Police believe the robbery at Lewis Market and the Friday night robbery at Bootlegger's Liquor Store in Dollar Bay may have been orchestrated by the same person. Anyone with information can call the Torch Lake County Police Department.

Below the article about the robbery was a picture of Paul Lewis and a prompt that his obituary could be found on page four. Mark fumbled through the pages and found the obituary about his friend.

PAUL LEWIS

Paul Lewis, 38, of Hubbell, died suddenly on Saturday, Nov. 2, 1974, after a robbery in the store he owned, Lewis' Market.

Funeral services celebrating the life of Paul Lewis will be on Wednesday, Nov. 6, at St. Cecilia's Catholic Church in Hubbell at 10 a.m., with Father Arnold Hail officiating.

He was born Sept. 29, 1936, in Calumet, to parents John and Beatrice Lewis, and lived his entire life in the town of Hubbell. He has one living sister, Laurine (Anthony) Maxwell, 40, of Lake Linden, and his mother, Beatrice Lewis lives in Hubbell. He is preceded in death by his father and sister, Janie Lewis.

He graduated from Lake Linden–Hubbell High School in 1956, and joined in running of the family business, Lewis' Market. In 1960, He married high school sweetheart, Barbara Allen, 38, and they had two children, son, Randy, 10, and daughter, Rachel, 8.

He was a member of St. Cecilia's Catholic Church, serving as an altar boy in youth and a Knight's of Columbus member for the past eight years. He played football for Lake Linden–Hubbell High School and lead them to two state team championships in 1955 and 1956. He has volunteered as an assistant coach for the high school since his graduation. He was a devoted husband and father who enjoyed singing in the adult choir at church, playing his guitar, camping, fishing, and deer hunting and cooking.

Memorials may be sent to the: Lewis Foundation, 2402 Yates Ave., Hubbell, MI 49934.

Mark put the newspaper down and shook his head in confusion.

"This cannot be happening. Mike, Mike come here quick!" he hollered to his brother who was in the living room.

Mike rushed to the kitchen and asked, "What is it?"

"There was a robbery at Lewis' Market last night. Paul Lewis was killed and Ernie is in the hospital in critical condition."

"No way. The newspaper says that?" he said, grabbing the newspaper from Mark's hands so he could read the devastating news for himself. His eyes scanned the front page and read that the news was true.

How could a nightmare like this be happening in our small town? they both wondered.

Paul Lewis was a neighborhood friend to everyone. Always pleasant with a joke or two to tell when you entered the store. He made the townspeople want to frequent his store just for his company. He had helped the football team that Mark and Mike currently played on, the Lake Linden-Hubbell Lakes High School football team. They were at the end of the football season and the team had made the playoffs. Paul was expected to help the team win the playoffs and state title.

Paul had been a mentor and role model to many kids on and off the field, the boys thought. He helped countless kids get off the wrong path, and instead get involved in football and work at his store. He lived his life with purpose and wanted other kids to feel their purpose, too. Paul loved his wife, Barbara, and adored his children, Randy and Rachel. The kids would often come to football practices with their dad and bring water to the thirsty players. Paul had said he was just waiting for the day when he could coach his son, Randy, in football.

Mark and Mike's thoughts then went to Ernie.

Ernie was probably the most upright man they knew. He led his life with integrity, compassion, and commitment. He worked hard at the service station, was a music mentor to them and helped the poor and needy children of the town experience a Christmas year after year.

Mark thought about the upcoming Christmas party that Ernie arranged every year, and he felt immense sadness. He leaned over the table with his arms folded under his chin and stared at the calendar on wall in front of him. The party was scheduled six weeks from today. Ernie's condition and the time needed for healing would prevent him from continuing with the Christmas party.

How was the Christmas party going to happen this year? Mark could not imagine cancelling the party. Kids -- and their parents -- counted on this celebration, year after year. Mark knew that the Christmas party must go on. But that it would require a team of people to pull it off.

I will do this for the children. And for Ernie, he silently resolved. He grabbed a piece of paper and starting writing down his ideas.

First, he would need to see what toys Ernie had already completed and finish the work on the toys that needed fixing at the service station. Second, he would need to arrange a toy drive, and tell the community his intentions to make this year's Christmas party happen. Third, he would need volunteers who could help devote time to cleaning, repairing, sewing, and painting the toys. Lastly, he would need assistance with the party itself, working with the church ladies for food and developing the music program with the children's choir. Luckily, the children had already been singing Christmas songs since late September. He would just need to take over where left off with the planning and teaching of songs. He had six weeks to try and pull of what Ernie had been perfecting his entire life, year round. It would be no small feat.

Mark would discuss the plans with Ernie when he was feeling stronger. He would talk with Father Arnold later this week about his interest and plans to save the Christmas party and help bring a town together that had been struck by tragedy. They needed joy in a time like this.

Mark yelled again for Mike, who was again in the living room.

"What do you want now, Mark?" Mike asked, bothered by the interruption, as he was trying to watch a television program.

"I want your help hosting Ernie's Christmas party with me," Mark yelled.

"What? Host a birthday party? Who's birthday is it?"

"No, Ernie's Christmas party!" Mark yelled back.

Mark grabbed his pencil and paper and stopped the nonsense of the banter back and forth. He charged into the living room with new purpose. He had a Christmas party to put together and Mike was going to help.

Chapter 7

Two long days had past since the shooting, and Ernie was slowly recovering from his injuries. His body was extremely weak, and he could not leave his bed. Mentally, his mind kept working overtime; he thought about the robbery every waking moment. Physically, the doctor said that he was a miracle, as the gunshot wound missed pulmonary arteries.

The surgeon removed the lower lobe of Ernie's left lung successfully. He had suffered pneumothorax, a growing air pocket between the pleural cavity that causes increased pressure and the collapse of the lung. Ernie also incurred a mediastinal shift, where his heart and major blood vessels shifted to the opposite side of his chest when his lung collapsed. He had substantial injuries, and it was by the grace of God his life was saved.

He would need to be hospitalized for another ten to fourteen days and continually monitored to assure his lung did not collapse again and also to ward off any infection. If all went well, he would be in intensive care for another four days and then moved to the rehab floor.

Harry and Greta remained at his side for countless hours, but Ernie knew they had a young family of their own to tend to, so he insisted they go home. Soon he would be able to see more friends, but in the meantime, he spent much time reading the stacks of cards and letters.

Spiritually, Ernie grappled with why his life had been spared but Paul's life had been taken. He knew the answer. But he was still perplexed and afraid. If he shared with anyone the experience he had had, they might take him for having a breakdown. He knew of one person he could talk to about it, though. Father Arnold. In time, he would share with Father Arnold how he went home to heaven.

"How are you, handsome?" Nurse Beverly asked Ernie, as she bounced cheerfully into his room.

Ernie, ashamed for a moment about how he looked, smoothed back his hair and managed a smile.

"Fine. How are you?" he responded.

"I am much better now that I get to come to work and see my favorite patient," she said.

Ernie felt his cheeks hot, blushing like a schoolboy. He was never one to get much attention from the ladies and her comment took him by surprise. He knew she was only being sweet because he was her new patient, but nonetheless, he liked the compliment.

"I have a menu for you. You can now eat solid food for dinner, or at least give it a try."

She put on her reading glasses and opened up the menu. "Let's see. For dinner, there is kielbasa sausage with roasted potatoes, peas, applesauce, and tapioca pudding. Sounds better than my ham sandwich in a brown paper bag."

"I love ham sandwiches," said Ernie.

"Then why don't we switch dinners?" said Nurse Beverly with a laugh.

Kielbasa, Ernie thought. That was what he wanted for dinner on Saturday night when he went shopping at Lewis' Market and walked into this unimaginable nightmare. At the moment, he no longer wanted the kielbasa, as the thought sickened him.

"Please just bring me some chicken noodle soup, bread, and the tapioca pudding. Can that be done?" said Ernie.

"Not much of an appetite yet, huh?" she asked.

"No. Just something light for now."

"I can get you whatever you wish. I see you still want the tapioca pudding, though. I can never pass up tapioca pudding either. It is my favorite."

"My favorite, too," whispered Ernie and grinned.

Nurse Beverly propped up his pillow and adjusted his blankets. She checked his vitals and his IV drip bag and all was stable.

"Your dinner tray will be here in less than an hour. Try to get your rest. You'll heal faster with some shut eye," she winked and then exited the room.

He has beautiful blue eyes, she thought to herself.

Ernie closed his eyes and then opened them slowly. He closed his eyes again. Minutes later, he opened them quickly and looked around the room. He panicked a little. He felt te tightness of his chest, with tubes going every which way. He wanted to be sure of his surroundings, because in his slumber, he went to extraordinary places and experienced things that made him doubt his sense of awareness of time and place.

———— ((◉)) ————

At 7:30 a.m., Barbara was awakened by the annoying buzz of the alarm clock. She rolled over and with the slam of her hand, stopped the noise. Today was Wednesday morning, and today would be the toughest day of her life. Paul's funeral was today and braving the hundreds of people at the church and reception would be daunting.

Before her feet hit the floor, she prayed for strength, and asked God that an extra reserve be supplied to her children. The children had been quiet and kept close to Barbara since their loss. They had lots of questions and Barbara did her best to answer every little detail. The kids worried that they would never be happy again.

"Mom, will I ever stop feeling sad?" Randy asked.

"Randy, you mustn't think that you cannot ever be happy again because your daddy died. That is not true. It hurts badly right now, but in time you will need to choose to be happy or be miserable," Barbara explained. "For instance, this morning, I knew today would be a tough day, saying goodbye to my husband and seeing all the people at the funeral. But I prayed to God for strength to get through this day."

She paused to touch his shoulder.

"I am not going to continue to be angry and full of sorrow every day," she continued. "My reaching out to God is a big step toward moving on to healing and happiness. I know that today will have its beautiful and tender moments. Many people will tell stories of how great your dad was and how he touched their lives. It is a time to remember a wonderful person, to celebrate his life, and to thank God for the time that we got to spend with him. And besides, our love for him will never leave our hearts."

Rachel spoke up now.

"Mommy, I know I told you last night that I didn't think that I could sing my song at the funeral today but I now think that I can," she said. "I am not going to be afraid. I think daddy would be proud of me for singing it."

"Are you sure of this, honey?" Barbara asked.

"I will ask God to help me sing the song. It is a song for daddy, and I will be okay," Rachel said with reassurance in her eyes.

Barbara hugged her daughter, and was proud that she had made this tough decision on her own. She was pleased, too, that Randy had decided to be a pallbearer and help carry his father's casket at the funeral.

Barbara's parents arrived and helped the kids put on their dress clothes for the funeral while Barbara got herself ready. Her "little black dress" that she wore for a cocktail party last year had now become "the funeral dress." She donned a black sweater over the dress and put on the gold cross pendant that she had worn on her wedding day. Tears flooded her eyes and she blinked quickly before it fell onto her made-up face. She took a couple of deep breaths, walked downstairs to meet the family, and then they all drove to the funeral home to follow the hearse to the church.

When they pulled up to funeral home, they saw the hearse with its back doors open. Barbara felt a lump in her throat and felt the tug of the children's little hands on her wool coat. She kissed them both on the forehead as her father parked the car. They exited the dark blue Monte Carlo car and slowly walked toward the hearse. Randy met other men who would help carry Paul's casket into the church. Harry was one of the pallbearers, and he met Randy with a big hug. Randy appeared proud to be appointed to do a job one last time for his father.

"Pallbearers, it time to bring Paul's coffin to the hearse. Please follow me inside," Harry directed.

The six pallbearers followed Harry into the funeral parlor, back to the room where last night's showing had been. A room where hundreds of people had made last night their final farewell to Paul and showed their support to Barbara and her grieving children.

Randy walked up to the casket hesitantly. Last night, he found it difficult to approach his father, unsure of what he would look like lying there so still. But he looked at peace, like he was sleeping, and it did not frighten him. It was real. His father was really dead, and he would no longer hear his laugh, see him smile, or be comforted by him. And when that casket closed, he would no longer see his face.

Will I forget what he looks like? Randy worried.

"I will close the coffin now," Harry said, pausing for a moment, looking at Randy.

Randy walked a few steps closer and looked intently at his father. He looked at his father's strong hands folded together across his chest with rosary beads weaved between his fingers. He looked at his father's face and studied it for a moment, not wanting to forget it. People always told him that he looked like his daddy and at this moment, he hoped he grew to look and be just like him.

"Goodbye, daddy. I will be strong and take good care of Mommy and Rachel."

The grown men tried to stay composed, but thoughts of their own sons and daughters being in the difficult predicament as Randy, and a glimpse of their own mortality, overtook them with sadness.

Harry gently lowered the lid on the casket while Randy watched the view of his father decrease to no more. He would never see his father again, this side of heaven.

He reached for the handle, as the other men had, and lifted his father up as high as his ten-year-old muscles could stand. He had a job to do today and it was honor to serve his father this last time. They walked slowly outside of the building to the waiting family and hearse. Barbara covered her mouth with one hand, afraid a gasp would be heard by little Rachel, who stood at her side.

She was so proud of Randy. Her little boy didn't seem so little any more, as he worked with the other pallbearers to hoist Paul's coffin into the hearse. It seemed Randy had aged ten years in the last few days. He was now the man of the house, and it showed in his posture and the muscles of his cheeks. Barbara stepped up to the coffin and laid the flower spray of red and white roses on top. She moved aside and Harry shut the hearse door. The thud of the door startled Barbara's heart and seemed to resonate in her empty chest.

The family assembled into the waiting processional cars and followed the slow black hearse to St. Cecilia's church. Upon arrival, the family entered the church and waited while the pallbearers retrieved Paul's body from the hearse. Father Arnold blessed Paul again with the sprinkling of holy water. The water beaded on the red mahogany casket like tears.

The organist opened with the playing of the processional song, "Make Me a Channel of Your Peace (Prayer of St. Francis)." The casket and pallbearers entered first, followed by the grieving family and then Father Arnold and the altar boys, Scott and Darren Muljo. Barbara grasped Rachel's hand and they walked humbly to their seats, along with her parents and Paul's mother and sister. As Barbara gazed around, she saw that the entire church was full, all the way up to the balcony. Paul was loved and it was evident by the showing of people who wanted to see his farewell.

Father Arnold led the funeral mass, and then Greta approached the podium to give a reading. Greta began, loud and steadily, "The God of peace will be with you."

The congregation responded, "And also with you."

Greta continued, "A reading from the Letter of Saint Paul to the Philippians." (Philippians 4:4-9 NIV)

Rejoice in the Lord always. I will say it again: Rejoice! Let your gentleness be evident to all. The Lord is near. Do not be anxious about anything, but in every situation, by prayer and petition, with thanksgiving, present your requests to God. And the peace of God, which transcends all understanding, will guard your hearts and your minds in Christ Jesus.

Finally, brothers and sisters, whatever is true, whatever is noble, whatever is right, whatever is pure, whatever is lovely, whatever is admirable — if anything is excellent or praiseworthy — think about such things. Whatever you have learned or received or heard from me, or seen in me — put it into practice. And the God of peace will be with you.

She finished, "The is word of the Lord."

The congregation responded, "Thanks be to God."

Father Arnold then spoke the gospel and welcomed Paul's sister, Laurine, to the podium to give her eulogy.

The stocky woman with short salt-and-pepper hair approached the podium. She fanned herself with the papers she had in her hand.

"Hello, I am Laurine Lewis Maxwell, and I am Paul's older sister," she said with confidence. "Today we honor a man who touched our lives with compassion, kindness, and laughter. As I talk about Paul as a young boy, I mean no disrespect. You all know how growing up with siblings can be. Fighting one minute and loving each other the next. Growing up with Paulie, I found him to be always on the prowl for makin' mischief. Momma, don't you agree?" Laurine looked in her mother's direction. Her frail mother spoke out with an "Uh huh." The congregation together laughed, knowing Paul's wit.

"Paulie liked to build things. He went from building Lincoln Logs to building treehouses. His treehouse had a level ten feet off the ground before he turned ten years old. By age eleven, he convinced daddy that he needed a penthouse, so they build another level."

Her arms stretched high up in the sky. She continued.

"One day Paulie and his friend, Louie, were playing in the penthouse, up to mischief again. Louie carried a mason jar full of grasshoppers up wooden board steps while Paulie carried a nearly empty gasoline can. Once in the penthouse, they emptied the jar of grasshoppers onto the floor. Many grasshoppers jumped in fright, others stayed stunned and did not move. I know you are all familiar with using a magnifying glass and sunlight to melt things or burn up bugs. Paulie an Louie and had another idea. Now this next part might frighten you a little." She paused for dramatic emphasis. "While Louie poured gasoline on the grasshoppers, Paul dug into his denim overalls for a book of matches he had taken out of the kitchen. I remember Paul telling the story; he then said, 'You grasshoppers are going to fry.' Louie was smart and stood back against the wall of the treehouse. Paul lit the match and threw it on the grasshoppers and flames erupted with a loud boom, throwing Paul off his feet and out the opening of the treehouse."

The eyes in the audience that had been teary moments earlier were now wide with anticipation.

"Paul fell from the penthouse, past the first floor and down to the hard earth below. Louie didn't know what to do -- fan the flames or help his friend, Paul? He raced down the boarded stairs to find his friend not moving. Louie ran into the house yelling for our mother, opening doors until she was found. The next door he opened was the bathroom, and he heard her humming in the shower. He yelled, 'Mrs. Lewis! Come quickly! The tree is on fire and Paul fell from the penthouse.'"

Laurine knew this was a nontraditional eulogy, but Paul had been no ordinary man. She knew he would rather see the town laughing at his funeral than crying, so she continued the story.

Mother, caught by surprise, didn't hear Louie correctly and became angry.

"Paul found some Penthouse? You tell him to come in here right now!"

"No, Mrs. Lewis, he can't. And it's not Penthouse magazines. He *fell* from the penthouse of the tree house! Call the fire department! The tree is on fire!"

"Oh, dear Lord," Mrs Lewis replied, nearly taking down the shower curtain with her as she rushed out of the shower.

The fire department and ambulance sped to the Lewis home. The firemen managed to completely douse the fire in the large oak tree without the fire spreading. The next morning, Paul woke up with two broken arms and some explaining to do.

Laurine's mind briefly flickered to the image of another ambulance hauling off her brother. Only this time, he had not awaken the next morning. She pushed the painful thought out of her mind and smirked at the audience.

"Paul's antics served him well. He had two full-length arm casts, and I got to help feed him, bathe him and tend to his daily bathroom needs. As a thirteen-year-old boy, you don't want your sixteen-year-old sister knowing your *business,* if you know what I mean!"

Laughter replaced the melancholic atmosphere in the church.

Laurine paused and took a deep breath. The next few moments would be difficult.

"Paul, it was a joy being your sister. You brought laughter to my days, usually at your expense, but nonetheless, you made life joyful. Thank you for sharing that love and joy with me. I will miss you a ton, little brother. I love you so very much." She turned her head toward Paul's coffin, blew him a kiss, and went to take a seat in the front row near Barbara.

If the congregation was hit hard in the heart by Laurine's words, they couldn't see what was coming next.

It was time for Rachel to sing her song.

"I would like to ask Rachel Lewis to please join me at the altar. Rachel is Paul's daughter and she is eight years old. Please come here at my side, Rachel." Father Arnold directed, motioning her with a wave of his arm.

"I would like to say something special about this little girl," Father Arnold said.

Rachel let go of her mother's hand and bravely walked toward Father Arnold. She stood with Father Arnold right behind her father's casket. Her innocent eyes gazed at the long box adorned with flowers. She found it hard to imagine that her father lay there when her mother said he was in heaven. The father who played dress up, called her a little princess and always sang sweetly to her.

Father Arnold placed his hand gently on the curly head of sweet Rachel.

"Rachel has always enjoyed singing, especially singing songs with her dad. The song she wishes to sing today is a song they used to sing together, a favorite of theirs."

The pipe organ's rich sound began, as Rachel's small hand hugged the microphone. Her big eyes looked out amongst the crowd and she tried to remember what her mother had said, that these people were all friends and family of daddy's and she should not be afraid. She opened her mouth to sing the familiar song originally sung by Kitty Wells, but sang lovingly with her father time and time again.

A little girl was waiting for her daddy one day;
It was time to meet him when she heard her mommy say;
Come to mommy, darling, please do not cry;
Daddy's gone to heaven, 'way up in the sky.'

CHORUS:
How far Is Heaven? When can I go?
To see my daddy, he's there, I know;
How far Is Heaven, let's go tonight
I want my daddy to hold me tight.

He was called so suddenly and could not say goodbye;
I know that he's in heaven, we'll meet him by and by;
The little girl trembled, her tears she could not hide;
She looked up towards heaven and then she replied:

CHORUS:
How far Is Heaven? When can I go?
To see my daddy, he's there, I know;
How far Is Heaven, let's go tonight
I want my daddy to hold me tight.

There was not a dry eye in the church as Rachel finished her song and leaned in to touch the coffin.

"You are no longer singing with me daddy, but now you are singing with the angels and with your closest friend, Jesus," she whispered.

Father Arnold heard her tender words though the congregation did not. His heart ached for little Rachel.

She courageously wiped her tears and Father Arnold helped her step down again to meet her mother. She leaned into her mother crying softly, while Barbara held her breath, feeling like she might explode with emotion.

If words could be heard in heaven, I know you would be proud of Rachel, Paul, Barbara thought to herself.

The funeral mass continued with Father Arnold blessing the Holy Eucharist and reciting the Lord's Prayer. He held the host, representing Christ's broken body, and then took the chalice of wine, representing Christ's shed blood, and he held them high above his head. He offered prayers of thanksgiving for Christ's amazing sacrifice that washed away all of our sins.

Father Arnold addressed the congregation. "Whoever is holy and in a state of sanctifying grace, let them approach. Whoever is not, let them repent."

The pews emptied for Communion, while the organist played a light instrumental hymn.

Following Communion, Father Arnold began the final commendation of committing Paul's soul to our Lord and into his tender care. The song, "May the Good Lord Bless and Keep You," a favorite of Paul's by Jim Reeves, played over the church's loudspeaker, while the family bid farewell to their son, brother, husband, and father.

May the good Lord bless and keep you, 'til we meet again.

Father Arnold incensed the body, waving the hot vessel on all sides of the coffin. He circled the coffin waving the vessel back and forth. Its aroma penetrated the air and the smoke rose up, symbolizing the departed soul rising to heaven. And for the mourners left behind on Earth, just as the smoke rose, so could their prayers rise to heaven.

Father Arnold instructed the congregation to stand.

"May the Lord bless you and watch over you. May the Lord

make his face shine upon you, and be gracious to you. May the Lord look kindly on you and give you peace. In the name of the Father, and of the Son, and and of the Holy Spirit."

The Congregation replied, "Amen" and made the sign of the cross.

The pallbearers assembled around the coffin. Randy stood straight, head high and lifted the casket above his right shoulder. The pallbearers moved slowly and solemnly down the lengthy aisle to meet the hearse waiting outside. The family followed the coffin outside into the sunshine, until it rested safely in the hearse that would drive it to the cemetery. There, Paul would be laid to rest in the plot that Barbara had chosen just three days ago.

On the ride from the cemetery to the reception hall, the hearse and processional cars stopped at a train crossing for an oncoming train. The horn blasted from down the track and Barbara could feel the rumble of the locomotive. The conductor must have seen the funeral procession of cars, because he quickly quieted his horn. Barbara rolled down her window halfway for fresh air.

Seconds later, in flew a beautiful blue butterfly that rested gently on Barbara's shoulder. This amazing creature fluttered its wings and stayed for moments on her shoulder without hesitation. As it perched there confidently, she and the kids marveled. *How could a butterfly still be around this late in the fall season and when the weather had turned so much colder?*

Barbara looked away from the butterfly and tried to brush the symbolism of the butterfly from her mind. She knew that the life cycle of the butterfly went from the birth of a caterpillar who crawled upon the earth, to an emerging cocoon in its restful state, and then finally into the beautiful butterfly that could be free to soar. Christian myths believed that butterflies represented rebirth and immortality, and Native Americans believed the butterfly was a symbol for guidance and happiness.

Just like the butterfly, in life we experience twists, turns, happiness, uncertainty and disappointment. It is through these life changes, we transform and grow, Barbara thought. *The path we start with does not always start and end the same. It moves along, taking detours as we go, often taking a path not taken before. We adapt, sometimes immediately, sometimes more slowly. but we move on.*

She looked back at her shoulder. It was still there. It fluttered its wings and amazed her. Its magnificent wings were as blue as the sky above -- and as blue as the memory of Paul's astonishing eyes, she thought. As soon as her thoughts shifted to Paul, the butterfly lifted off of Barbara's shoulder and flew out the window.

Barbara sighed loudly, wishing it wouldn't leave just yet. She wanted it to remain closeby, longer. She held her breath and remained still, hoping it would enter the window again and gracefully land on her shoulder once more. It remained hovering just on the other side of the glass window, as if pausing for a moment to look one last time at this family. It then flew away, into the sunshine, and out of sight.

Thank you, Paul, Barbara smiled to herself. She couldn't help but think he had brought this awe-inspiring gift their way. The butterfly gave her instant hope that she would be guided on her new journey of renewal and would one day soar again.

The train passed by and the car moved on toward the reception hall.

—((O))—

Ernie spent a good part of his day in prayer. He longed to be with his friends at Paul's funeral and pay respect to a man he dearly respected and loved. Yet, he was confined to the hospital bed and would be remain this way for another couple of days.

Ernie was now able to have more visitors. Even with this allowance, not many had stopped by in the last two days, as they were busy with the funeral, assisting Barbara, and helping run his service station. Ernie was stunned by the outpouring of thought and attention people expressed in response to his hospitalization.

One man, Ted Benson, who had been out of work since the university's layoffs six months ago, worked a full day's shift at the service station, relieving Ernie's worries about how the station could stay open in his absence. Mark had stopped by yesterday and was excited to tell Ernie that he was going to take over the Christmas party planning. Ernie was delighted, as he did not want to disappoint the children. Ernie offered Mark as much help and advice as possible, from his bedside.

Mark explained that he was going to assemble men and women to help repair toys, a team to chop down Christmas trees to sell at the service station just like Ernie did each year, and Mark and Mike would prepare the music with the children's choir for the party and Christmas Eve mass. Lots to do in a short time, but the party was still on. Ernie was delighted.

After dinner, Father Arnold visited Ernie at the hospital. Ernie was jubilant to see him and to have company. He also had wanted to talk with Father Arnold about his bewildering experience -- his encounter with the afterlife.

Ernie tried to sort through the experience step-by-step in his mind. He was certain that everything that he saw and felt had not been a dream; he had visited heaven. He had read stories of people who had out-of-body experiences on their deathbed. Then, he had believed that they could be true. But he never believed that he would be one to profess them for truth.

"I want to talk to you about something that has been on my mind since the robbery. I want your spiritual guidance and opinion on this."

Ernie paused, still questioning if he should yet be telling anyone about his experience.

"Do you believe that people can experience an afterlife or heavenly encounter in the moments following their death?" Ernie asked.

"Hmm. I have heard of this happening, but honestly, the Bible does not refer to it," said Father Arnold.

Ernie responded, "That is what I thought, too. I am almost afraid to talk about it, but I am with certainty that it happened to me."

"Go on," Father Arnold said with curiosity, leaning in.

"One minute I was lying on the table at the hospital, and the next I was transported through a narrow tunnel into a bright light. When I got to the end of the bright light, I was standing in a bright room with vivid colors. All around me was splendor of unimaginable beauty. My mother and father were waiting for me. We spoke, hugged, and walked. Father Arnold, they led me to the pearly gates."

"I can only imagine heaven's awesome splendor," Father Arnold admiringly said. He searched Ernie's eyes, and he had no reason to doubt his friend. Ernie's confidence swelled when he realized Father Arnold believed him.

"I could see things, hear people, and feel the touch from others when they touched me. I could even talk to them. Everyone appeared younger, livelier, and very happy!" Ernie exclaimed. "My parents talked about their joy to see me, and they were the ones selected to ask me if I wanted to stay in heaven or return to Earth. As much as I wanted to stay with them and go on to meet my Lord and Savior, I was puzzled and desired to return to Earth."

"Hmm, why so?"

"It is not easy to explain, but I felt like God's plan for me was not complete here on earth. Does that sound strange?"

"It does not sound strange at all. You have a wonderful life here and you are so needed in the lives of many. God says our days are numbered but apparently you have some time before you're finally resting in heaven," Father Arnold said.

"Why was the decision left up to me then, as to stay or go?"

"That is a question we will never be able to answer this side of heaven," Father Arnold replied.

"What I am going to say next is even more surprising," Ernie continued. "I knew Paul died, even before I was told of his death the next morning."

"What? How? What are you saying?"

"I heard my doctor announce that I was clinically dead at 7:55 p.m., but I awoke suddenly after that. In my death experience, I spoke with my mother and father but I also spoke with -- I spoke with Paul," Ernie said.

"You spoke with Paul? Where? At the store before the ambulance came?"

"No," Ernie hesitated. "I spoke to Paul -- in heaven."

Father Arnold repeated Ernie's words again, "Spoke to Paul in heaven?"

He could not believe it. Well, he believed it, in heaven and all of its mystery, but Ernie was talking about seeing and speaking to a friend who was dying nearly at the same time he was dying.

"So what you are saying is that you spoke to Paul in heaven after he just died and *you* just died?"

"I saw Paul walking to the heavenly gate with his mother and father. I yelled his name and he turned and walked toward me happily, not at all fazed to see me. It was if he expected to see me there. It was so strange. He was wearing a white billowy robe and was not soiled of blood or sweat. I looked down at my own clothing and I was wearing the green dress shirt and black slacks that I had worn to church that evening and onto Lewis' Market. I noticed my hands were rough and my fingernails still soiled from grease, despite scrubbing, from working at the service station! I also had blood on my clothing. My wet blood."

"How can that be?" said Father Arnold, learning in again.

"Paul then asked if I was 'coming or going.' Paul told me that he was to stay in heaven," Ernie said. "Let me repeat that again: He was *told* that he was to stay in heaven because God's plan with him was *complete*. Paul asked what my decision was, whether to stay in heaven or return to Earth. I told him that God's work was unfinished in me. So I returned to my earthly home."

"That is amazing," proclaimed Father Arnold, as it all started to sink in. "You spoke to Paul. In heaven."

"Yes, and we embraced. He had no pain and no injury from the injury. In fact, I did not feel any pain either, even though I had blood on my clothing. We both appeared very much alive," Ernie said.

"If what you are telling me is true, and I do believe what you say, it really is possible to experience a glimpse of heaven! For you to see your parents again must have been complete joy. How difficult it must have been for you to make a decision as to whether you should stay in heaven or return to Earth. I can only say that I underestimate God and all He has in store for us. His ways are truly amazing," Father Arnold said, exasperated.

"No eye has seen, no ear has heard, no mind has conceived what God has prepared for those who love him. I would like to think that I caught a glimpse of heaven, but I believe there is so much more in heaven than we can ever comprehend. And until that time when I take my final breath and rest in the arms of my Lord forever, I will never waste a day of my life. I believe the best is yet to come, and I can only wait with bated breath. Besides, life here is not so bad," Ernie smiled. He added, "You know how I said I was met by my mother and father? Well, guess who was with Paul in heaven?'

Father Arnold said, "I have no idea. Paul's father, John?"

"Yes, his father, but also his sister, Janie."

Father Arnold felt his face go cold. He remembered little Janie. She had been a beautiful, inquisitive child whose life had been swept away by the current of the water down by the lake.

"Janie. Yes, I remember her. Did you talk with her?"

"Yes, I did. I cannot express to you how surprised, yet happy I was to see her. I found forgiveness there, Arnold. I have carried with me years of guilt, feeling responsible for her death. She wasn't angry at me. She hugged me and giggled and called me silly for carrying this burden of guilt," Ernie said, elated at the lightness he felt.

"That is amazing! I am so happy for you and know how her death troubled you so."

Ernie continued, "Paul also spoke about Barbara and the kids and how much he loved them. He asked me to look after them. When he spoke of them, Paul's emotion was real and authentic. He was confident that God would provide for his family, and that it was okay for him to remain in heaven. And you know what else I keep thinking of?"

"Yes, go on."

"Could it be that, before I gave my decision whether to stay in heaven or go back to earth, the decision was already made? I mean, think about it. Paul was in a heavenly white robe, and I remained in my street clothes. His robe was as white as snow, no blood, and pure, while I remained stained and soiled from a sinful world? Wouldn't I have donned a white robe, too, if I was to remain in heaven? Perhaps God's plan was perfectly clear and he knew what answer I would give before I even made it."

"God is omniscient. He knows all things before a word is even spoken from our tongues. God is omnipotent. He has infinite and ultimate power. It is through Him that everything is made and completed. God is omnipresent. He knows our innermost thoughts and knows each person's heart. I am sure he knew what answer you would give, Ernie."

"But God could have trumped my decision and taken me to heaven anyway."

"You are thinking about it too much, Ernie. Yes, He could have done that but He didn't. Again, what was your reason for returning to Earth?"

"Work still to do here on Earth, I suppose."

With that, Ernie announced, "And I do have more work to do. I need to arrange a visit Barbara."

Chapter 8

Greg Atkins lay on his dormitory bed counting the money he had pulled out of his lock box. Each small bill and loose change added up to $1,242. It was a good start, but not nearly the amount needed to make the second semester tuition and books at Michigan Tech University.

He would be receiving one more paycheck from work as a busser at the Kaleva Café before the tuition payment was due. Even with that extra $200, he would still be short. He needed at least $400 more and then he would be set.

He picked up the phone and called his mom in Farmington Hills, Michigan, in hopes that she could come to his aid. It had been a couple weeks since they had spoken and he knew that she would probably again be insistent that he come home and leave college for a while. He did not want to go back home when he was so close to graduating.

In May, only a few short months away, school would be over and he could finally look forward to a future where he was in control of his own destiny. He wanted to be a mechanical engineer and maybe have his own business someday. His father was a mechanical engineer and did well for himself, making a decent living for his family. He made enough money to afford a home in Farmington Hills, near Detroit, and own a timeshare in Florida. He was able to put Greg's sister completely through college. Greg had a year of school to go when the accident happened.

Greg could not allow himself to think about that awful night with his father. He was forever changed that evening and reliving it again, well, he just couldn't go there in his mind. Incomprehensible anger! He was tormented by his past and by the recent decisions he had made.

The phone rang four, five, six times, and then his mom's out-of-breath voice answered the phone.

"Hello?"

"Ma, this is Greg. How are you, Ma?"

"Greg. I am doing okay. How about you?" she asked.

"Ma, I was calling to see if you could help me out with tuition on my last semester of school. I need $400," Greg said, going straight for the point of the phone call.

"Four hundred dollars? I don't have that kind of money, son. I am so sorry. I am doing what I can just to afford keeping the house after your father died. I have returned to work and times are tough."

Anger bubbled in Greg, and he tried not to show it in his voice.

"I don't know what to do. I don't want to quit. Do you think Lynn would help?"

"I doubt if your sister would be able to help you, as she is saving for her wedding in June. I suppose you could try," his mother said, with a shrug in her voice unconvincingly.

"Nah, I won't bother her. It was a dumb idea. It just ticks me off; I am so close to graduating and feel so *stuck*. I can't stand it! I have no one to turn to, Ma. Somehow I got to make this work. I gotta go, Ma," Greg said and hung up the phone quickly.

He punched the pillow in anger and tried to think of what he could do next. He was not used to having empty pockets. He had grown up in abundance, getting what he wanted when he wanted it. He was well liked in high school and was known for being "the kid with the T-bird." He always had money to spend, a good-looking girl on his arm, and he dazzled everyone with his handsome good looks.

Greg was used to the lavish lifestyle his father had provided for him. Despite having everything he desired growing up, he still had a rebellious side to him. He had his share of small petty crimes that he took responsibility for by completing community service hours, but his father had a way of paying off some of the fines with a wink, a smile, and a tuck of some cash into a coat pocket. His father always seemed to watch Greg's back and got any charges diminished or erased. His record looked squeaky clean when he applied for college, and he looked like the model teen any university would be glad to have.

Greg could have had it all, still, if his father hadn't died suddenly and missed the last payment on his life insurance policy. This frustrated and angered Greg, who often misplaced his anger at his father onto others.

Greg remembered the day his mom called the life insurance company following his father's death, in hopes of collecting the life insurance money. She was told the grim news that the last payment had not been received and was past the thirty day grace period. His mother investigated further to find, indeed, her husband did not pay the bill and the remittance payment slip was still attached to the premium booklet in the drawer of his desk. The insurance company would not budge and kept their rigid rules providing nothing to the grieving family.

Greg could not take it. He called up the insurance company and went crazy with accusations and insults, almost daily for two weeks. The insurance agent even told Greg that charges would be pressed if he continued to harass them with phone calls. The life insurance company did help somewhat and basically covered the cost of the funeral, but Greg's mom could not collect the $1 million policy amount.

Not having that money devastated their family. Where his mom was sensible by cutting expenses, going back to work, and getting a female roommate to help pay the bills, Greg expected to live life as he always had: with plenty of money in his pocket.

I could do it one more time and probably get the money I need for school.

Greg wrestled with the idea in his mind for some time and thought back to how bad the last attempted robbery went. He hadn't been caught but he did leave two victims in a ghastly scene. The word "victim" stuck in his head. Wasn't he a victim, too? Victimized by the sudden death of his innocent father? Victim by an insurance company who could not find compassion for a family who was hurting following the death of their loved one, who had absentmindedly forgotten to pay his policy payment before he met his demise?

Greg wouldn't be in this mess if it weren't for the death of his father and the bullies at the life insurance company who were probably happy not paying out more than they should have. It wasn't fair, and he could not be blamed for what he knew: He had to do again. If others suffered, so what? He had suffered, too, beyond anyone else's suffering.

The Lakes' football team had its playoff football game tonight, Friday night, against the White Pine Warriors in White Pine, Michigan. The game would be broadcast on the radio, and Ernie planned on listening to the game from his hospital bed. Nurse Beverly came into Ernie's hospital room carrying a handheld transistor radio that she had brought from home. She handed the radio to Ernie with these instructions:

"You are to keep the volume under control. If you get caught with this radio, you will most likely get it taken away. If anyone asks where you got it, keep my name hush."

Ernie already felt like a child about to get into trouble for something he knew was wrong.

"No cheering too loudly, as it will disrupt others and call attention to yourself. Plus, cheering could hurt your stitches."

"Here is the on/off switch and the volume. Have fun," she said.

"Thanks a bunch. You are the best," Ernie said and took the transistor radio and hid it under his top sheet until 6:55 p.m., when the broadcast would start. He ate the few last bites of his pasta dinner and watched the local news on television.

"There are still no leads in the two robberies that happened last weekend, in the small towns of Dollar Bay and Hubbell. Friday night police say a gunman entered the Bootlegger Liquor Store in Dollar Bay and held up an employee, who was ordered to empty the cash register. The very next evening the gunman, believed to be the same man, entered Lewis' Market in Hubbell, shooting the owner, Paul Lewis, and shot a store patron, Ernie Price, police say. Lewis died. Price remains hospitalized for his injuries. The gunman left with money from the cash register. The suspect is believed to be a young man in his twenties to thirties and is about six feet tall and 175 pounds. If you have information, please contact the Torch Lake Police Department," reported a news broadcaster.

Ernie thought for a moment about the robbery and the shooting. He wondered if the suspect ever thought about him or Paul? Was the suspect some kind of monster that would strike again? Was he sorry for what he did? The newspaper and radio announced that he was thought to be in his twenties. So young, Ernie thought, to be a criminal. What would possess a young man to commit crimes and terrorize neighborhoods by his wicked ways? Regardless of the reasons, Ernie had been always taught that he should pray for his persecutors. Holding onto hate, anger, or the desire for justice is not from God; it is of the devil, Ernie believed. So he bowed his head and prayed for the young man who had days earlier killed a good friend and left him to die. Ernie silently recited Matthew 5:44.

But I say unto you, love your enemies, bless them that curse you, do good to them that hate you, and pray for them which despitefully use you, and persecute you.

———————⊰«◉»⊱———————

Mike and Mark arose Saturday morning jubilant about their football playoff win the night before. It was another close game, but the Lakes pulled off a victory, 17-10.

The win meant they were playing in the state semi-finals next Friday night. The team members had their hearts in this last game, as it was dedicated to Paul Lewis, Ernie Price, and their grieving town. The team showed that they were strong and the spirits of everyone in the town had been uplifted. It seemed strange to feel joy so quickly after experiencing feelings of fear and grief, but people were determined not to wallow in the what-ifs and what-could-have-beens. They wanted to move forward by pulling together and being there for one another.

Today, Mike and Mark, with the help of little Scott and Darren, had plans to ride their bikes around the entire town, delivering flyers to houses announcing the upcoming toy drive. Their hope was that each person would be touched to give with loving kindness.

COMMUNITY TOY DRIVE!

Sunday, November 17th, noon to 5 p.m.
Please drop off your new and gently used toys, bikes, sleds, games, dolls or cash donation to Ernie's Service Station. All donations help provide

for the annual St. Cecilia's Children's Christmas Party scheduled for December 15.

Helping hands are also needed to fix toys and wrap presents. Stay and help and enjoy tasty cookies and hot chocolate. Thank you!

Following the delivery of flyers, Scott and Darren went back to Ernie's gas station to help fill cars with gas and pump air into tires. Mike and Mark went home to pull out sheet music for song selections that Ernie had given them for the first Christmas children's choir rehearsal tomorrow evening. Bringing out the old Christmas hymns and familiar children's classics brought excitement to the boys and they could not wait to share them with the children's choir.

It would be strange for Ernie not join them this year for the festivities, but all would pray that he would be well enough to sit back and enjoy the party. Ernie had faith in Mike and Mark's ability to orchestrate the party and Christmas Eve mass, as they were both talented and mature young men who had watched him plan and deliver programming for the community and church for years. Mike and Mark had been working with Ernie in the choir for about six years and it was Ernie who had first taught them to play guitar and bass.

When Mike and Mark first started learning guitar, all they wanted to do was jam and do boisterous rock star moves. But slowly, they toned things down and began participating in the singing, too, soon realizing that they had talented voices. Not to mention, they noticed that the young ladies in choir liked a boy who could sing.

Tonight the boys would be playing their instruments and singing with the children's choir at Saturday evening mass, alone, without Ernie. It would be a good test to see how ready they were for moving forward in the rehearsals, Saturday masses, upcoming Christmas party and Christmas Eve mass. They needed to be prepared in the event that Ernie would not be with them. As they had been forced to learn firsthand, nothing in life is certain.

The children performed beautifully at Saturday night mass. Mark and Mike were relieved that the children quieted down whenever they instructed them and followed every move with attentive eyes, ready to do as asked. The kids understood that Ernie would be not able to join them until he was stronger and that he had put Mike and Mark in charge. The kids also understood that they needed to cooperate, as they were getting into such a busy time of year and they would have many singing commitments. They were excited that tomorrow night they could begin singing Christmas songs and already bickered over desired solos.

After mass, the choir stayed for a few minutes afterward to make "Get well" cards for Ernie. A few of the girls brought in colored paper, scissors, markers, and Crayons, and they got busy making beautiful cards and cutting out snowflakes that Mark and Mike would bring to Ernie in the hospital. Mark knew that Ernie would appreciate the thoughtfulness of the children and it would definitely cheer him up.

Overnight, extreme cold air set in, with an average high of just fifteen degrees. The weatherman forecasted forecasted snow by Monday morning. It had been a glorious fall season, seasonably warm but the cold weather was likely here to stay. It was time to start hauling out the winter coats, boots, warm gloves, hats, and scarves. Snow shovels and snow scoops, too.

The kids never seemed to mind the cold weather. They looked at it as opportunity to play in the snow and hope for school to be cancelled by a sudden blizzard. Snow in November also would get everyone thinking about the holidays to come. Some people were already eagerly dangling holiday lights on the outside of their houses and on pine trees in their front yards. The downtown business district was bustling with shoppers trying to get a head start on their holiday gift-buying.

But not Barbara. She found it difficult to think about the holidays after just losing her husband a week ago. No doubt this would be a difficult time for the Lewis family, as the holidays often are for people who have lost loved ones. Barbara and the children were invited to share the holidays with her sister and family, but Barbara was uncertain if they could attend. She still had the market to tend to and she needed more time to grow stronger.

This past week, she had asked other employees to work extra hours so she could remain at home with the kids, trying to put their lives back together, while she made plans for continuing the business. Barbara would continue to work at the market but would need to change her hours a little to be able to be with the children after school and in the evenings. She would need to hire a butcher, as Paul had done that work himself.

She was determined to keep Lewis' Market open and in operation, as it had for more than sixty years. Paul had loved the market and the family tradition of small-town, friendly service. Barbara had grown to love it, as well, and invested many years of retail and gourmet cooking experience in it to make Lewis' Market a sought-out place to shop and entertain. Her local employees were like family, and she couldn't close the doors and force them to find other work. Especially not this time of year.

Tomorrow morning, Barbara would step foot in the market for the first time since Paul's death. She was apprehensive, but asked the Lord to be at her side.

⸻ ◦(◐)◦ ⸻

Ernie's strength and optimism grew each day. He had moved out of intensive care to a post-op room. Doctors removed his chest tube as he was now able to keep his lung functioning normally without accumulation of fluids in his lungs. His breath sounds were no longer shallow and rattled. He worked with a physical therapist and a respiratory therapist everyday to increase his activity, walking, and breathing.

The respiratory therapist was impressed that he was able to blow the ball on his incentive spirometer higher each day. Ernie was increasing his lung volume and able to cough, which showed good progress. He was making slow strides, but each day showed promise that he would recover in time for the upcoming Christmas party. He would still need oxygen on occasion, but he was relying on it less and less as time went by.

He looked forward to walking with Nurse Beverly and was excited to make the walk from his room and around the nurse's station loop. The nurses smiled and waved as he walked by, and Ernie loved the attention. Ernie was able to sit up for periods of time in his room in a chair and play Scrabble and cards with visitors. It made the time go by. But never fast enough.

Ernie was a little impatient, thinking of the all the things he should be doing. He missed working at the service station, church, and the hours of time he put into preparing for the children's Christmas party. He knew his body should rest, but his heart and mind wouldn't allow it. He asked Nurse Beverly if he could have someone bring in his guitar but was told that he was denied privileges to playing in his room. Ernie took that as a "No," meaning there was no way he would get his guitar until he left the hospital. Nurse Beverly thought otherwise.

She knew that Ernie could not play his guitar in his hospital room but she couldn't see any reason why Ernie couldn't play his guitar in the family room at the end of the hall. That way he could play for himself, as well as others. She made arrangements for Ernie to walk down to the family room after dinner tonight, where a few of his friends would meet him. She would invite ambulatory patients to join in, too.

Father Arnold, Harry, Greta, Scott, Darren, Barbara, and her children, Randy and Rachel, hurried into the family room down the hall from Ernie's hospital room. Father Arnold had taken Ernie's guitar and music book from the church with him to present to Ernie. Ernie no doubt would be surprised by seeing his friends, but he would be delighted to see his oldest friend, his guitar.

Ernie received the guitar as a gift given from his father on his twenty-first birthday. Ernie had just returned from World War II and was rehabilitating from a staph infection in his leg when his birthday came along. Ernie's father knew the guitar would help pass the time and probably heal his son's restless heart too, Ernie learned the guitar quickly. He never worked with a teacher and was proud to say he learned everything on his own. He was a natural talent with the guitar and soon wanted to play for other people. He started playing church hymns and country songs for the senior citizens at the nursing home. The seniors enjoyed the sweet music and Ernie's company. They marveled at the songs that he played and soon they started remembering lyrics to songs that they thought their fading memories had forgotten. The music made them feel alive. Some residents would dance and some would sit in their wheelchairs and rock back and forth. Tears would be shed too.

Ernie also played his guitar for children in schools. The children learned many folk songs and silly songs that kept their attention, and many wanted to know how they, too, could play the guitar. Ernie started giving guitar lessons and taught many children to excel at loving and playing the guitar. He instilled in them an appreciation for music and a lifelong skill that could soothe their souls, and entertain their friends and families.

Nurse Beverly cleared Ernie's dinner tray and fetched Ernie's bathrobe and slippers.

"C'mon Ernie, we are going for a walk. We are going to work off that extra chicken leg you ate!" she laughed.

"I guess my appetite is back," he chuckled, shifting his weight to the side of the bed. "Sure, I would love to take a walk with you."

He sat at the edge of the bed, and Nurse Beverly donned his slippers. Then he stood up and she helped him with his robe. They walked slowly out the door, while Ernie pulled the IV drip pole beside him. At the end of the hall, he saw a little face peek out from the doorway. He thought for a moment that it was Darren Muljo. A smile crossed Ernie's face, and he kept walking to see if it was, indeed, a familiar child he knew.

Then he saw little Scotty's face peek out, too. Scott put his hand over his mouth and quickly withdrew into the room. Ernie was sure of it now. He had visitors. He almost ran to the end of the hall to see the boys. He joyously waltzed into the family room and to his surprise, there was more than just Scott and Darren in the room. He saw Harry, Greta, Father Arnold, Barbara, Rachel and Randy, too. His heart leaped with excitement and he gently extended his arms for hugs.

"What a wonderful surprise! Just the cure for the hospital blues," exclaimed Ernie.

"We have missed you, Ernie," said Scott and Darren, clutching onto Ernie's waist.

"Barbara, it is so good to see you. Oh, how I have thought of you." His arms reached for her and he felt her melt against his chest. Whatever frailty Ernie had in the moment was lost, as his arms now were as sturdy as an oak tree, cradling her. "I am so sorry. I loved Paul like a brother," said Ernie, his heart aching inside, since it was the first time that he had seen Barbara following Paul's passing. Though she was heavy in grief, she did not know the happiness Paul was now experiencing. Ernie had witnessed it.

Barbara hugged Ernie and sobbed quietly, tears falling onto the collar of his bathrobe. Rachel and Randy walked up to Barbara and Ernie and hugged them both, patting them on their backs. The tender moment struck the hearts of everyone in the room. Father Arnold sniffled and Greta shuffled her feet, gazing away, as she knew she would cry. Scott and Darren nuzzled into Harry's side, as Harry comforted the boys by stroking their fine hair.

Nurse Beverly was touched by the healing she witnessed, happening right before her eyes. Barbara and Ernie both faced the same fierce battle: overcoming the boulders in life that could consume them, but bravely, they would find comfort, understanding, and peace. They would fight it out together. In their embrace, everyone could see that they would not let the other's future be one of forgotten loneliness or incessant worry.

Barbara's life would truly never be the same, but God could make beauty out of ashes. Ernie was given his life to move forward, and he was still coming to grips with that. Why was Paul's life taken and not his? Now Barbara would be facing days and years ahead making decisions that were supposed to be made by a husband and wife, together. It didn't seem fair. While Barbara buried her husband last week, Ernie was hoping to bury his grief and guilt of surviving and trying to make sense of what purpose he was to serve on earth. He knew he had to talk to Barbara. His soul would not find peace until he told her of what he had seen.

Nurse Beverly thought back to five years ago when she lost her husband, Charlie. He died of lymphoma, a cancer of the lymph nodes. Charlie passed away within three months of his diagnosis, and Beverly could remember that she almost died with him -- of a broken heart. Feeling alone, since her children had grown and moved out, she cocooned into a catatonic state. She couldn't eat, sleep, or work and lived in a depressed stupor for about a year.

Finally, her good friend, Mary, got her the help that Beverly desperately needed; she brought her to a support grief group and picked her up for church the next Sunday morning. What helped Beverly the most with her grief after Charlie passed away was connecting again with God.

She had been a new Christian at the time Charlie had passed

away, and at first, she felt betrayed by God. *How could He let this happen in her life? I am changing my life for You and You rearranged by life by taking my husband out of it?* Rather than drawing closer to God and finding refuge in His grip, she chose to walk away from Him. She denied her friends' attempts to help her. She withdrew and slowly withered away, emotionally and physically from anything that might connect with her heart in any way, for fear that even one more crack might crumble it like dust.

It took nearly one year to shake Beverly out of her fraught state. One night, feeling lonely and afraid, Beverly cried herself to sleep. She awoke in the middle of the night and looked straight ahead to the moonlight coming into her room. The light in all its glory was bright and filled up the room. She sat up in bed and looked at the moon and its incredible light. She rubbed her eyes for a moment, as she saw what appeared to be a cross on the moon.

She looked again and sure enough, the moonbeams appeared to go north and south, east and west across the moon and into the night sky. In all her life, she had never seen the moon appear like this. The moonlight radiated brightly and comforted her. She lay back down in bed and continued to be mesmerized by the moon, until she fell asleep again.

In Beverly's dream, God told her that she was meant to see the cross in the sky. This was to reassure her that His mercy would be enough and He would give her rest. She saw herself in her dream, sitting at the feet of her Father God and Him saying these beloved words to her, from 1 Peter 5: 7-11:

"Cast all your anxiety on him, because he cares for you. Discipline yourselves, keep alert. Like a roaring lion your adversary the devil prowls around, looking for someone to devour. Resist him, steadfast in your faith, for you know that your brothers and sisters in all the world are undergoing the same kinds of suffering. And after you have suffered for a little while, the God of all grace, who has called you to his eternal glory in Christ,

will himself restore, support, strengthen, and establish you. To him be the power forever and ever. Amen."

Beverly awoke from her dream feeling completely light of pain, anger and regret. Suddenly, she understood that this immense peace could only come from God, Himself. She vowed to return to loving her Father God and walking in His ways. No longer would she carry feelings of remorse or anger; instead she would exchange it for good and allow God to use her familiarity in grief to help others. God kept His promise and restored Beverly to be able to start a support grief group in the hospital for people who struggled with the loss of loved ones. Beverly lovingly approached Barbara and invited her and the children to participate in her family grief group when she was ready.

Father Arnold stepped forward smiling and said, "We have something for you Ernie." He pulled his arm from behind his back to reveal Ernie's beloved guitar. Ernie's eyes opened wide with anticipation.

"Well, hello there dear friend," he said to the guitar, and the group laughed.

Ernie took a seat in the recliner and Father Arnold placed the guitar in his lap. Everyone took a seat around Ernie and he began to play softly, strumming his guitar and thanking God in his heart for this moment of friendship and healing. Beverly led the others in singing, Let There Be Peace on Earth:

"Let there be peace on earth,
and let it begin with me..."

Soon, other patients began streaming into the family room to allow the sweet sound to fill their souls. Doctors and nurses passing by popped into the room for just a moment to sing a verse or two, and then returned to work happier and more content.

"I thank you all for the wonderful surprise of your visit and the time we could spend together singing. I am a very lucky man to have you all as friends," Ernie said, misty-eyed.

"I hate to be the one to break up the party, but Ernie must get back to his room and rest," Beverly interrupted.

"Would it be alright if Barbara walked with me back to my room? I would like to speak with her alone if I could," Ernie asked.

"That would be fine. Visiting hours end in twenty minutes though," Beverly reminded.

"I'll will sure to leave on time," Barbara winked.

"Hey kids, how does an ice cream sundae sound to you all?" Harry offered.

"It sounds really good. Can we, huh?" Scott blurted out, excited.

The children did their little happy dance, and Father Arnold joined in the fun, too, throwing his arms high in the air and wiggling his hands.

"Barbara, why don't you stay and talk with Ernie, and Greta and I can take the kiddos and Father Arnold out for sundaes, then stop by your house with Rachel and Randy afterward," Harry insisted.

"That sounds fine, Harry. Thank you," Barbara grinned.

"Well then, madam, will you take this arm and lead me down the hall to room 316?" Ernie asked Barbara, offering the arm without the IVs dangling. She smiled and took hold of his strong arm and escorted him down the hallway.

Barbara helped Ernie sit on the edge of the bed and then took a seat on the chair at his side.

Ernie reached to pick a piece of paper off of his nightstand and held the paper delicately in his hands. He had spent quite a deal of time thinking about how he could start this important conversation with Barbara. He had rehearsed it over and over again in his mind, making sure that what he said would be of comfort to Barbara and that would not confuse or upset her. He relied on the famous poet T.S. Eliot to help him with the right words, the words printed on the paper now in his hands. He guided the paper toward Barbara, who took it gently into her hands and focused her eyes on the words on the page.

"It is worth dying to find out what life is." -- *T.S. Eliot*

This time she read the words out loud, "It is worth dying to find out what life is."

She looked up into Ernie's gentle blue eyes and said, "I am not sure I understand. Did you just read something from T.S. Eliot? Is this message for me?"

"Yes, the message is for you. What do you think these words mean?"

The word "dying" jumped off the page and pierced her heart. She immediately thought of her beloved Paul. She was drawn to the word "life" and tried to find the connection between the two words. Dying. Life.

"I suppose its relevance to me could be that, in Paul's death, I have a new life? I dunno," she guessed, stumped by what answer Ernie was looking for.

"Yes, that is true. Your life is forever changed by his passing, but you will move on. I promise you. And I promised Paul --" Ernie stopped, realizing that he mentioned the promising Paul part a little prematurely. This was not going as he planned.

"You promised Paul? Ernie, what are you talking about?"

"I promised Paul that I would look after you and the kids."

"When did you agree to do this? At the market when he was dying?" Her eagerness for his answer made her unsettled in her chair. She wrung her hands with apprehension.

"No, Barbara. It wasn't the market, ambulance or hospital," Ernie paused. "It was in heaven."

"Heaven? You spoke to Paul in heaven?" Barbara's voice was a soft whisper, as she choked back emotion. "Ernie, help me here. I am so confused."

"After the shooting, there were a couple minutes where I left this Earth and passed away, as well. I went to a place that can only now be realized by its incredible beauty and peace, as heaven."

"Oh my gosh, Ernie. You died? And can remember being in heaven? How can you be so sure?"

"Barbara, it was magnificent. No words can describe what I saw or felt. I was enveloped in a love that could only be the love of God. I never saw God but did see other people there," Ernie excitedly remarked.

"Ernie, you saw Paul there, didn't you?"

"I did see Paul, and he was overjoyed to be there with his father and sister, Janie. He actually met me and my mother and father at the gate of passing."

Barbara felt like all air would escape her chest. Unbelievable surprise and happiness filled her body where the air had departed. There was no doubt in her mind that Paul would be in heaven, but hearing Ernie say that he saw him there brought feelings of incredible distance spanning between Paul and herself.

"Barbara, he looked radiant in a long, white gown, pure and clean. I stood before him, still in my church clothes from that day. I was not given a white gown at my arriving. I soon realized that I was not staying. It was impressed on my heart that the decision to stay in heaven or go back to Earth would be mine. But God knew already what my answer would be, so he never got the white gown from the chest, I guess. I realized that I need to return to Earth to finish up some things for our Lord."

"So, you got to chose to return to Earth rather than stay in heaven?" Barbara asked.

"I did. Paul did not have a choice, as the decision was made for him. He did know that his life on Earth was over and that heaven would be his new home. He was overjoyed! He spoke of you and the children with immense love and concern, asking me to watch over you. He was confident that our good Lord would take care of you, too."

"It means everything to me to hear that he is in heaven and is so happy," Barbara said, feeling tears of love and relief in her eyes. Her beloved was more than okay; he was *overjoyed*. "My grief lightens knowing that he is home. It may not be the home on Maple Street with me and the kids, but heaven is his home now. Don't we all want that someday? To be in heaven for eternity?"

"Jesus said, 'Anyone who believes in Him will live, even after dying. Everyone who lives in Him and believes in Him will never die,'" said Ernie, quoting John 11:25-26. "You will see Paul again someday, Barbara. Since Jesus lives in you and you believe in Him, the Lord will fulfill his promise. We will all live with Him in paradise someday."

"I believe in His promise, I do. Until that day, I must keep living here, trusting and serving God."

Ernie nodded and smiled.

Barbara looked down at the crumpled piece of paper in her hand. She opened it, flattening the rumpled page. The words, "It is worth dying to find out what life is," now rang clear to her. Paul was alive again. More alive than he had ever been.

Chapter 9

The Lakes football team traveled two hours by bus to their next playoff game in Marquette, Michigan. A parade of cars holding Lakes fans followed the bus in support of their high school football team. It looked like the entire towns of Lake Linden and Hubbell had been emptied and were attending the game.

The Lakes team colors, blue and gold, were visible on every fan from head to toe. Banners waved and pom-poms shook. Screams and cheering roared in the stadium, like a freight train passing by. The hometown pride and spirit was at an all-time high. This was the furthest their football team had ever gone in the history of the high school. If a win happened tonight, they would play in the state finals next week and that would mean another road trip seven hours away.

The team was thankful that they would play the game indoors in a dome with turf, instead of playing outside where the temperature was eighteen degrees Fahrenheit and there was snow on the ground. The team had never played on turf before and would get some warm-up time to try it out before the game started. The players went into the locker room, got suited up, and then walked onto the enormous field.

They were in awe of the size of the stadium, eyes open wide with unimaginable delight. Some threw high-fives, reveling in the reality of a place this incredible. Others, stood dumbfounded with mouths open wide like large Cheerios. The bright fluorescent lights shined above and the fans marveled at the colorfully detailed scoreboard with their team name, the Lakes, positioned as the away team. The enormous stadium had seating for two thousand, plenty of enough room for fans, as compared to back home. The tiny field would pack them in like sardines and then take out the lawn chairs and blankets for late arrivers. arrivers.

The coach got them warmed up, and they started running some plays. Running on turf was a lot different from running on natural grass. The turf had a hardness and stiffness to it and certainly hurt more when you fell on it. When you fell, it felt like getting a carpet burn. The team was aware that there were more incidents of injuries on turf than on natural grass, and they hoped that would not be the case here today.

The opposing team, the the Frankfort Panthers, used this field for all their practices and games, so that would leave the Lakes at a disadvantage. The coach admitted that the Panthers experience with the turf was a bonus but he was not going to allow anyone on his team to think of making up excuses or creating self-fulfilling negative prophecies before the game had even begun. That was bad luck and he wouldn't hear of it.

The opposing team aggressively stormed the field. The players grunted as they got stirred up and started pounding on each other's shoulder pads. Sizing up the team members, they looked like a good match for the Eagles.

Ernie lay in his hospital bed holding the transistor radio that Nurse Beverly had brought in for him to listen to the game. It was now the middle of the second quarter. Still not points. Suddenly, the Lakes scored with a forty-yard touchdown pass. The fans went crazy and cheered again when the extra point kick was good.

Ernie's grit teeth transformed to a wide grin and his feet kicked with joy as the Lakes pulled ahead. "Way to work it, Lakes!" he yelled and then shuddered, knowing he needed to keep his cheering to a quiet roar in the hospital.

The score remained seven to zero at halftime, when the teams resorted to the locker room for a break. The Lakes' coach was pleased at his team's great start but warned them about getting overconfident. He knew from experience that once you start getting cocky about your playing, the tables turn.

The coach went on to quote all-time football great, Vince Lombardi, former coach of the Green Bay Packers: "The price of success is hard work, dedication to the job at hand, and the determination that whether we win or lose, we have applied the best of ourselves to the task at hand."

The coach continued, "We have had a great football season, and your hard work and dedication has brought us to this point today. Be proud of your success, despite the challenges that personally have affected our friends, family, and town recently. Paul Lewis was a great assistant football coach and he helped prepare you for where you are today. He is greatly missed for his talent and friendship, and we still mourn his passing. You all have shown me great service in your acts of mercy for others and the Lewis family, and you are all winners."

He paused and looked around the room into the faces of his young athletes. The boys were stoic.

"Whether we win or lose tonight, I think this team is pretty special. You have shown me perseverance through heartache and steadfastness by coming together as a team. Thank you for a great season that goes down in my playbook as remarkable in every way."

The players bowed their heads in prayer and for several moments of silence, until the referee whistle blew to begin the second half.

The Lakes remained ahead until the fourth quarter. At the top of the fourth quarter, the Lakes were forced to punt the ball. The kicked ball soared forty-five yards, and the Panthers returned the ball twenty yards, before stopping at the thirty-yard line. On the first down, the Panthers' quarterback bulleted the ball, only to be caught by a running back with legs of steel. The running back broke three tackles from the mighty Lakes' defense, and he managed to run the length of the field for a Panthers' touchdown. The kick was good. The score was now tied up at seven to seven.

When it was finally the Lakes' turn, the players were forced to punt after only three plays. With four minutes left in the game, the Panthers now had the ball on the Lakes' twenty-five-yard line with a first down. The fans were nervous and concerned, hoping that their great season would not come to an end. It was a knuckle-cruncher and nail-biter.

The Panthers surprised everyone by trying three plays, going for the end zone each time, and each time coming up empty. With a little over two minutes left, the Panthers still had a chance to put the game away with a field goal. The Panthers' kicking team lined up to attempt a forty-five-yard field goal. With a perfect snap, the placeholder nervously placed the ball on the ground, ready for the kick.

The kicker approached the ball with everything he had and the ball sailed toward the goal post. Knocking the right post, the ball bounced inside the uprights and through for a successful field goal. Heartbreak overcame the Lakes' supporters and the team let out a moan. The Panthers now had the lead at ten to seven with less than two minutes to play.

However, the Lakes quickly got to the Panthers' forty-yard line and almost within field goal range. On the third down, Mark Alcott, the Lakes quarterback, eyed a receiver wide open twenty-yards down the field. Mark cocked his arm back, ready to throw -- when out of the blue Mark took a hit from both sides, throwing him forward like a rag doll and jolting the ball loose. A Panthers' defender quickly snatched the rolling ball and the Panthers' fans went wild.

Mark did not move on the field and lay there still. He struggled to catch his breath; the hit had knocked all of the air out of him. Mark started to gasp for air. The coach ran out to the field to check on his valuable player. He encouraged Mark to slowly inhale and exhale and not get excited or try to talk. After a few tense moments, Mark was able to stand with the help of his coach. He felt better physically, but knew the grave consequences of the hit: the loss of the ball and the game was now over, as the Panthers had control of the ball with only ten seconds left to play. The Panthers' coach and teammates sprinted onto the field in celebration. The Lakes' coach congratulated the Panthers' coach with a handshake and the team applauded the winners. It had been a great game. Just not the outcome they had hoped for.

Ernie sighed in the last few seconds, when he realized that the Lakes football team would not be advancing to the state championship. Their season had ended tonight with a valiant effort, and though they played with determination, it was not their fate to secure a win.

"Did the game end?" Nurse Beverly asked, as she entered Ernie's hospital room.

"Yes, the final was ten to seven," Ernie mumbled. "The Lakes lost."

"Oh, rats! Was it a good game though?"

"Yes, the Lakes team played their best and would have won but just ran out of time."

"Huh? That was a joke, eh?" she laughed.

"Yes. But not a good one I am afraid," Ernie laughed.

Nurse Beverly changed Ernie's IV bag and checked Ernie's vitals.

"You are doing so well Ernie. I bet in a couple of days you will be allowed to go home."

"Really? That would be wonderful. I will be home before Thanksgiving. And when can I go back to work?"

"Hold your horses now, mister. Work will need to wait a couple more weeks. You will still need physical therapy and respiratory therapy at home. Do you have anyone at home or nearby that can help you with cooking, cleaning, and some light nursing duties?" she asked.

"No, I don't have anyone that can be there on a daily basis. Possibly a few friends that could stop by. Will I really need that much help?"

"Unfortunately, you will need the help, and if you do not have someone lined up to assist you, you will not be discharged from this hospital and be sent directly to a rehab facility for a couple of weeks."

"I don't want to do that!" Ernie exclaimed.

"I wouldn't want that for you either," she said. "If you do not have anyone reliable to help, maybe I can be of assistance to you on my off days. I do work home healthcare hours occasionally outside of this job, and I could take on some hours caring for you. That is, if you are interested. My friend Mary works as a nurse's aide and most likely could be of help, as well."

"You would do that for me?" Ernie said with eagerness.

"Absolutely. We can work out the details and let your doctor know so there is no hesitancy in him sending you home on your planned discharge day of Monday," Nurse Beverly said, as she reached over Ernie to prop up his pillow.

Ernie breathed in and could smell lilacs. Lilacs on a cold winter day. Beverly's perfume lingered in the otherwise antiseptic smelling hospital room, and he found himself almost blushing when her arm brushed across his chest. He found himself looking at this beautiful women and all she had done for him, and he was somewhat smitten by her.

Her salt-and-pepper-sprinkled gray hair lay neatly in a chignon upon the nape of her long neck. Her large green eyes and warm smile radiated her lasting beauty long into her middle-aged years. He liked her spunk, sense of humor, and her small but mighty stature. She was a petite gal, probably just making the five-foot-tall mark. Every time she entered the room his heart beat a little faster. He was not accustomed to feeling like this. There was only one other woman he ever had strong feelings for and she broke his heart long ago.

Ernie was relieved by the news of being able to go home soon. He was thrilled that Beverly would be able to help him at home, too, with chores and cooking. It would be wonderful to have his new friend near his side in the next couple of weeks while he recuperated.

Sunday morning arrived. Today was the day of the Community Toy Drive that Mike and Mark had organized. They opened up Ernie's service station at 11:30 a.m. and took out the tools, paint, sewing supplies, and other materials they would need to repair the toys that came in for the toy drive. Their mother had made a few dozen of homemade gingerbread, fudge, sugar cookies and shortbread and equipped the boys with carafes of hot water for hot chocolate. The boys had arranged with Harry to use the barbershop next door also as a place to repair the toys in case many people showed up to help. At a little before noon, cars started pulling up to the service station and people started unloading their trunks and back seats of new and used toys. People pushed bikes and pulled wagons full of toys to the service station. Some people were able to stay and work on the toys and others grabbed a cookie and were on the way. Christmas music was playing in the background, and everyone was getting in the festive spirit. They told stories of Christmases past and shared their fondest memories.

Harry took out the Christmas lights and got busy decorating the eves of the roofline of the service station. A few ladies wrapped gifts and put tags on them, designating if the gift was for a boy or girl and the age of the child. Greta and her daughters, Sarah and Claire, got busy knitting handmade hats and mittens. Their handiwork was beautiful. They had diligently been knitting throughout the year in preparation for this event. In total, they had already made forty hats and forty pairs of mittens. They also donated two crocheted blankets that would make a wonderful gift for a family at the Christmas party.

Some visitors, who did not have children of their own with used toys to give or time to shop for toys, offered cash donations toward the purchase of new toys or to buy Christmas dinners for the needy. So many people opened their hearts with loving kindness that they made the toy drive even bigger than past years.

Many people stayed all day to help repair the remaining used toys. Soon the entire back room of the service station was packed full of gifts. Some people moved over to Harry's Barber Shop next door, because they still had more work to do but had no more storage space for toys at the service station. With one hour left to go in the toy drive, they could all say that they had been truly blessed by the community's response. More than one hundred children would receive toys and many families would receive holiday baskets and a big ham for Christmas day.

Nurse Beverly stopped by the toy drive in its final hour with a large pot of chili and hot cornbread for the workers. She explained that she was Ernie's nurse at the hospital and he had told her yesterday that friends were working on the toy drive. Ernie was a bit melancholy about not being able to be a part of the festivities, and he had his friends and the toy drive on his mind.

Beverly had taken it upon herself to make the delicious chili and cornbread and bring it by the service station on Ernie's behalf. Everyone was overjoyed by the token of her grateful heart and Ernie's thoughts of them together on this day. Beverly could see that Ernie had a wonderful collection of friends who deeply cared for him. Some of the friends had been at the guitar-playing social the other night at the hospital, and she was glad to reconnect with them again.

By 5 p.m. everything was cleaned up and put in place at both the service station and the barber shop. Harry locked up the shop and Mark locked the service station, checking the lock twice. The toys would sit tight for another three weeks until the Christmas party commenced.

⸻ «()» ⸻

Greta arrived at the hospital at 1:00 p.m. the following day, the day after the toy drive was completed. She had received Ernie's telephone call earlier in the morning that he was ready to be discharged after lunch. The news caught her by surprise, as it was a day earlier than expected, but she was delighted nonetheless. Ernie had his bags packed and had already met with the doctor who advised him of his follow-up instructions.

Ernie was to continue receiving physical and respiratory therapy at home for three weeks, use oxygen when needed, have a chest x-ray in two weeks, and no working or physical lifting for three to four weeks. If any illness, fever or signs of infection should occur, the doctors instructed him to come to the hospital immediately. So Ernie would be taking it easy through the entire Thanksgiving and Christmas holiday season.

Greta entered Ernie's hospital room and he was sitting on the edge of the bed waiting for her to arrive. Nurse Beverly was in the room putting Ernie's shoes on and grabbed his coat. She was sad to see her favorite patient go home but she knew she would be seeing him soon. She helped Ernie with his coat and then sat him down in the wheelchair. She wheeled him down the hall with Greta following to the nurse's station. The nurses and doctors at the desk stood up, clapped and cheered for Ernie -- for his brave recovery, for the miraculous news of his departure, and for the lives he had touched through his kindness and sweet smile in the hospital.

"Are you that eager to see me leave?" Ernie laughed.

"Don't be silly! We are sorry you are leaving. You have been a joy to know," another nurse said.

"Aw, don't make an old man cry now," Ernie said, pretending to wipe a tear.

"We wish you all the best, Mr. Price. Be healthy and do not rush your healing time. No changing tires on a big-rig eighteen-wheeler for a few weeks, okay?" said Ernie's doctor.

"It might be tempting, but no, I will take it easy," Ernie smiled. "Thank you all for your care. You have restored a lifeless man to his feisty old self again. I will miss you all. God bless." Ernie waved goodbye.

Nurse Beverly helped Ernie into the awaiting car. She gave him a hug and said, "I am glad this is not goodbye for us. Tomorrow, you get to see me barking my nurse's orders at you from your own living room. I will stop by around 2 p.m., promptly," she said, winking at Ernie.

"I'm not quite sure what to say in response to that," said Ernie, shrugging his shoulders. In his heart he felt elated at seeing his new friend again and so soon.

"Goodbye, Ernie."

Greta slowly drove away and Ernie turned his head and waved goodbye to Beverly, who was waving back from the hospital entrance. There was that sweet smell again. Lilac perfume permeated the shoulder of his jacket. Ernie breathed in the wonderful fragrance and smiled.

Greta got Ernie situated at home and then put the pan of leftover stew in the refrigerator for Ernie to eat for dinner later. She laid out his medication on the counter in the kitchen and set up his portable oxygen tank near the couch. Greta filled his hospital drinking cup with ice and cold water and put it on the table near the couch where Ernie was sitting. Ernie snuggled up with the afghan his mother had made and got comfortable. He was going to rest for a while and told Greta that she or Harry could come back in a couple of hours and check on him.

It sure is good to be home, Ernie thought, and he quickly drifted off to sleep.

Greg stormed into his apartment and threw his book bag on the floor. He had another frustrating day of tests, work, and the constant nagging worry of how he was going to come up with the $400 he needed to pay for his upcoming tuition that was due on Friday, the day after Thanksgiving. He hated that the responsibility fell on him and that there was no one to help him.

As always, he grew angry at his father, who was supposed to take of his his wife and children. In a way, Greg felt abandoned and betrayed by his father's death. He felt desperate. His mother felt guilty for not looking after the bill-paying. She had witnessed her husband's forgetfulness firsthand, and she regretted not offering to help him more. She knew he would only grow angry if she pointed out his weakness, so she withdrew and no longer looked over his shoulder. Now the messy future was hers. If only she had spoken up.

She put her son in a difficult situation, too, by not having enough money to give him to finish college. She felt the only solution was for Greg to come back home and live with her and return to school at another time when they had the money. But Greg refused to quit with only six months left. He was definitely not going to return home for good either. That would kill him.

The bank had foreclosed on his mother's house last month, and she moved into a two-bedroom apartment in Pontiac, Michigan. He no longer could return to the home that he grew up in, the big house in Farmington Hills. Greg experienced too many changes in a short time and he couldn't handle the disruptive turn it had taken with the way his life was supposed to play out. Where was God when he needed him? God would not have let this happen! God deserted him and took away the good life he was used to living. Life was not fair and God was not real to him anymore. He had been told growing up that God would never desert you in your time of need.

That was bull! he thought. *All the religious acts, going to church, and praying was just a complete waste of time.*

Yes, he was certain that he had to pull off another robbery if he was going to get ahead in life. There was no other alternative. He had already sold his eight-track stereo, tapes and some clothing, but made less than expected -- only $108. Getting another job would be nearly impossible, as he was already putting in many evening hours and weekends bussing at the restaurant. Nobody was watching his back or looking out for him. He needed to take action again on his own.

Greg opened up the phone book and scoured through lists of businesses where he might commit the next crime. How about a restaurant? A car dealership probably would have ample checks but not much cash. Knock off a Salvation Army bell ringer? He kind of laughed at that ingenious idea. A pet store? Barking dogs. A bank? Hmm. He thought more about the possibility of robbing a bank. Robbing a bank would be a big hit where he certainly could get more money than $400 needed. If he timed it right, the bank not be busy with customers. In and out, quickly. Yeah.

He decided he would drive through small towns tomorrow and look for possible banks that could be his target. It would be a good idea to find a small bank and stop inside and take a good look around before he decided to make the heist. He ripped out the phone book page for banks and folded the page into a neat square and tucked it away in his wallet. He cooked a TV dinner and while eating, thought of his plan to get his life back again.

***

Ernie had physical therapy and respiratory therapy early Tuesday morning, ate some soup for lunch and took a short nap before Beverly arrived close to 2 p.m. She walked inside, brushing the snow off of her face that had accumulated from the walk from her car to the house. It was the first hard snow of the season and it was beautiful to see. The air had been much chillier those past two weeks and the hard freeze was setting in. It looked like the snow was going to be staying awhile and would no longer just melt after hitting the warm ground.

She removed her winter coat, boots, and mittens and walked with Ernie into the kitchen to put away the few groceries she had picked up. She had stopped at the market to pick some fruit, vegetables, milk, eggs, and ingredients to make homemade spaghetti sauce that she would make Ernie for dinner. Beverly did a check of Ernie's vitals and all were within normal limits. She paid close attention to his breathing and his breaths were not labored. His skin coloring was good. No need for all the machines he had while in the hospital; he was making good progress at home with oxygen at night and if needed when he was tired in the day.

Ernie sat at the kitchen table and cut up the onions and mushrooms while Beverly stood at the stove cooking the Italian sausage and boiling the spaghetti noodles. They chatted about Ernie's therapy appointments earlier in the day and about the snow that starting coming down yesterday and into today. There would definitely be snow on the ground for Thanksgiving.

"Do you have plans to spend Thanksgiving with family?" Ernie asked.

"I will spend Thanksgiving with my daughter Carol, her husband Todd, and their three children. She lives in Baraga, only an hour away from me. I will drive there on Thanksgiving day and stay that night and return on Friday morning," Beverly said.

"That sounds very nice. Do you usually spend the holidays with her?" he asked.

"My son Carl lives in Seattle and occasionally I will visit him and his family. This year Carl and his family will be coming to stay with me for Christmas. I can hardly wait. My daughter-in-law Lucy had their first child six months ago, a little boy named Charlie. I haven't seen Charlie since he was born and it will be wonderful to see him again."

"His name is Charlie? Was that your husband's name, as well?" Ernie asked.

"Yes, he was named after my late husband Charlie. Charles Daniel Foster."

"It seems that you have a wonderful family. I am so glad for you," Ernie said.

Beverly continued to stir the sausage in the pan and wondered if Ernie had ever married. His home was lovely but it certainly did not have a lady's touch about it. She noticed that there were no pictures of Ernie and a woman or children on the wall. Should she ask or was that too sensitive or nervy? she wondered.

"Do you have any family?" she asked after a long pause.

"If you mean by family, as a wife and children, well, no, I do not. I never did marry or have children. I wanted to marry but she --" he paused, swallowing hard, and then finished. "Oh, I won't bore you with the story."

"I am not bored with anything you have to say. If you wish to share, I will listen," she said encouragingly.

"Anna was my highschool sweetheart and we planned on getting married once I finished my enlistment with the Navy Seabees during World War II. I left in early February to go to Camp Allen in Virginia for boot camp and then had more advanced and specialized training at Port Hueneme in California for two months. I learned skills in pipeline installation, building of petroleum facilities, highway construction and placing of pontoon causeways."

Beverly raised her eyebrows, impressed. Ernie continued.

"Anyway, I was shipped out to the area of the Society Islands and the Philippines in the Pacific Ocean. I would be gone another year and she promised me that she loved me and would wait for my return so we could finally marry. I received weekly letters from her and I felt her love for me was strong and could withstand the distance and time apart. The love that she sent me in letters was enough to keep me going strong, despite the awful conditions I was subject to in the Seabees. Soon the letters started getting fewer and farther between and then they just stopped altogether."

Ernie stopped, the sharp sadness returning. He pushed it away so he could go on.

"At first I thought it was because my battalion was traveling a lot from place to place and maybe her letters were not catching up with me. But I received a letter from my mother one day and she told me that she had spoken with Anna face-to-face. Their conversation upset my mother a great deal but she knew that she must tell me the truth and the truth was not going to come from Anna lips. The news devastated me! Anna had not been faithful to me, and she had decided to no longer wait for my return and our planned future together. She eloped with another man and moved as fast as she could out of this small town before I returned home from the Navy. I have never spoken to her since," Ernie explained.

"I'm not sure what to say. I am sorry," Beverly quietly said, feeling terribly embarrassed that she had asked Ernie to share.

"It was very difficult when I returned home. But luckily, with the support of good friends, family, and God Almighty, I did get through it. I never met another woman who I wanted to share my life with. Some people said that I was too heartbroken to ever fall in love again but I don't think that is true. I got over the broken heart and I did court again, but I felt I could not trust someone so completely another time," he said.

Ernie handed the chopped vegetables to Beverly, who added it to the cooked Italian sausage and tomato sauce and spices.

"Trusting someone means being completely vulnerable and allowing your whole heart to be accepted -- or toyed with. Unfortunately, not all people are authentic in who they are or profess to be. You learned early on and the hard way about Anna and her feelings for you. Sadly, some people stay married for years and think they know someone and trust them with their whole heart and then find it to be a facade," Beverly said.

"I hope that did not happen to you, Beverly?"

Beverly walked to the sink, sniffling, and washed her hands nervously. She hesitated. He had been honest with her. She could be honest with him, too. So she began.

"A year before Charlie found out he had lymphoma, he had had an affair with his secretary at work. It wasn't until after his funeral that I found out the truth about a man who kept secrets and led another life. His mistress walked up to me on the way to my car following Charlie's burial and told me that 'she loved him, too.' At first I took it as 'we all loved Charlie and he will be sadly missed.' I had been hearing that over and over again from people giving their condolences. But she repeated it to me again, 'I loved him, really loved him and we shared a relationship together.' I was stunned. Here this woman, whom I had known to be Charlie's secretary for more than ten years, was in love with my husband and she was telling me this minutes after I buried the man!"

Ernie studied the face of the woman before him. Beverly still carried hurt that no words he could say would erase. His heart ached for her. He wanted to stand up and throw his arms around her, but he mustered the will not to, and listened on.

She continued, "My world fell out from under me and I lived the next year of my life in deep despair and depression. I had given everything to this man and felt so deceived by him. I was angry and wanted to tell him off, but I couldn't! I questioned why he didn't love me enough that he would have to cheat. *Sigh*. It was my darkest hour. It took a long time to work through my hurt and loss. The sting is still there today. I, in a sense, had to come to grip with an affair and a death, at the same time," she said.

"I am sorry to hear that your married life with Charlie was not always happy," Ernie quietly said, questioning if these words were enough to calm her soul.

"Don't get me wrong, I was very happy and he was very good at hiding his double life. I never had a clue that something was going on while we were married."

"And I didn't know that Anna wasn't going to wait for me and had been seeing someone else while I was away at war. Life sure throws some curve balls, huh?"

"Yes, but you just need to get up, dust yourself off and get back in the game of life," Beverly said.

"Hmm, looks like the pasta noodles are about done," Ernie said, changing the subject.

"Let me drain the pasta then, and why don't you just have a seat?" she said.

"Beverly, would you like to join me for dinner? There is plenty of pasta, and I would love your company. You are so easy to talk to, and I feel like we have opened up and talked about some pretty tender things. Seems strange for you to hurry off."

"Yes, I am surprised by my openness. Golly, I would love to have dinner with you. I will just get to the cleaning after we finish dinner. I promise not to be too late so you can get a good night's rest."

Ernie smiled and grabbed another plate, fork, knife and glass of water and placed them on the table. Beverly served the pasta and meat sauce and placed the two plates on the table. They both bowed their heads and Ernie said the blessing.

"Bless us, oh Lord, and these thy gifts, which we are about to receive, from thy bounty through Christ our Lord, Amen."

They made small talk about the weather, hobbies they enjoyed and trips they had taken. Ernie spoke more about his time spent in the war in the Pacific Islands and Beverly spoke about when she went to college to become a nurse and her nursing jobs over the years. They laughed a lot and conversation flowed freely, as if they were old friends. Beverly noticed Ernie's great sense of humor and smiled at his contagious laugh. Ernie was fond of how Beverly threw her head back when she laughed, and how she would tilt her head and smile when listening to him talk. It was good to make a new friend, and he was thankful that such a wonderful woman had come into his life under such unexpected circumstances. As he sat there listening to her talk, he realized that he would have never met Beverly if he had not been in the tragic shooting at the market. He would have never expected such joy could come out of such pain. But there he sat, with the widest grin on his cheeks.

Together they cleaned off the kitchen table and Beverly started the dishes. Beverly told Ernie to go rest while she cleaned the dishes and did some vacuuming and dusting, too. She needed to get caught up on some chores tonight because she was not working at the hospital tomorrow. She agreed to bring Ernie by the service station to check in with Ted, who had questions about ordering and inventory. Plus, Ernie heard so much about the number of toys that were brought in during the toy drive last Sunday that he had to see the mountain of toys for himself. Ernie also wanted to stop by the bank to make a business deposit tomorrow.

Beverly was delighted that she would drive to her daughter's house for the Thanksgiving holiday. Ernie was excited to solidify his plans to attend dinner on Thanksgiving Day with Harry, Greta, and their children. Ernie had so much to be thankful for this year. God's loving grace and mercy would allow him to spend another Thanksgiving Day here on Earth. Every day felt like a true blessing to him and he wanted to live them all to the fullest.

Chapter 10

At 8:10 a.m. the next morning, Ernie awoke to coffee brewing downstairs. Father Arnold had let himself in and was making coffee and breakfast for them both. Ernie could also smell bacon cooking, and he knew he had to rush downstairs before Father Arnold started snitchin' all the bacon. He got dressed and walked downstairs to see Father Arnold clad in an apron, standing at the stove stirring the scrambled eggs.

"Aren't you looking lovely this morning, my dear," Ernie laughed, motioning to the apron that Father Arnold was wearing.

"Are you making fun of me for wearing an apron or because you didn't know I could cook?" Father Arnold laughed.

"Both," Ernie laughed. He took a seat at the table and poured himself a glass of orange juice.

They sat down to breakfast, said the blessing, and shared the newspaper in pieces. Father Arnold took the front page and Ernie got the cartoon page.

"Since you think you are so funny, you can have the comics first," Father Arnold joked.

On the front page, Father Arnold noticed a write-up about the burglaries; there were still no more leads on the two recent robberies. No other robbery incidents had been reported since Lewis' Market. Detectives believed the robber might not be from the area or had been just passing through the small towns on that dreadful weekend. Ernie read the write-up, as well, and it stirred within him. He hoped that these had been connected incidences and the robber had moved on, but there was unsettling feeling in Ernie that he could not move past. He wondered if he ever would. Even if the suspect had been caught.

Father Arnold cleaned up the dishes and Ernie went to get cleaned up and shaved, knowing that the respiratory therapist would be stopping by for his treatment. Following Ernie's therapy, Beverly would pick him up to run errands.

He laughed to himself when he said "run errands" in his mind. He was far from running anything! He was moving still at a snail's pace but he thought that leaving the house would be good for him. Plus, he needed to deposit a month's worth of money from the gas station that was collecting under the counter - not a safe storage place, especially not in light of the recent robberies. He needed to get the money to a safe place so he could focus on recovering and not worry about it.

He would bring his oxygen tank with him today when he ran his errands. The respiratory therapist agreed that would be a good idea, especially with the cold air, as breathing could be more difficult. Still, Ernie was using less oxygen each day and was becoming less dependent on it. He continued to take the prescribed antibiotic and would do so for another two weeks. He also had pain pills to take if he was uncomfortable or the pain caused unrestful sleep.

The doorbell rang and Father Arnold answered the door to see a lovely lady standing there before him.

"Beverly, I presume?" he said and extended his hand.

"Yes, and you must be Father Arnold," Beverly said, extending her hand for a handshake.

"The collar gave it away, huh?"

They shared a laugh and he welcomed her inside his warm and

cozy home, which smelled of smoked bacon and maple syrup. She stayed at the door with her jacket and boots on, while Father Arnold helped Ernie with his jacket and boots. He grabbed a scarf for Ernie to wrap around his face to keep him from breathing in the cold air outside. Father Arnold locked up the house and they all went outside into the lightly falling snow of the late morning.

Father Arnold returned to the church to work on plans for the mass and Ernie and Beverly drove to the service station. When they pulled up, they saw Ted pumping fuel into two lined-up cars. Ernie waved happily and walked slowly inside the station, with Beverly alongside him. Ted entered the service station and shook hands with Ernie.

"So good to see you, Ernie," Ted said.

"Likewise."

"How are you feeling?" asked Ted.

"I am getting better every day. Let me introduce you to the nurse who helped me along the way to getting stronger. Ted, this is Beverly. She was my nurse at Torch Lake Hospital and is also my nurse doing home health care."

"Very nice to meet you, Ted," Beverly said warmly.

"Beverly, why don't you have a seat right here while I talk with Ted about business stuff. I shouldn't be long."

"No worries, take your time. I am here if you need me," Beverly offered.

Ernie and Ted discussed the ordering of new supplies and more tires from a distributor. They went over the accounting and bank deposit information and Ernie was pleased to see that business had not slowed down. Business was doing very well, in fact, and there had been a twenty percent increase in tire sales due to the snow's arrival.

Ernie followed Ted to the back storage room and saw the enormous display of toys, all wrapped and ready for the children's

Christmas party in December. Ernie immediately felt overwhelmed with emotion at the community's generous support. *This must be what the children feel like when they open an unexpected Christmas gift,* he thought. For the first time, he really got it. He felt the humbling, warming power of community help for something he couldn't manage to do on his own. He was astonished at the many gifts on the shelves before him. Ted informed him that there were just as many toys in storage at Harry's Barber Shop next door. Ernie couldn't wait to see the look on the children's faces when Santa Claus came to the party and called out their names. Oh, the many gifts they would receive.

Ernie realized that he still needed to work with Mark and Mike to assign gifts to the names of children who would be attending the party. He peeked inside a few of the bags at items that were too difficult to wrap and found a pair of ice skates that he knew Lisa Muljo would definitely love. She had mentioned not long ago that she needed new skates, as she had outgrown last year's pair. He spotted another pair of girl's skates that might fit her sister Linda, too. On the bottom shelf, he touched a pretty baby doll and buggy that would be perfect for their little sister, Kimmy. He would have to search for extra special gifts for Scott and Darren. The boys had been such a big help to Ernie throughout the year, and he thought they were such great kids.

For the second year straight, Scott and Darren would not be able to attend the Christmas party as guests, because they would be acting as Santa's elves at the party; both would be dressed in red and green costumes, hats and pointy slippers with jingle bells. They would remain with Santa until the jolly man made his big entrance. Somehow Santa always remembered to pack extra gifts for his two elves to unwrap and enjoy, too.

Ernie locked up the back room and returned to the lobby of the service station. He talked a bit more with Ted and then returned to the car with Beverly. They still needed to stop at the bank, and then Ernie needed to get home, have lunch and rest. As much as he enjoyed being out of the house and socializing again, he was growing tired.

As Beverly and Ernie drove away, a blue Chevy Nova car pulled in behind them. The Nova stopped and a blonde-haired young man of about twenty years old asked for $10 worth of gas. Ted had never seen him before; he must be driving through, Ted figured. The young man asked Ted if he sold cigarettes at the service station.

"No, we don't," Ted answered, while wiping down the car's windows. "But you can get them at the store across the street."

The young man looked across the street and down away and his eyes latched on the sign out front. Lewis' Market. He froze. It was a deja vu. Ted noticed the expression on the young man's face.

"Do you see it? Down the road about 300 yards. Lewis' Market?" Ted asked.

"Yeah, yeah I see it. Lewis' Market." He paused. "Isn't that the place where a robbery took place?"

"Yeah, that is the place. Sad story there. I lost a good friend. And the guy who lived, this here is his service station. I am filling in for him while he recuperates," Ted said.

Greg could not believe his luck. Meeting the friend of the man he killed made it suddenly so real. Maybe he couldn't go through with this again. But what was he supposed to do? He was already here and he still needed the money. He may as well drive over to the bank and check things out. He wouldn't hurt anyone. Just in and out. No one would feel it but the bank, a rich institution with no worries like the ones he was dealing with. The bank would never even feel the loss.

Ted returned to the gas tank to top off the gas. The young man was still and silent, so Ted's eyes wandered through the window into the back seat of the car. He saw a book bag, some empty pop cans, candy bar wrappers, gloves and an Arctic Cat ski mask. Ted put the gas nozzle back into the pump, collected the $10 and wished the young man a good day.

Greg waved back and left down the road, deciding not to stop for cigarettes at Lewis' Market after all. He had a couple cigarettes left and that would get him by until he could pick some up later tonight -- anywhere other than at Lewis' Market. That robbery had gone all wrong. No one one was supposed to die. Guilt rattled him, for he had taken another man's life. This time, it would be a robbery and nothing more. *Get the cash, move out quickly and without a trace. Pay your tuition, graduate, get a job, and get on with your life, Greg. And never look back.*

He drove about three miles down the road to the bank he had scoped out the day before. It was a little bank branch on the south side of Lake Linden. He noticed only one car parked near the bank, and it was probably a good sign that not many patrons were there at this time. Rather than park his car in the parking lot, he parked his car a little bit down the road in front of the bowling alley.

He went over the plans inside his head -- how he would provoke the teller and then brandish a gun. But he did not want the incident to get out of hand, like the last robbery. He hadn't wanted to shoot two people last time, but the younger guy had come after him with a meat hook and he had to shoot him. The man had probably had gotten a good look at him when he tried to pull off his ski mask, anyway. The older guy had come into the store suddenly and had to be shot, too, to be hushed up. He could have just fought the old guy, but with his mask all messed up, he was sure that the old man had gotten a good look at him.

The mask must stay on this time, and he would only pull out the gun if provoked. Yesterday when he scoped out the bank, he noticed a young female teller who appeared to be new and training, as identified by her name badge. She appeared confused by a transaction a customer was trying to make and needed help from the only other teller. If the young teller was working today, he would be sure to go to her.

He took the ski mask and stuffed it in the front of his down jacket. He checked the pistol again for bullets. He had six. He took out his wallet with his identification from his right back jeans pocket and threw it in the car. He walked a normal pace toward the bank, rehearsing everything in his mind. He looked around to see if anyone was watching. Not a soul.

He sneaked behind an evergreen bush and pulled the ski mask on top of his head. As he stood before the glass door ready to open it, he could see that the bank, indeed, had people being waited on by the tellers. He spotted a pregnant woman and an older man and older woman, and the two bank tellers. None of them would stop him. He could have just stopped and walked away. But he felt confident that he could still be in and out of the place quickly with bags of cash in grip, despite the three patrons in the bank. He pulled down the Arctic Cat ski cap over his eyes, grabbed the gun from his pocket, opened the bank door, and yelled.

"Everyone hit the floor! Now! Give me the cash in the drawers and don't do anything stupid. I have a gun" he scowled, throwing two bags on the counter in front of one of the tellers.

He taunted the patrons to the floor by frantically waving his arms and throwing his voice in a loud, husky threat. He saw the shock and horror in their eyes. The pregnant woman started screaming.

"Shut the hell up. If you keep screaming, I will kill you!" Greg growled, rushing at the pregnant woman.

She grabbed her swollen stomach and slowly lowered to the floor. The older man and woman hugged one another, and the woman cautiously helped the old man to the floor. The tellers stood at their stations, pulling money as fast as they could from the drawers and piled it into the bags. They exchanged nervous glances with one another, and the younger teller started to cry. The other teller had been on a telephone call before the gunman entered. He hadn't noticed. She gently pushed a piece of paper over the phone that lay off the hook on the counter. She prayed that the caller on the line was patient, did not hang up, and was listening to every word the gunman said.

"Quit sniveling and hurry up," Greg commanded the young teller. "When you are finished, I want you both to come here with the others and get on the floor. Do you hear me?"

The gunman looked down at the patrons and saw the older man staring him right into his eyes. His glare was deliberate and the gunman aggressively responded, "What are you staring at, old man?"

That man was Ernie. He lowered his head immediately.

"Are you trying to take a good look at me? What do you see, old man? You can't see much but the shape of my eyes and mouth under this ski mask. But go on. Take a look," the gunman warned.

Ernie raised his head and his weary eyes again met the gunman's cold steel-blue eyes. Perhaps he was stunned that this was happening to him -- again. Perhaps he was no longer afraid of death, having already conquered it once. Or maybe this was his time to go. He accepted that, as he bravely cried out, "Why are you doing this?"

Beverly squeezed Ernie's hand and whispered, "Shh!"

The pregnant woman screamed out a loud moan, and covered her head and face quickly with her arms, expecting the gunman to kick her -- or worse yet, shoot her.

Her noise, combined with the strange old man's question, made the gunman shift on his feet nervously.

"Shut up if you want to ever see your child, lady," he yelled to the pregnant woman. The gunman quickly stepped to the front doors and turned the deadbolt lock.

Once the doors were secure, the gunman turned back to the old man who sat still on the floor. He studied the old man's face. What was it about this man that bothered him so much? Ernie remained quiet and lowered his eyes. The gunman walked up to Ernie and lifted his face with the barrel of the gun. The others in the room silently whimpered in desperate disbelief of what was happening.

Ernie, again, stared at him wide-eyed and spoke in a low voice.

"The Lord is my helper; I will not be afraid. What can man do to me?"

The tellers crept toward the gunman and placed the bags of money at his feet. Then they quickly kneeled down on the floor.

The older teller said, in solemn desperation, "Now please go."

Greg smiled underneath his mask. He did it. He reached down to pick up the bags -- and at that very moment, he heard a different voice on a loudspeaker. Then sirens. He heard it clearly now: "Come out with your hands up. We have the area surrounded!"

He dropped the money bags, startled by the sirens and his unexpected apprehension of a job done wrong. Police rushed through the front doors, and Greg ducked behind the pregnant woman. In a desperate reflex, he dragged her up onto her feet by his right arm strongly hooked beneath her chin.

He heard the other patrons gasp and cry out, "No!" This made him nervous, but he planted his feet, determined to stand his ground and not give himself up. There had to be a way out of this. He was smart and savvy, and this was just a small and simple town. He would take hostages to negotiate his demands and release them when he was satisfied.

The cops again commanded, "Come out now with your hands up!"

"Hell, no!" yelled the gunman. He again instructed the restless patrons and tellers to remain on the floor.

Moments passed and the phone rang at the young teller's station. Everyone, including Greg, shuddered. It rang. Rang. Rang. Everyone looked at the gunman, wondering what he wanted to do next. The gunman ordered the young teller to go to the phone and answer it and repeat back everything that was said. She hesitantly got to her feet and reached for the ringing phone. She held it up to her ear and tears started streaming down her face. Choked up tension in her voice, she stuttered, "Hel-lloo?"

"This is Lt. Sheriff Bob Sheeves. Who am I speaking with?"

"Carol Butler," she nervously answered.

"Ms. Butler, please remain calm. If you look out the windows and the front doors of the bank, you will see many policeman and police cars around the perimeter of the bank. Please tell me how many robbers are in the bank?"

Carol repeated the information to the gunman and he told her to answer that there was one robber and that he had a gun and was not going to come out of the bank.

"Sir, there is one robber and he does have a gun with him. He says that he is not coming out of the bank," Carol said.

"How many people are in the bank besides the gunman?" Lt. Sheriff Sheeves asked.

"Myself, another teller, an older man, and woman and… a pregnant woman. The gunman has the gun pointed at the pregnant woman!" she cried.

"Okay, I need you to listen. We will be observing what is happening by binoculars and by talking with you on the telephone. Do not hang up. I will be in touch in a bit as we discuss strategies," he said.

Lt. Sheriff Sheeves and the other policeman at hand talked about the safety of the hostages; that was their number one priority. They needed to find out the demands of the gunman, who the hostages were, and what each of their general conditions were. If the standoff lasted long, they would then discuss how to protect the hostages and take aim at the gunman. Good communication would be necessary between the police and Carol. They would encourage her to be calm and compliant and to listen very carefully. She needed to create normalcy, if that were possible, in a chaotic atmosphere.

Carol told the gunman everything Lt. Sheriff Sheeves had said, everything but the possibility of taking a hit on him. She hoped that the standoff would not head in that direction. Carol could not believe that this was only her eighth day on the job and now she encountered a bank robbery. At the moment, she thought she was crazy for wanting to work in a bank and thought that she should have stayed at her old waitressing job. She wondered what she could do or say to calm the gunman down. For the time being, she would be available when needed as the mediator between the police and the gunman.

Carol sat down next to Ernie and Beverly and rubbed Beverly's back with her hand. Her comforting touch, though sweet, did little to ease Beverly's nerves. Ernie tried to keep his emotions under control, as he did not want his breathing to start becoming irregular. *Deep breath in. Slow, little breaths out.* The pregnant woman was gripped in the clutched arm of the gunman. She kept still with her eyes closed, as if praying. The other teller kept watching through the window at the police outside and wondered when they would step it up and rescue them.

Ernie remained quiet as flashbacks to the shooting at the market raced through his mind. Though only a blur in his mind, the likeness of the man at the market and the man before him was similar. Same stature, same quick, erratic movement of his arms, like he didn't know what to do with them. He was certain that the gunman in the bank was the same man who shot Paul and himself more than two weeks ago. He remembered the Arctic Cat ski mask being the same in color and style and the gunman was wearing the same down jacket. What he remembered most was the pistol. The gun that the gunman had waved in front of him just moments ago was the same one that sprayed the bullets that took Paul's life and nearly took his own life, as well.

Ernie questioned God in his thoughts. He wondered why he

again was at the wrong place at the wrong time? How could this be? *Why me, Lord?*

His thoughts then traveled back to a more peaceful place: heaven. He remembered the moment he passed from this world and into God's heavenly kingdom. Instant joy. But he chose to return to his earthly home and finish God's plan. His eternal home would wait.

Did God really send him back to Earth to have him walk right back into danger again? No, because God's plan was for good, not evil. Ernie vowed in his mind to trust God's plan, knowing it would be revealed in time. With certainty, he knew the Lord would not abandon him.

Ernie could hear the voice of God loud and clear, resonating in his heart and mind, saying, *"Talk to him. Tell him that he is a lost child of mine and that he is loved. He can turn away from the evil that consumes him and turn again to me."* Fear built inside Ernie. He knew that he must be experiencing a spiritual struggle between doing what God asked him to do, and the field day that the devil must be having, creating fear within Ernie's soul.

Ernie prayed to God, admitting that he was scared but wanted to be obedient to God's calling. God's gentle voice reassured Ernie that he would never leave him or forsake him. God would help guide Ernie in his thoughts and his words to be an instrument of peace where peace was needed desperately.

Just then, a booming voice echoed through loudspeaker again, alerting the gunman that the police wanted to speak directly on the phone with the gunman. The gunman told Carol, the young teller, to get up and answer another phone ringing nearby and instructed her that she would do the talking between the police and the gunman. Carol rose to her feet and went to the phone, as commanded. She lifted the phone to her ear.

"This is Carol."

"Carol, we want to speak directly with the gunman," Lt. Sheriff Sheeves said.

"He has instructed me to talk and will not come to the phone," she nervously replied.

"Okay then. Carol, I need you to stay calm and listen carefully. I understand that there are five people held captive, is that correct?

"Yes, there are five."

"What are the conditions of the five people?" Lt. Sheriff Sheeves asked. Carol repeated the question to the gunman and he gave her the signal to answer.

"We are trying to remain calm. No one is hurt. The pregnant woman is still held in restraint from the gunman," Carol apprehensively answered.

"Carol, I need to know the names and ages of the people that are held captive." Carol relayed the message to the gunman and he ordered everyone to give their names individually.

"Carol Butler, age nineteen," Carol repeated it and listened for the next captive to give their name and age. The other teller spoke up and said, "Marsha O'Toole, age forty-four." Carol repeated and waited for the next person to speak.

The pregnant woman cried out, "Jodi Wilkens, age twenty-three." Carol repeated and looked at the two remaining people to answer.

"Beverly Allen, age fifty-four," Carol repeated and then looked at the remaining person in the room to answer.

Ernie paused for a moment and looked at the gunman eye to eye. He kept looking at the gunman as he knew there would be a reaction from him when he released his name. "My name is Ernie Price, age fifty-one."

Carol started repeating the name when the gunman rose to his feet and threw the pregnant woman from his grasp to the floor. She rolled hard onto tile floor and sobbed, coiling up on her side in the fetal position.

"Say your name again!" he shouted.

"Ernie Price."

Carol quickly told the police, "Ernie Price." She heard a gasp on the other end of the phone. The gunman moved away from the teller window and with a slow, deliberate stride, stood over Ernie and said, "I left you for dead over two weeks ago. I should just take you out right now!" He planted the gun firmly into Ernie's right cheek.

Ernie swallowed hard and responded, "Are you the kind of man who would try to kill the same man twice?

The words penetrated the gunman's ears, and he tried to block out the sound by covering his ears, flailing the gun uncontrollably overhead. Beverly grabbed Ernie and they crouched down closer to the floor.

The pregnant woman started moaning and rocking back and forth. The gunman got distracted by her moans and could not answer Ernie right away.

"I think I am starting labor! Please help me," she pleaded. Her body had not taken the violent fall the ground easily. She didn't know what was happening, but she felt excruciating stabs of pain shooting through her midsection. She clutched her stomach in agony.

"Oh, dear God!" the gunman exclaimed.

Beverly spoke up quickly, offering, "I am a nurse. Can I go to her?"

The gunman said, "Yes and shut her up." Beverly quickly moved over to the pregnant woman, leaving Ernie's side.

Carol spoke up. "The police want to know what your demands are?"

The gunman found that question to be amusing. "I suppose they won't valet drive my car up to the curb and let me get away with the bags of money and forget this ever happened, will they?" he said sarcastically. "I don't know," he continued. "I suppose we will need some blankets, food, and water. We could be here awhile."

Carol relayed the information to the police, and they responded, "We can get you the blankets, food, and water but we need the gunman to release a hostage."

The gunman thought about the deal, and it was not difficult for him to decide what hostage should go first. He ordered the pregnant woman, Jodi Wilkens to be released. Beverly helped Jodi to her feet and walked her closer to the exit door.

"Stop, that is far enough, old lady. Unlock the door and she can leave on her own. Tell the police that she is coming out," the gunman alerted.

Carol told the police that Jodi was on her way out of the bank. Jodi opened the glass door and waddled out of the bank, doubled over in pain. At the end of the sidewalk was a gurney where a paramedic and ambulance awaited her. Paramedics worked quickly; strapping Jodi down to the gurney, covering her with a blanket, and then whisking away in the ambulance.

The others in the bank watched through the front glass windows and sent thoughts and prayers with Jodi and her precious baby. The blankets, food, and water were left at the front door, and Beverly cautiously walked over to retrieve them. She carried the items over to the others but no one reached for food, drink or a blanket, as they were too afraid to make a move. Besides, they didn't know how long they would be kept hostage, and they needed to ration food and water for a more critical time of need.

The gunman pulled a chair abruptly over to Ernie, sat down, opened up a can of 7 Up and said, "It is quite the irony to run into you again! I stopped by your service station just before coming to the bank and was told by the gentleman there that I just missed you. Little did I know I would run into you minutes later, here at the bank. More than a coincidence, wouldn't you say?"

"I'd like to think, rather, that it is divine intervention," Ernie mustered.

"Ha! Divine intervention! Do you really think God had any plan in this?"

"I mostly certainly do. It is not a mistake that I am here."

"I am intrigued. Go on," the gunman said with a laugh, leaning down and looking over Ernie while taking a gulp of 7 Up.

"When you shot me and left me to die on the floor of the market, I died that night, along with the other man named Paul," Ernie admitted.

"What are you talking about, old man? You seem alive to me."

"I was actually dead for a couple of minutes and brought back to life."

"Lucky for good medicine, huh?" the gunman said, unconvinced.

"No, I don't see it that way. Life is about making choices. You can chose to impact someone for good or for bad. Every day you are given the opportunity to do God's work and it is up to you to either use your time wisely or waste it away. I stood before the glorious gates of heaven and could have entered happily into the arms of Jesus, but I chose to return to my life and its unfinished business."

"You are spooking me out, old man! And this happened the night that I shot you?" He paused. "So what you are saying is that you died, went to heaven, and you came back to Earth?" He couldn't believe it.

"That is correct. And I came back to do unfinished business."

"You are an angel," Beverly whispered, hearing this for the first time. She smiled at Ernie, who returned a smile back to her.

"Unfinished business? And what might that be?" questioned the gunman.

"I have thought about nothing but that question since the day that I opened my eyes in the hospital room following my surgery. It did not make sense to me then. But it makes sense to me now," Ernie realized with conviction. A tear fell down his cheek, as he was wrought with emotion. "I think my life was spared so that I could reach you." He spoke directly into the heart of the gunman.

"What? You are talking nonsense. You are freakin' me out," the gunman said restlessly.

"I am not trying to upset you," Ernie said, and then paused for what felt like hours, but was only a few minutes. "What is your name?"

The gunman wondered if he should tell Ernie his real name. He decided to tell him his first name only.

"Greg. My name is Greg," he reluctantly said.

"Well, then, Greg. I am not trying to upset you. I am just sharing with you the revelation that has just occurred and is starting to make sense to me."

"It makes sense to you, how? And how does it involve me?" Greg asked nervously, looking into Ernie's convincing eyes. There was something about this man that Greg could not understand. His soft and gentle demeanor perplexed Greg. How could this man remain so calm when faced with danger? Or maybe he didn't think that Greg could fully carry out the mission. Perhaps this man would be helpful to Greg to get out of the bank and be free.

"I believe that God's plan is perfect, and he planned for us to meet again. I believe, too, that he will protect me and everyone in this room. He will protect you, too."

"Maybe I won't surrender. I could just shoot you all and take my life," Greg angrily said, suddenly agitated. All this talk about God and His plan was messing with Greg's mind and his plan to rob the bank and get on with his life.

"Greg, you said, 'maybe.' *Maybe* you won't surrender. I hear in that word alone that you are unsure of what to do. I would be willing to bet that you never wanted the robberies to happen, but you didn't see another way out of some predicament in your life. Am I right?"

"Of course I wanted the robberies to happen. I need the damn money. But I never meant to kill someone; it just got out of hand!" he screamed. "He came after me with a meat hook, I had to shoot him!" Greg cried, referring to Paul coming after him in the market robbery.

Greg's reference to Paul made Ernie recoil a little, at the painful memory. But he didn't want Greg to notice, so he continued.

"I understand, really I do. It must have been a frightening experience and you acted defensively. But then -- why did you shoot me?" Ernie said, asking the question he had been spinning over and over in his mind since that night. He had not provoked Greg. He couldn't have stopped him, either.

"I didn't think there was anyone else in the store and you surprised me," Greg said quickly. "You saw me shoot the other man and I knew you might be able to identify me. I had to leave no witnesses. So I shot you."

Ernie felt his chest tighten. Maybe it was the shock of the gunman's answer -- hearing it from Greg's very lips -- or maybe it was just his body still weak and recovering. "Please, I need my oxygen. May I use the mask over my face to help me with my breathing?" Ernie pleaded to Greg.

"I am his nurse. I can help him with the oxygen and mask," Beverly added.

"Go on," Greg said, watching that they wouldn't do anything foolish.

Beverly placed the oxygen mask over Ernie's ashen face and adjusted the flow of oxygen to be given. Beverly took the blanket, rolled it up and placed it under Ernie's head and covered his body with another blanket. Greg struggled, watching the old man breathing heavily, knowing he was the cause of his shortness of breath and his weakened condition in the first place. Greg watched Ernie's labored breathing and remembered months earlier, after his father was in his car accident and lay dying on the hospital table. Greg was at his father's side at the hospital only minutes after the accident. He saw his father struggling to breathe from severe internal injuries suffered in the crash. He watched his father's chest rise and fall rapidly. And then stillness came over him. He breathed his last breath.

Watching Ernie with his oxygen mask on disturbed Greg so much that he could not look at him anymore. He turned his head and attention to the two bank tellers, who watched intently.

"So, do you believe in heaven?" he asked the younger bank teller, Carol.

She was caught off guard by his request and paused before answering. She was trying to read the gunman's temperament. Should she tell him the truth that she loved the Lord, her God with all her heart, her soul, her mind, and strength? Would the gunman be angry that she was a believer? She spoke what she knew in her heart to be the truth.

"I believe in heaven."

She then continued with a well rehearsed prayer that she knew well and believed with all her being. "I believe in God, the Father Almighty, Creator of Heaven and Earth, and in Jesus Christ--"

The gunman suddenly cut her off.

"His only Son, our Lord, who was conceived by the Virgin Mary, blah, blah, blah! The Apostles' Creed, I know that one."

Ernie's eyes opened wide. So did everyone else's in the room. The gunman was a believer -- or had been one. They tried to make sense who this gunman was. What was his past? What had led him to the dark course in life he was on?

"So, are you a believer?" Carol guardedly asked.

"Me, a believer? Ha! All my life I went to church, and grew up in a good Christian family. But everything is different now, and I would not consider myself a believer today. Far from it," the gunman expressed with protest. He looked away, hoping that their questions stopped there.

But Beverly chimed in. "What is it that hurt you so much that you would turn your life away from God?" she questioned.

"I am sure you all would like to know that, but I don't think I want to go there," Greg said, looking away, uncomfortable with the question "May I say something?" Marsha O'Toole spoke softly. Everyone looked at her, surprised that she spoke, as she had remained nervous and quiet the entire time of the standoff.

"I am not a believer," she said convincingly. "But if I survive this robbery, I will commit my life entirely."

That is interesting, thought Beverly. She looked at Marsha with surprise and conviction, saying, "You would be willing to commit your life to the Lord only after you were faced with sudden obstacles or a brush with death?"

"My whole life, I have been too proud and stubborn to believe in anything outside of my own control. I thought I called the shots and had the ability to make my life good or bad. But hearing you all talk about God and heaven has me questioning if there isn't something more to life and beyond. Rather than call the shots, maybe I need someone who calls the shots. Someone who knows what is best for me, beyond my own foolish choices. If I survive this day, I think I will have God to thank," Marsha confirmed.

Greg was quiet, taking it in. He did not respond. He did not appear agitated by Marsha's words. He just sat still.

Ernie was feeling much better and removed the oxygen mask from his face. Beverly helped him sit up, and she took his pulse and checked his breathing rate, which appeared to be normal. Greg looked at Ernie and found himself grateful in the moment that the old man was coming around and looking better.

"Just as Marsha held onto pride and stubbornness, Greg, do you hold back from returning to God for the same reasons?" Ernie asked the tough question.

"Maybe. I dunno. Mostly anger and fear. God has let me down, and I don't know if I can ever forgive him," Greg murmured.

"God doesn't do anything that is not for the good of those who love him," Ernie said.

Greg jumped up from his seat. "I did love God, but he still took my father in *death!*" he screamed, throwing his arms in the air, and a bullet fired suddenly from the pistol into the ceiling.

Frightened outbursts came from everyone in the room, and they crouched down for cover. Greg, himself, was even surprised by the gunfire, but he tried to regain composure.

He took a deep breath and with his voice quivering said, "My father died in a car crash in June. Our family lost him and all our assets upon his death. And he left us penniless without life insurance. He didn't pay the *damn life insurance premium!*" He was screaming now. He then added quietly, "We have no money and no future."

"I am sorry," Ernie said. He sat in silence for a moment. "You lost your father, and you felt you lost everything. You feel God is responsible for that?"

"Damn right I do."

"Scripture says, 'The Lord gives and the Lord takes away.' God gave your father life, and God, in His time, took your father in death. You may not understand the purpose in why God called your father home, but you should recognize that God was the one in control. God's suffering always has a purpose. You simply did not wait for God's plan to unfold and took matters into your own hands," Ernie relayed.

"I was desperate! We had no money, and I did not want to drop out of college with only six months to finish. I wanted to forget the pain and move on with my life," Greg cried out.

"Perhaps, God wanted you to experience the hardship longer. A favorite Bible verse of mine comes from James 1:2-4. 'Consider it pure joy, my brothers, whenever you face trials of many kinds because you know that the testing of your faith develops perseverance. Perseverance must finish its work so that you may be mature and complete, not lacking anything.'"

"I don't think I like the idea of a God that produces suffering," Marsha chimed in.

"God creates suffering not for evil, but for good. Evil exists because of man's selfish ways and because man turned his back on the creator of everything. That is why man still suffers. Pure suffering, with no greater purpose, does not even exist, from God's larger perspective, knowing the bigger picture of a wonderful good that will come of every challenge. Suffering only exists insofar as the limited human mind allows itself to accept God's plan -- and trust God. In a world with perfect faith, there is no such thing as pain or hurt or sadness or frustration. Faith eliminates all of those. When we ask, 'Why does God let bad things happen?' we should really be asking 'Why do we doubt that this thing is not, in fact, good?' Those are the only the real problems in this world: the ones we create for ourselves, by not seeing the world as God sees it -- as God makes it. God gave us free will to make choices to serve him or walk away. I think the suffering happens when we walk away. You see, Greg, after God took your father home to heaven, you rebelled and created evil from your suffering. It was God's plan to take your father at that time for his life on Earth was complete. God's gift is that your father will suffer no more and is rewarded with the ultimate gift of heaven."

Greg sat dumbfounded but patiently listened to every word Ernie said. It kind of made sense to him, but yet he still felt justified in his anger and his actions. Maybe he was still too proud to admit the error of his ways. Greg was confused and not sure what to say or do next. And what was he going to do with the circumstances that were unfolding at the moment? *My God,* he thought, *I have made a mess of things!*

The telephone phone rang at the teller station and everyone's eyes looked back at the gunman for a response. The phone continued to ring, as Greg thought of what his next move should be. He finally told Carol to answer the phone, and she jumped up to answer it immediately. Lt. Sheriff Sheeves spoke to Carol and asked about the danger inside of the bank. Carol responded that everything was calm and that they all had been talking with the gunman. She was careful with what she said, as she did not want the gunman to get upset and change the course of the conversation. Lt. Sheriff Sheeves had said that they were looking for ways to isolate the gunman and possibly take a shot at him.

"No!" Carol yelled, before she realized what she was doing. She tried to continue more calmly, but her voice was still loud enough to catch the gunman's attention. "Don't do that. We are doing fine."

The gunman rose to his feet.

"Don't do what? What is he saying?" the gunman quickly asked.

Carol hesitated. She was shocked that she had released the words from her mouth. She asked the officer, "Do I tell him what you said?" Lt. Sheriff Sheeves told her to repeat his words in complete calmness.

"The police may shoot at you," Carol said with remorse.

"I am not surprised by that. But I won't let them take me out. I would rather shoot myself," he said as he raised the gun to his head.

"No! Stop!" Carol cried.

"Please don't shoot yourself. It can't end this way!" Ernie yelled, fearful that this might end in sudden gunfire. This was not how Ernie envisioned a conclusion to the gunman-and-robbery story.

After making a connection with the gunman who had once tried to take Ernie's life, Ernie could not see it ending with another death. If Ernie thought he was supposed to live to make a difference in someone else's life, and clear up unfinished business, it couldn't end this way. His work was not complete. But was God's work complete through Ernie and what he had accomplished to this point? Ernie did not know. But he still felt compelled to try more.

"Greg, what good would killing yourself bring? I beg you to stop and put the gun down," Ernie pleaded, reaching his hand out to Greg.

"What has become of me? I don't know what to do. I don't know if I can stand living with myself and the mistakes I have made. It would be easier to end it all," Greg screamed.

"No, you need to forgive yourself for what you have done. God will forgive you. Please give me the gun, surrender to this standoff and, most importantly, *surrender* to *God!*" Ernie cried.

"God would forgive me? I am wretched with sin. I cannot even love myself."

"Sin is in the heart of all people. God does not see degrees of sin. He will not love you any less than he loves me. I am a sinner, too!" Ernie yelled back. "God can still love you as you sit in a prison cell, but do not eternally separate yourself from God by killing yourself."

The others in the room began crying, watching the tortured internal struggle within Greg. He wrestled with two terrible choices: giving himself over to the law and sitting for the remainder of his life in prison, or dying and going to hell. The torment of each option weighed heavily in his heart. Even though they were his prisoners, victims of his cruelty, and even though he had put their very lives at risk, the gunman's captives prayed silently for him at this moment. They prayed that he would do the right thing and surrender himself to the law -- and surrender himself to God, so he could be free of his wrongdoings and mend his broken relationship with God. They knew that no discomfort and sadness in prison would ever compare to the agony of a soul severed from its Maker -- a soul never to return to its home. If he took his life like this, it would be too late. There would no recovery.

Marsha thought about her own life -- the fears and pride that had kept her from fully accepting God's love before now. Her life seemed so trivial, but that changed once she looked death in the eyes. She vowed to make a major life change once she made it through this ordeal. Her brain was spinning, yet she had never understood life and love more clearly than now. What she saw happening before her and in her was nothing short of a miracle. Her heart was changing.

"Can you help me prepare my heart for Jesus?" Greg suddenly asked, turning to Ernie. The room silenced. Marsha perked up, intentionally listening.

"Greg, I need to understand what I am preparing you for?" Ernie answered cautiously. "Are you preparing to live? Or die?"

Tears brimmed in Greg's eyes. "I guess it is both," he mercifully said. "I need to die to my old self so that I can live. I need to surrender and stop the madness."

Hope filled the room and God's presence was felt by all. Marsha's heart tickled with warmth she hadn't felt before. Carol smiled, knowing that her new friend and coworker, Marsha, was realizing for the first time who this Jesus was, who she often spoke of. Beverly looked admirably at Ernie for what he was able to accomplish in the bank. He not only was changing the gunman's heart, he was also changing all of their hearts for God's greater good.

Ernie's hands trembled with emotion, with hope. Not just for his chances of getting out of here alive, but for this stranger who had put him through so much pain. As God's beautiful plan more clearly revealed itself, he could feel God's physical presence, much like he had felt when he stood in heaven's doorway. He had never felt God's presence so profoundly on Earth before.

Greg walked over to Carol at the teller station and laid down the gun on the counter. He took the phone from Carol and began to speak to Lt. Sheriff Sheeves.

"Just give me a couple more minutes, and I will come out. I will not harm anyone or myself, and I have turned over possession of the gun and will surrender."

"That is the right thing to do, son," Lt. Sheriff Sheeves called back from outside.

Greg pulled off the Arctic Cat ski mask and threw it on the floor. Everyone in the room looked at his stunningly handsome face, his sweaty golden blonde hair and deep blue eyes. He was clean cut, shaven and had a baby face of unblemished skin. He looked nothing like the stereotypical gunman; dirty, mean and rough. He looked like he had walked out of a magazine. Like a golden angel. Not an evil madman.

Lt. Sheriff Sheeves wanted to believe this was the beginning of the end. But he would remain cautious until he saw the gunman com outside with his hands over his head in total surrender. And right now, he could see the gunman through the window, and was not moving.

Greg walked over to Ernie. He placed his hand gently on Ernie's shoulder, and then they bowed their heads.

Ernie spoke, "Greg, repeat after me." He paused and looked Greg squarely in the eyes. "I believe that Jesus is the Christ, the son of the everlasting God --"

Greg repeated, "I believe that Jesus is the Christ, the son of the everlasting God." His voice cracked with emotion, he hung his head and closed his eyes, listening for Ernie's next words.

"He is my Lord and Savior, and I am His."

"He is my Lord and Savior and I am His."

The police could not make sense of what was happening through the bank window. But they did not sense alarm. One police officer called back to the others, "It appears that they are praying, Lieutenant."

Lt. Sheriff Sheeves could not believe his ears. *Praying?* he thought. *Couldn't be.*

He kept his hand on his pistol in the holster, just in case. He had to see it with his own eyes. He rubbed his eyes for a moment, as they stung from the bright sunlight. The cold and gray day was now bursting with rays of sunlight, penetrating through the clouds and down to the Earth in an awesome display of wonder. He took his sunglasses from his coat pocket and put them on. Removing them rather quickly, he looked again at the rays of light, wanting to take a picture of this very moment. But he suddenly came to grips of where he was and what he should be doing. There was still a gunman in the bank.

"Jesus suffered and died on the cross for my sins so that I may live."

"Jesus suffered and died on the cross --" Greg stopped. Everyone around him froze, too, wondering what he was going to do. Was he going to run? Pull a weapon? Instead, heavy tears began spilling from his blue eyes, and he finished his sentence, "-- for my sins so that I may live."

Ernie continued, "I know that sin separates me from God."

"I know that sin separates me from God." Greg extended his arm and placed his hand on Ernie's shoulder. He squeezed Ernie's shoulder, fully aware of the pain had had caused this great man on Earth, and the sins against his Father God, in heaven.

"I surrender my life to you, Lord, and will walk in your ways, always."

"I surrender my life to you, Lord, and will walk in your ways, always."

"Amen."

"Amen."

With that, Greg fell into Ernie's arms. The old man wrapped the young gunman in his embrace, Ernie's weak frame wobbling under the weight of the surrender. Greg emotionally collapsed, weeping. Ernie cradled the man in his arms like a mother rocks her baby. Complete forgiveness spilled through both Ernie and Greg's hearts, and all hurt dissipated. They now wept tears of joy.

The police and captives all began gathering closer around them, in a surprising celebration of life and renewal. Lt. Sheriff Sheeves watched through the binoculars at what was transpiring inside the bank and could not believe his eyes. Everyone was embracing!

"Let me walk you out, Greg. Are you ready?" Ernie asked.

Greg let out a big sigh and rose to his feet, extending his hand to help up the gracious man. "Yeah. I am ready. Let them know that we are coming out."

Ernie towed his oxygen tank behind him and his other arm rose to gently guide Greg forward into a life where he was now accountable for his reckless choices. Greg lifted his arms over his head and slowly moved forward through the front doors of the bank. The police still had their guns cocked and ready to fire if need be, but it appeared that the standoff would not end in that misfortune. Greg did not say a word until the police took his arms behind his back and cuffed him. Ernie stood at his side and they walked together into the rays of sunlight.

Greg's tear-filled eyes looked into Ernie's eyes, and he said, "I am so sorry. Please forgive me?"

Ernie watched as the police looked the silver handcuffs on the young man's wrists and gently guided him to the back seat of the police car. Ernie could not imagine what would come next for Greg - how many years he would spend in prison, what would become of his still-new life on Earth- but he did know one thing. He knew where Greg would end up, after his time on Earth was through.

He caught the back door, before the police could shut it behind Greg.

"Greg," Ernie whispered, "You are forgiven. '*For if you forgive others their tresspasses, your Heavenly Father will also forgive you.*' (Matthew 6:14). Our God is a God of peace, and I hope you can find that peace in Him, Greg."

Greg looked one last time into the gentle eyes of his new brother before the door slammed and the police car whisked away. Ernie stood on the side of the road, his heart wildly pounding. Long after the car had driven out of view, he was still praying for Greg.

Suddenly, the peaceful tranquility of a perfect moment passed when the paramedics rushed toward Ernie, full of questions. Paramedics started giving him the lookover to make sure he had not been injured.

"I'm fine," Ernie reassured them. "I have never been more alive."

Policemen entered the bank and released the other hostages for questioning. Soon, they were released home to their families. Beverly rode with Ernie to the hospital in the ambulance as doctors wanted to examine him further. Ernie was weak, but his heart was strong, and he would recover.

In the solitude of Ernie's head, an old African-American slavery song from the nineteenth century filled his mind and eased his worries of the day:

I am weak, but Thou art strong,
Jesus, keep me from all wrong,
I'll be satisfied as long
As I walk, let me walk close to Thee.
Through this world of toil and snares,
If I falter, Lord, who cares?
Who with me my burden shares?
None but Thee, dear Lord, none but Thee.
When my feeble life is o'er,
Time for me will be no more,
Guide me gently, safely o'er
To Thy kingdom's shore, to Thy shore.

———— ((O)) ————

Marsha O'Toole happily exited the bank and yelled, "Hallelujah! Where is the nearest church?"

Chapter 11

The next morning, sunlight streamed through Ernie's bedroom window. Another beautiful day to be alive and rejoice in. Ernie could smell coffee brewing and knew that it was Father Arnold messing around in the kitchen.

Ernie yawned and stretched, then got himself dressed, before heading downstairs to meet Father Arnold and the gazillion questions he surely had lined up.

Ernie thought about the day earlier and almost felt like it was a dream and had questions of his own. Did a bank robbery really take place? Did I really experience a second encounter with a man who almost took my life? Did I help this man give up the robbery, and stop him from hurting more innocent people? More importantly, did I witness Jesus into the heart of this lost man? Ernie shook his head in awe of how God had used him to do good work for His kingdom. He could almost feel God looking down on him, saying, "Well done, good and faithful servant."

"Good morning Ernie. Happy Thanksgiving," Father Arnold exclaimed.

"And glad tidings of goodness and joy," Ernie laughed.

"That is a Christmas scripture, but nonetheless, isn't it great to be alive?"

"Yes, my fine man, but I did not have a Thanksgiving scripture or a quote from the pilgrims and Indians on the top of my head to use," Ernie smirked.

They both laughed and sat down at the table to share coffee and conversation. Father Arnold took the newspaper that was on the table and held up the front page for Ernie to see. In bold letters across the top of the front page, it read:

Service station angel, Ernie Price, talks 'sense' into bank robber, the day before Thanksgiving.

"It really is quite a story, Ernie," Father Arnold said. "It is said that you prayed and witnessed with the alleged same robber who shot you at the market and got him to surrender in the midst of a bank robbery."

"Yes, that is true. It is so remarkable I cannot even tell you the height of it in words! He not only surrendered to giving himself up in the bank robbery, but he also turned his life over to God. He was a lost kid who made some seriously stupid mistakes out of grief and a lack of patience. He just needed to find his way home again," Ernie said.

"It would be hard for some to believe that you could be so tolerant of this man a second time when he almost took your life. Did you ever just want to lunge at him and scratch his eyes out?" Father Arnold asked honestly.

"First of all, I am an old weak man who, two days earlier, was released from the hospital. So no, I did not think of taking him on in a rumble. Secondly, I felt reassured by God that I was supposed to be there in the bank to see my assailant again and make things right. I was calm and steady with God at my side the entire time," Ernie replied. "Remember when I told you about my life-after-death experience in heaven? I did not stay in heaven because of unfinished business; God's life for me on Earth had not been fulfilled. I believe that the unfinished business was encountering the gunman again, getting him to surrender to his crimes and, above all, to surrender his life to Jesus."

"That is the most selfless act that I have ever heard. You really did lay down your life for your brother," Father Arnold said in awe.

"We are all called to lay down our lives for our brother, but fortunately, it is in other deeds, maybe not as drastic as a gun shooting or bank robbery." Ernie paused. He continued humbly, "I feel God's purpose for me has been realized. His beautiful plan unfolded. I feel very blessed."

"That blessing has a trickle-down effect doesn't it? You saved the lives of the hostages in the bank yesterday, you put at ease the minds of worried, fearful people who were affected by the robber's crimes, and you gave hope to the man who committed these crimes in the first place."

"Yes, he has hope for a future again with Jesus Christ. A 'Prodigal Son,' so to speak, returning home. I am sure that my encounter with him does not stop here and it is only the beginning," Ernie said.

The rest of the day and evening were filled with laughter and love as Ernie spent the Thanksgiving holiday with his friends Father Arnold, Harry, Greta, and their children. Ernie had much to be thankful for and was grateful for good people surrounding him, their influence in his life and God's continued provision.

Still, Ernie was not with one person this day who had made such an impact recently on his life. Ernie felt lonely without her tonight. He thought of Beverly and her beautiful smile and thanked God again for bringing her into his life. He would tell her someday just how much she meant to him.

Beverly had had a wonderful dinner with her daughter, son-in-law and grandchildren. She was thankful for a day to be among people who loved her and was especially grateful that yesterday's bank robbery had ended in peace. She founded herself rattled about the encounter off and on throughout the day but tried to focus on the good outcome rather than the what-could-have-beens or what-ifs.

She thought of Ernie and how proud she was of him. He had

been instrumental in bringing about a beautiful ending that was far from her expectation of how the day would end. She found herself thinking of Ernie in a way that was unexpected, as well. She admired him for his bravery, his grace under pressure, and his loving kindness that radiated to everyone he encountered, even a gunman whose life was out of control. She had never met anyone like Ernie and was intrigued. In fact, if she was completely honest with herself, she could feel herself falling for him. Someday she would let him know just how much he had changed her life.

Ernie was becoming quite a celebrity again in town. Everyone was talking about the bank robbery and how Ernie had happened to be at two of the three robberies. Some called it bad luck. But Ernie called it a blessing. People started calling Ernie an angel, and he would just laugh, because he was too humble to believe any of the talk. He felt fortunate that he had been of help in the bank robbery and that no one had been harmed.

On Friday morning, Mark and Mike stopped by Ernie's house to visit and share breakfast with him. The boys made buttermilk pancakes and venison sausage, and settled at the table to enjoy Ernie's company. They sat around and talked about the robbery, the gunman, and the connection Ernie felt he had with the young man who had terrorized the small towns in the past few weeks. Many people even felt sorry for the gunman, after hearing his story of losing his father earlier in the year and the pain and desperation he must have felt to lead him to rob the bank.

When the police found the gunman's car a couple of blocks away from the bank, inside the car on the front seat, they found a stack of unopened mail. The police brought the mail to Greg in jail. Later, police found him weeping on the floor after opening one particular letter. The letter was from his sister Lynn and it read:

Dear Greg,

Mom told me that you were struggling financially to make your final semester's tuition payment at the university and that the payment was due the day after Thanksgiving. I pray that you receive this letter and check in time to be able to pay your tuition bill! Just think, you will be graduating next May! I am so proud of you! I know this year has been a difficult one for you and that you are taking Daddy's loss very hard. I, too, am struggling with my own grief, but my fiancé is helping me through it immensely. It will take some more time for our hearts to heal and adjust to the loss.

Our plans for a June wedding next year continue, and I am so excited! I have taken out a second job to help pay for the wedding, but I still was able to put some money aside to help you. Please accept this check for $430 with all my love. I know that your tuition is $400 but I included $30 extra so that you will have gas money to come home at Christmas this year. Please say that you will be able to be home! I will be home Dec. 23-27, and I hope to spend some time catching up with you.

All my love,
Your sister,
Lynn

The wails from Greg could be heard from one end of the jail to the other. If only Greg had opened the mail he had picked up the day he went to the bank, he would have never needed to go through with the robbery.

But Greg did realize, too, that he needed to be held responsible for the other robberies. For killing a man, young Paul Lewis, who in his death left behind a wife, son, and daughter. Children, just like Greg, widowed from their father. He now carried his own loss of his father, compounded with the loss of their father; their pain with his. He understood too intimately the anguish he had caused. He wrestled with his sin again and cried out to God to hear his plea.

—————)«(0)»(—————

Ernie answered the door at 5:00 p.m. and welcomed Beverly inside. She was carrying a bag full of goodies for Ernie, including homemade turkey noodle soup, rolls, and a pumpkin pie. Ernie licked his lips with delight at the home-cooked food, but he was even happier to simply see Beverly. Ernie couldn't help but notice how neatly her hair was pulled back in a bun, above a purple cardigan sweater that made her emerald green eyes sparkle.

First things first. Beverly checked Ernie's surgical wounds, checked his vitals, and had him withstand some breathing in his spirometer. She was eager to talk with Ernie more about Thanksgiving with her family; she also wanted to talk about the bank robbery. She and Ernie had not had much time to talk following the end of the standoff, because they had gone straight to the hospital and then had to meet with media. Before she realized, it was getting late in the evening and she had to still drive to her daughter's house for Thanksgiving. Beverly had not yet had a chance to talk to her daughter about the bank robbery, and she knew she would be up for some time telling the story.

Ernie's vitals appeared strong today. In fact, Ernie said he was feeling vigorous, both mentally and physically. Spiritually, he felt more alive than ever; he felt more connected to God than he could explain. He and Beverly pulled up a chair at his kitchen table and began talking about the spiritual battle that the young gunman had faced, and how Ernie seemed led to reach him.

"I still am in awe of how you handled the communication with the gunman yesterday," Beverly said, playing with the hem of the lace tablecloth.

"Well, I have had some time to think about it. It's practically all I think about. I did talk with Harry and Greta at their house yesterday, too. The whole ordeal is quite astonishing."

"Miraculous, I would say," Beverly added.

Ernie smiled. "That, too. I suppose, I spoke from my heart and truly felt led by God to make a difference in this man's life," he said. "When I realized that he was the same man who had shot me at the market, and we met again under these unbelievable circumstances, I knew God was giving me a wake-up call. Even amid the chaos, it made perfect sense to me that I was to reach out to this man for God."

"I really don't know how you could speak so lovingly to him and show him so much mercy -- the same man who tried to kill you! Didn't you want to, I don't know, jump up and hit him over the head with your oxygen tank or something?" Beverly laughed, trying to lighten the heavy conversation.

Ernie laughed and replied, "No, I didn't want to hurt him at all. Quite the opposite. I felt moved to show him the power of God's love and for him to know that he could be forgiven."

"I got nervous for a bit thinking that the gunman would take his life. He was pretty distressed, and I thought that was how it would end," Beverly confessed.

"I never felt he had it in him to kill himself. I was confident that it wouldn't end that way," Ernie said. "I was surprised, however, that he allowed me to witness to him and that he ultimately took Jesus back as his Lord and Savior. I think he just needed to stop resisting God's grace -- and quit thinking that God deliberately hurt and deserted him through the death of his father." Ernie rose from the table and walked to the refrigerator. He swung open the door and grabbed a glass pitcher of iced tea.

"Would you like some tea?" he asked, then walked over to the cupboard.

"Sounds good. Thank you."

He grabbed two glasses from the cupboard and placed them on the table, then poured the amber liquid into the glasses and placed the pitcher on the lace tablecloth.

"So basically, he committed these crimes out of anger after his father's death?" Beverly asked. "Out of the fear of dropping out of school and feeling that no one, not even God, could be relied on to help him physically, emotionally, or spiritually?" She reached for her glass of iced tea and took a sip of its goodness.

"That sounds about right. He was in a real dark place, felt he was alone with no one to help him," Ernie said. "He was such a lost soul. I pray that his faith can continue to be strengthened as he draws closer to God, even in a jail cell. I don't think it is over for me and Greg. I believe it is only the beginning."

"What do you mean? What do you plan on doing?" Beverly asked.

"I plan on visiting him in jail and following his court case. If he will see me, I will continue to help him grow in his spiritual journey," Ernie smiled.

Beverly heard herself gasp and nearly spilled her iced tea. She blushed at her audible response and clumsiness. *Ernie's soul was so transparent: beautiful, forgiving, and loving,* Beverly thought. She had never met anyone like him. Her heart danced with a flurry of emotions just being near him. Ernie was quickly filling a void in her life. Companionship.

"You, my friend, are amazing," she said, boldly reaching her hand to touch his. "You are an angel. I get misty-eyed thinking of how useful you are for others and mostly for God. You are one or a kind and you inspire me to be my best."

Ernie looked down at her small hand inside his and he smiled. Her hand was warm and soft and he did not want to let it go.

"You are the best, Beverly. With you by my side in the hospital and here at home, you have given me such great care and have made me stronger. You are a loving friend, and I cannot thank you enough. And despite the trouble I have caused, bringing you to a bank that got robbed, you are still by my side," Ernie said, then raised her gentle hand to his lips.

Beverly was pleasantly surprised by his gesture but also felt quite giddy. She smiled feeling Ernie's comforting hand in hers and quickly realized that she probably held onto it longer than a fleeting moment. She withdrew her hand from his and stood up, appearing flustered, "Let me get that soup warmed up for you. I hope you like turkey noodle."

"Sounds delicious and just what my nurse ordered," Ernie grinned.

Beverly put the pot of soup on the stove and turned the burner on. She reached into the cupboard for the bowl and then paused. *One bowl, or two?* she wondered. Without asking, she took out two bowls and laid them both on the table. Her glance met his. Ernie grinned, pleased that she would stay for dinner and that she felt comfortable enough to make herself at home.

<hr />

On Sunday morning, Ernie received a phone call from Mark and Mike, who announced that they would like to take Ernie to choir practice that night. Ernie loved the idea and eagerly accepted. He felt overwhelming joy that he would get to spend some time with the children, as he had missed them. Many of the kids had sent him cards and letters while he was in the hospital, but he missed their sweet chatter and innocent stories.

Ernie wanted to get back to singing with the kids, because

being around them always brought smiles and contagious laughter. Especially this time of year, with Christmas coming, it had always been such a fun time working with the kids in preparation for the Christmas party and the beautiful candlelight Christmas Eve mass. He felt relieved that Mark and Mike had taken on the planning for the Christmas party and the music that would entertain the guests. He was also amazed at these two young men's ability to orchestrate the connections with the other people who, too, would be a huge part of the party's success. Invitations had been sent out and RSVPs were spilling in. It looked like this would be the largest Christmas party that St. Cecilia's Catholic Church had ever held.

Ernie spent a good part of Sunday preparing his Christmas cards, as he certainly had the time on his hands to do so. He pulled out the Christmas box that contained cards he had bought on sale last year after Christmas, in preparation for this year. He was glad that he had bought these cards in advance and there was no need to rush to the store to buy some. Ernie was feeling a little anxious about going to another store, even though he knew the gunman was behind bars.

Ernie turned on the radio station that had started playing Christmas music, and he hummed along to the tunes. He lifted the new cards out of the Christmas box to reveal tucked underneath many old cards that he had received from friends and family from previous years. He kept every card, probably hundreds, and cherished looking through each one as a reminder of how time had changed, little people grew up, and others were no longer alive. He picked up a card from Mark and Mike -- sent ten years ago. The boys had each written a sentimental note to Ernie in their beginning handwriting stages, complete with misspelled words and chicken scratch.

I hop you have a hapee Chrissmass Ernie! Love, Mark

Hapee Chrissmass to my frend Ernie. I hope Santa brings you lots of gas and tyers. Love, Mike

Ernie smiled and laughed at Mike's sentiment. He certainly

hoped he wouldn't get any gas - of any kind. He chuckled again. He picked up another card. *From the Lewis family, Paul, Barbara, Randy, and Rachel.* In the picture, Rachel was just a baby in Barbara's arms and Paul had a full head of hair.

Ernie sat still, staring at the picture. He felt his tears rise at the sight of Paul's happy face. He missed his friend so much and was still dealing with the loss. His heart ached during the day and his dreams kept him up at night. He knew it would take time to get over the trauma of his encounter and the untimely death of his friend. He prayed constantly about this. He often wondered how people without faith get through hurts, hardships, and difficult circumstances. He was thankful that God was always near.

He reminded himself that Paul was in heaven; he had seen him there himself. Ernie was certain that Paul was smiling even bigger in heaven than in the picture that he held in his hand.

"I miss you, my friend," Ernie said out loud, and he gently placed the card on the table.

Ernie dug way deep inside the box and his hand caught a red card adorned with silver glitter. His heart dropped. He didn't realize he still had it. He hadn't dug this far into the Christmas box in years, and seeing this card took him by surprise.

It was a card from his lost love, Anna.

She had sent Ernie this card the first Christmas they did not spend together, while he was in the Navy during World War II. He hesitated to open the card. He feared that the sting in his heart was still there. Through the years, he tried to fight the lingering heartache and resist thinking of her, but he couldn't. He had never loved another woman and how could he after pain like this? He had grown to forgive Anna, but he could never forget her love.

I should be thankful that I was blessed to have one good love of my life, he thought to himself, trying to push away the sadness. Yet underneath it, he felt like God had shortchanged him by not giving him the chance to completely fall in love with someone else, for life. Of course, he dreamed of having someone by his side through the good and bad, sharing hopes and dreams. Someone to grow old with. Growing old alone was lonely at times, and he longed for companionship.

His hands opened the card before his heart could protest. He read:

Merry Christmas to the One I Love!

Christmas is the perfect time to tell you how much I love you! Though we are far apart, the love I have for you stays special in my heart. I remember our last Christmas together and the miracle of our love awakening. Dreaming of Christmases near when we can be finally together again. Be safe my darling and let our memories embrace you today and always.

My darling, Forever,
Anna

P.S. I won't step under the mistletoe with anyone else but you!

The last line pierced Ernie's heart. Anna did not cheat on him that Christmas; it was two months later. As much as Ernie wanted to trust that their relationship was not, again, a part of God's plans, it still stung with hopelessness.

The radio played a familiar song that Ernie knew and it was one of his favorite Christmas songs, An Old Christmas Card, sung by Jim Reeves. The lyrics caught his attention, as they were painfully poignant at this very moment.

Ev'ry Christmas Eve, when Santa's work is thru,
I tip-toe thru the little attic door;

LISA J. SCHUSTER

Thru my souvenirs, I turn back all the years,
Until I find what I am looking for;

There's an old Christmas card in an old dusty trunk,
And it brings back sweet mem'ries dear to me;
Tho' it's faded and worn, it's as precious as the morn
When I found it 'neath our first Christmas tree.
I thrill with ev'ry word, ev'ry line;
Guess I'm always sentimental 'round this time;
Pardon me if a tear falls among my Christmas cheer,
It's the memory of an old Christmas card.

I don't know why I get to feeling sentimental
about this time, every year, but
every time I see a Christmas card,
I just can't help reminiscing
about that first Christmas we spent together.
What a beautiful card you gave me.
Why you must have looked thru thousands of them
To find that wonderful poem that still brings tears to my eyes.
And the picture on the cover,
why it look exactly like the little white church where we wed.
And the line that you added in your own handwriting,
I'll remember it for as long as I live.
It read:
My darling, Forever.

I thrill with ev'ry word, ev'ry line;
Guess I'm always sentimental 'round this time;
Pardon me if a tear falls among my Christmas cheer,
It's the memory of an old Christmas card.

His eyes read and reread that final line of Anna's card, 'My darling, Forever.' The memory of this old forgotten Christmas card, and Anna's broken promise, burnt his eyes with tears and ached his heart with glimmers of repressed feelings that sneakingly resurfaced.

Ernie watched as the tear fell from his eye and trickled down the glittered card in his hands. The teardrop fell right in the middle of the word "love," almost breaking the word into two parts. LO / VE. Just as their love was...broken. He wiped his face and, though alone, felt embarrassed that he was feeling this way. He should have had more self-control. *My God, it had been years!* Nearly thirty years.

He stopped. He was not really mourning Anna's love. He was mourning the love of someone in his life.

Ernie jumped at the sound of the telephone ringing. He stood up and grabbed the receiver, relieved by the distraction.

"Hello?"

A beautiful voice spoke from the other line.

"Hello, this is Beverly. How are you doing today, Ernie?"

Ernie was pleasantly surprised to hear her voice. A warmth filled his chest. "I am doing fine. How are you doing, Bev?" he asked.

Beverly noticed his voice sounded a bit different than his usual happy voice filled with optimism.

"Are you feeling alright, Ernie? You aren't getting sick are you?" she asked, concerned.

"Sick? Oh no! No need for concern. I am just a little stuffed up from being, er, sentimental. I am looking through some old Christmas cards and they have taken control of my heart, I guess," he admitted.

"Yes, old Christmas cards and pictures can do that to you." Beverly paused. "I am impressed that you are set to do your Christmas cards already. Good for you. Let me know when I can run to the post office to get you some stamps to send your cards out. Well, I was calling to see if you needed any groceries or if I could do some Christmas shopping for you? I plan on doing some holiday shopping in the next week or so and would be glad to do your shopping as well."

"Hmm," Ernie thought. "Yes, I will need some holiday shopping but will have to give it some thought so I don't have you wandering aimlessly through department stores for me. That wouldn't be very nice," Ernie joked.

"Well, when you are feeling up to it, make that list and I will do the shopping. I wanted to remind you, too, that I will not be at your house today, as we discussed. Do you have someone lined up to help you?" she asked.

"Oh, everything is in place, don't you worry. I am having dinner with Mike and Mark and then they are taking me to the children's choir rehearsal."

"That sounds marvelous. But I need to warn you to still take it easy. You can play the guitar but no singing. Let your lungs get stronger, okay?"

Ernie agreed and they said goodbye. Ernie felt touched that Beverly had thought to check on him. Soon her nursing visits would be ending, as Ernie continued to get stronger. Ernie's growing strength was a double-edge sword. Every improvement brought him closer to the end of Beverly's nursing visits. He hoped her visits would continue, simply for their friendship, because he would miss her immensely otherwise.

Ernie reached back into the box of old Christmas cards. He sifted through the box and pulled out cards from his mother, father, and more friends. Oh such memories! Some made him smile and some made him sad. Sad for family and friends who now have passed on. Finally, he realized that he needed to get busy writing his own cards, so he tucked the stack of old cards again at the bottom of the box. He took out a folded piece of paper from his trousers and read this year's Christmas card list. He grinned seeing the first name on the list...Beverly.

Later that day, Mike and Mark brought over meatloaf, mashed potatoes, green beans, and apple cobbler for dessert. The meal was delicious; Ernie was thankful that their mother was such an excellent cook. The boys told Ernie their plans for the Christmas party and got Ernie's approval and advice on some questions they had. He was impressed with the work the boys had done and gave them both a hearty hug and pat on the back. Two fine young men who took Ernie's charity to the fullest.

Ernie kept watching the clock, waiting until he could go to the choir rehearsal.

They cleaned up the kitchen, and Mike retrieved Ernie's guitar from the closet. They loaded up in the truck and drove to St. Cecilia's School, where in a few minutes they would be met by overly anxious children. When they pulled up to the school, lights were already on. Ernie assumed that maybe Father Arnold was in the building.

They got out of the car and Mike chuckled. Mark shot him a stern look.

"What?" Ernie asked. "What's so funny?"

Mike stammered. "Oh, I don't know. I was thinking about a joke in school. Never mind."

Ernie shook his head, smiling and they began walking leisurely down the winding sidewalk to the school. Mike grabbed one double door and Mark, the other. At the same time, the boys flung the doors open and the air filled with cheerful voices.

Ernie stepped back in surprise, as the joy nearly knocked him to his knees. Two large nets dropped and dozens of colorful balloons spilled out, racing towards the ceiling. Hands waved and feet jumped. Voices half-sung, half-cheered, "For He's a Jolly Good Fellow." On the back wall, an oversized hand-written sign read, "YOU ARE OUR ANGEL, ERNIE!"

Ernie was overwhelmed with emotion, as he realized that he had unknowingly walked into a party in his honor. There were probably fifty people in the room -- not just the choir kids -- applauding and smiling back at him. Mike and Mark guided Ernie to a podium, where he was met by Barbara Lewis. Barbara hugged Ernie tightly and they whispered words back to each other that no one else knew. They both wiped a tear, and then Barbara spoke loudly above the crowd.

"Ernie, this celebration is for you. We celebrate the man that you are, the lives that you have touched, and the service you have given to this community. Through joy and sorrow, you remain steadfast in our hearts as a man who leads with integrity and are a shining example of God's love."

Father Arnold sashayed towards podium and rested his arm around Ernie's shoulder.

"Our friend, Ernie, is surely an angel impressing God's love on others. He has touched our lives through his generous acts of kindness in how he has served God's people in the church and the community. He also reaches the weary, the lost, and the broken. Days ago, he helped a young man who had made serious mistakes with the law and had taken the life of our dear friend and brother, Paul. Ernie loved this young man, Greg, past his grief, guilt, and despair and witnessed to him the greatest love he had ever known, the love of our Lord, Jesus Christ. I believe that Greg was entrusted to Ernie, who is an angel that walks among us. We are so fortunate to know and love you, Ernie. God bless you as you continue to bless others!"

Music began to play from the corner of the room. Mark and Mike were strumming their guitars and the crowd began singing the hymn, "Take My Life and Let it Be."

Take my life and let it be
Consecrated, Lord, to Thee.
Take my moments and my days,
Let them flow in endless praise.

Take my hands and let them move
At the impulse of Thy love.
Take my feet and let them be
Swift and beautiful for Thee.

Take my voice and let me sing,
Always, only for my King.
Take my lips and let them be
Filled with messages from Thee...

When the song ended, applause erupted, as Ernie made his rounds to thank the guests. Hugs and tears. High fives and handshakes. Ernie felt a soft tap on his left shoulder. He spun around to see Beverly, grinning back at him.

She reached forward and kissed him on the cheek and said, "I am so very proud of you. You have touched so many people's lives, including my life, and for that I am thankful."

Ernie blushed and they embraced. Beverly felt her heart leap. Her feet felt light, like a schoolgirl's in ballerina slippers, wanting to flutter across the room. She was beginning to feel that way around Ernie each time she thought of him, and especially when she was near him. There was an attraction that she could not deny. She loved Ernie's gummy smile and dimples, his hearty laugh and twinkling eyes. But she most of all loved his heart, so rich in giving.

Beverly was falling in love with this man.

Her mind started playing the question game. Should she let him know her feelings? When? Could he love her back? At this stage in her life was love foolish and forgotten? Her heart was restless but she knew now was not the time to sort through her emotions. She dismissed the questions of her heart and continued to have a good time among Ernie and his friends. Whether she was near Ernie's side or chatting with someone new across the room, her heart soared in his presence. and would not be perplexed of when to make her feelings known to him. God would prepare her heart for the right time.

Others entertained themselves with punch and cake and mingled for a bit before the party finished and the children's choir began their real choir rehearsal. Ernie played the guitar with Mike and Mark and marveled at how well the children were memorizing their songs. With two weeks left before the big Christmas party, they would be soundly ready by that time.

It was a memorable evening from start to finish and Ernie relished every minute of it. Looking back on the past few weeks, Ernie had experienced both sorrow and joy, and he thanked God for the ability to feel every second of it. Life was precious, because in a moment it could all change. The sorrow could be washed away, but he never wanted to forget this evening.

Ernie had seen a glimpse of heaven that not many people live to tell about. He had always believed in heaven, but now he knew with certainty that heaven was real. That changed things on Earth; in a way, it solidified his faith, the belief in that which you cannot see. Ernie had seen. He knew. He experienced the sights, sounds, and smells of heaven, and the awesome love and peace there.

He thought about the party tonight, easily one of the best nights of his life. He had felt so much love and joy, but not even a fraction of the love and joy as a few fleeting moments in heaven. Life on Earth was a gift, but it was still nothing compared with the next chapter, Ernie thought. And how exciting was that?

He realized that our temporary time on Earth really is minuscule compared with eternity in heaven. Ernie always led a virtuous life before the attack, but today he felt even more determined to lead a full life and show others the facets of God's unending love.

The weeks ahead were milestones. Ernie finished his physical and respiratory therapy, and the doctor gave him permission to run errands and do light chores around the house.

He went back to work at the service station, starting with just pumping gas, because washing windows and changing tires was still a bit too strenuous. Ted continued to work alongside him. Ted still had not found reliable work, and with the Christmas holiday approaching, well, Ernie did not have the heart to let him go. Besides, he still needed Ted to do the tires and windows. Ted had done a remarkable job managing the service station while Ernie was recuperating.

Ted was a kind, gentle, trustworthy man and Ernie enjoyed the slow time in the station shooting the breeze with him. He found out that Ted was a recovering alcoholic with three years of sobriety. Ted confessed how thankful he was for work, because the strain on his marriage and family was towering.

He had struggled to stay sober during unemployment, but never did touch a drop of alcohol, he said. However, the temptation was challenging every day, and he realized that it had a lot to do with not having work, a purpose, and something or someplace to occupy his time.

Ted had also aptly handled all the Christmas trees that were delivered in early December. That was another one of Ernie's traditions: He had been selling Christmas trees at his service station for years and did not want to disappoint the community on account of his absence. Nearly everyone in town got a tree for Ernie. He had trees of all shapes and sizes, and all types, too: Scotch pine, white pine, Douglas fir, blue spruce, and balsam fir.

Ernie picked out his own small, five-foot tree, and Ted tossed it in the back of his pickup truck. The tree was just the right size to place on Ernie's small pedestal table in the front window facing the street for all to see when passing by. Ernie hoped to get the tree decorated tonight.

At lunch time, Ernie and Ted drove the tree home and put it in the tree stand atop the table in Ernie's living room. Four boxes of ornaments and garland sat on the floor but he had already found his favorite ornaments and gently laid them on the sofa. He would put these on the tree first. Ornaments his mother had saved since he was a lad.

Ernie listened to the radio in his pickup truck on his way back to the service station and heard the weather forecast warn of a heavy snowstorm heading their way late this afternoon. He could tell that the forecasters could be right on this one, because snow was falling pretty heavily and the temperature did drop ten degrees since he woke up this morning. The roads were already a bit icy from the snow that had fallen earlier in the week. Not the best weekend to be out and about. Good thing Ernie had plans to stay home and decorate his tree.

The children's Christmas party was just two days away and this weekend would be a busy one, moving hundreds of gifts from the service station and from Harry's barber shop. Ernie wondered if the snow forecast might hamper attempts to bring all of the gifts over to the Catholic school for the party on Sunday evening. He figured he wouldn't worry about that now and just let God handle the details.

The afternoon at the service station was pretty slow, and Ernie decided to go home early because of the weather. Ted would close shop and walk to his home two blocks away. Really, Ernie just wanted to go home and take a good nap. He didn't want to admit that he stilled tired easily.

Ernie awoke from his nap with a growling stomach. He walked downstairs to the kitchen to make dinner. It was already past 6 p.m. and he had slept longer than he anticipated. *A two-and-a-half hour nap was good for him, though,* he thought with a chuckle.

He looked out the kitchen window. As the weather forecaster predicted, the snow was coming down hard. The winds had picked up, as well. Ernie was glad that he had no place to be on a night like this, and he felt comforted and excited by the idea of staying home to decorate his new tree.

Now what for dinner? The only thing that sounded good at the moment was bacon, eggs, and toast. Blame it on the snowstorm or a hard day at work, this trio was his comfort food. He rummaged through the refrigerator for two eggs, four strips of bacon, and two slices of cinnamon bread, and went to work busily in his little kitchen. The sizzle and smell of the bacon was heavenly and stimulated his appetite. He scrambled the eggs perfectly and added a little cheddar cheese to his liking. The cinnamon bread was a gift from Beverly and he enjoyed the last two slices of the loaf. A large glass of milk topped off his meal, and he leaned back in his chair, satisfied, and full.

Ernie cleaned up his dishes and moved into the living room to tackle untangling of the Christmas lights. Each year he vowed to put the lights back in a more organized fashion so the following year he wouldn't have to wrestle with them. He was anxious to see if he had remembered to do so. He pulled the lights out of the box and, sure enough, he had done the job right this year. He had neatly wrapped the lights around a piece of cardboard. He let out a sigh of relief.

Now he prayed that the lights all worked. He plugged the lights in. Each one glowed brightly, with not a single replacement needed.

"Whew!" he said, happy that the task was starting out right.

Ernie started stringing the lights from the bottom of the douglas fir and then moved up toward the top. He liked the clear-colored lights that reminded him of snow glistening on the tree. This year's tree was a little smaller and shorter than the tree he typically got, only because he still had to be careful with lifting and reaching following his injury. He took a break from hanging the lights to go put the radio on. What was missing was some Christmas music to make the mood merrier. The first song playing was Bing Crosby's "White Christmas." With the snow coming down so heavily outside, he certainly would have a white Christmas. No doubt about it. Ernie moved slowly, enjoying every moment of the decorating. He hummed along and sang a little bit, but avoided singing all out like he typically did.

After nearly an hour, the tree stood tall, completely covered with its twinkling lights. Breathtaking. Pleased with his progress, he moved on to rummaging through the boxes of house decorations. He pushed aside the Elf on the Shelf in his cute red outfit and found the big, artificial wreath with a bright gold bow and hung it outside on the hook of his front door. He moved rather quickly, as the snow blew furiously against his front door and he was not wearing a coat or boots. He shut the door, happy to be again toasty in his warm house, when the phone rang. He picked up the telephone and it was Beverly.

"Ernie, I hate to bother you but I am having a little trouble," she anxiously said. "I am in the town of Butterfield right now, only ten minutes away from you, but more than a half an hour away from my house. I was out shopping alone and the snowstorm took me by surprise. The roads and the visibility are pretty bad and I wonder if I can stay with you until the snow lets up?"

"Of course, Beverly, do you think you can drive safely to my house or should I come and get you?" Ernie asked.

"I wouldn't think of having you come out for me! I think I can make it if I go slowly and watch for all the accidents alongside the road. It is treacherous outside," she warned.

"Take your time and I will say a prayer for safe travels. Try not to fret," Ernie said and then hung up.

He walked back to the tree and whispered a prayer that Beverly would be safe and the others on the road would be free from harm, as well. *Send angels to protect everyone out tonight.*

Ernie eyed the clock every couple of minutes, waiting for a knock on the door. He continued to hang ornaments and tried not to worry. He walked into the kitchen and filled the tea kettle with water and waited for it to boil. He stood there waiting. Wasn't there a saying about a "watched pot never boils?" Or something like that? Watching the kettle made him more aware of each dragging second. He felt a nervousness inside, butterflies perhaps. He took out packets of hot cocoa and marshmallows and some tea bags. Beverly would probably enjoy something warm to relax her after driving on the icy roads.

Then there was the long-awaited knock at the door. Relief flooded Ernie as he darted to the door. It must be Beverly. He opened the door to see her pretty face dusted with snow, and she immediately stepped inside and threw her arms around Ernie's neck.

"Bless you," she said. "I am so glad that I could get off the road."

She quickly hung up her coat and removed her boots and rubbed her hands together for warmth.

"Where are your mittens, dear?" Ernie asked, taking her hands into his warm hands.

Barbara felt her cold hands warm in his at once. *Did he say, dear?* Barbara melted at his words.

"I stopped to help at an accident, and I left the mittens with the young woman who was without some. She was waiting for a tow truck and she needed the mittens more than I did."

Ernie made a mental note to buy Beverly gloves for Christmas.

"I have hot water ready for cocoa or tea. Would you like some?" Ernie asked.

"I would love some hot cocoa. I would never pass up chocolate."

"Wonderful, then grab the kettle and pour yourself some hot water. There is a cup on the counter and some hot chocolate packets, too. Then please join me in the living room. I was decorating the tree when you called. You can help me if you'd like."

"That sounds like a lot of fun. I would enjoy that very much," Beverly smiled.

Ernie would exchange a quiet night alone for one spent with Beverly, any time. It had been a long time since Beverly had decorated a Christmas tree with another man. Well, at least six years ago, when her husband Charlie was alive. They spoke of Christmases past, favorite traditions, funniest Christmas stories, and favorite Christmas songs. Two cups of cocoa and a decorated tree later they stood back and admired the finished tree. It truly was beautiful, Ernie thought, and he was thrilled at the work they had done together.

"I need to look outside and see what the weather is like. Maybe the snow is letting up," Beverly said, walking over to the front door to take a peek.

The cold air rushed in and she was hit in the face with swirling snow. She groaned. To her dismay, the snow was steady and strong and accumulating quickly. Ernie laughed, as she wiped the snow from her face.

"I guess you got your answer," he said. "Looks like you will not be going anywhere tonight." He laughed, shutting the door, with a whimsical grin on his face.

"Then I shall be a miserable house guest. You will wish you never saw the likes of me," she giggled and playfully threw a couch pillow at him.

"You could not make me miserable if you tried, Beverly. I'm just that happy of a guy to be around," he joked. "And now that you are so content with staying, why don't we try to find a holiday program on the television."

Ernie stood at the television and turned the knob to see what shows were available. Having only three channels, he hoped that something good was on. Sure enough. He found the movie, "It's a Wonderful Life." And it had just started. Perfect. It would be a beautiful ending to a beautiful night. They sat comfortably on the couch and Ernie gently covered Beverly with his mother's afghan.

"We can share the afghan. I don't bite!" she teased and pulled some of the afghan off of her to cover Ernie's lap.

"Now we are as cozy as two bugs. Snug in a rug," he smiled.

Ernie always enjoyed this movie, and he often paralleled it to his own. He never went for the finer things in life, and his only travels were when he was in the Navy. He lived and breathed in this small town of Hubbell and the people of the town came to rely on him. People often told Ernie that he was the cement that kept the town together. Humbly, Ernie had a hard time believing that, but it was nice to hear.

There were times when he wanted to leave and explore the world, especially after Anna broke his heart, but his father had become ill and Ernie took over working at the service station for him. Following his father's death, he worked at the service station, providing for his mother until she passed on two years ago. It was a good job and he could be self-employed; he really had nothing to complain about.

However, he was different from the main character, George Bailey, in that he never wanted to end his life. He always believed, through every heartache, there would be healing and hope. After the past few weeks, he knew that to be true. Maybe he had an angel like Clarence in the movie, watching over him? Ernie smiled to himself, as his friends had called an "angel among us" at his surprise party. Ernie did not feel like an angel; he just called it "loving your neighbor."

The movie was in the final minutes, and Beverly pardoned herself from getting emotional as tears welled in her eyes. She tried to rise to her feet to hide that she was getting teary-eyed but Ernie was quick and reached for her hand, prompting her again to have a seat next to him.

"My dear, you are not leaving this couch because you might cry from the sentiment of the movie. I will put up with your tears if you can put up with mine," he laughed.

"The ending of this show always brings a tear to my eye. I love it when everything works out for George Bailey and Clarence gets his angel wings."

Ernie just looked at her and thought how beautiful she looked with the glow of the Christmas tree lights on her face, and how her eyes twinkled from the tears she was holding back. He wanted to kiss her. He had been holding back the passion inside all evening. As they sat close to each cozying under the afghan, he felt the time was right. He prayed that his forwardness would not be too strong for Beverly, and that she would delight in his advances.

Beverly and Ernie turned to catch the remaining minutes of the show. Little ZuZu Bailey said the words, "Look Daddy, every time a bell rings, an angel gets his wings." Ernie peeked over at Beverly and saw that she was, indeed, crying now. He put his arm around her shoulder.

Beverly leaned her head into Ernie's chest and said, "I feel so silly for crying. Don't mind me."

Ernie lifted her face gently with his hand until their eyes met. She saw streams of tears on his face, too.

"I love that about you, Beverly. I love everything about you," he shyly said.

Their eyes studied each other. Both felt an overwhelming joy rush through their hearts, and their lips met with sweet softness. The kiss lingered warmly between them for a few minutes. A friendship was blossoming into true love. There was no resistance, uneasiness or question that this was meant to be. They both knew they were ready. They wanted to trust themselves and each other. They wanted to love again. Beverly wiped her eyes and bravely admitted her feelings.

"I felt something remarkable about you the moment I walked into your hospital room," she said softly. "Something I had never felt before, particularly while I was at work. I loved your sense of humor and kindness, and I was drawn to you, finding myself making excuses just to check in on you."

"I did think that you came around a lot, but don't get me wrong, I loved the attention!" Ernie laughed. "When feelings started stirring in me, I was taken aback. I hadn't felt that way in such a long time, and besides, you were my nurse. How was I to sense if your kindness and care were not just part of your job and I was just another patient?"

"I suppose that could be confusing. Can I tell you another confession?" she asked.

"Anything. Go on."

"I have prayed to God in the past year that he prepare my heart to love again. I asked him to break down the barricades of distrust that surrounded my heart and to help me find joy again. I can say that he has helped me here immensely. Then I prayerfully asked him to bring into my life a man who was honest and true." She paused, realizing the tremendous conclusion God allowed. "A man with an *earnest* heart."

Ernie's eyes perked open and his smile turned to a gasp. He took a deep breath, making the connection.

"God fulfilled his promise as he sent me a man named Ernie, who does have an earnest heart. You are my sign, my promise from

God, I am quite sure of it," Beverly confided, then pressed her head into Ernie's shoulder.

Ernie wrapped his arm around her tightly and kissed her head, whispering, "Oh great and glorious God, the creator of all things, and the God of love. We look with favor on your blessings. Thank you for days to start anew and love again. Guide us toward a love that pleases you, Lord. Help us to never forget that love is the gift we give each other because it came from you first. Amen."

"Amen," added Beverly.

Ernie wanted to stay up all night and talk to Beverly. Now that his feelings were flowing freely, he had so much to say. Yet it seemed nothing more needed to be said. It was known. He felt growing aches in his back and realized he hadn't stayed up this late since the shooting. Already past midnight. Beverly noticed it at the same time, and they both stood up, knowing this sweet night needed to end, but also knowing that tomorrow would be even sweeter.

Ernie told Beverly that she could sleep in the guest room next to his bedroom. The guest room was actually his mother's old room, and it would be perfectly comfortable for Beverly. Ernie would reside in his bedroom, as he had no intention of moving their relationship too fast. He had waited his entire life to meet Beverly. He could wait another lifetime, if needed. She was worth every moment of patience.

Ernie walked first up the stairs and Beverly followed behind, holding his hand. They got to the top of the stairs.

"This room here will be yours," Ernie motioned. "There are extra pillows and blankets in the closet if you need them. The bathroom is down the hall." He pointed across the hallway, "This room is mine, and I will be there."

She nodded, rubbing her eyes. The exhaustion was setting in.

"I will see you in the morning, sunshine," he said, kissing her tenderly on the lips and parting their interwoven hands.

"Thank you for making the night perfectly special in every way. I am so very happy," Beverly said.

"Lord knows how happy I am, too. Thank you." He walked to his room and shut the door, anxious for the break of dawn.

Chapter 12

The next morning, Beverly and Ernie shared breakfast together. Chairs side by side as the sunshine penetrated through the stained glass window, they lingered over hotcakes, warm maple syrup, and generous amounts of coffee. The snowstorm left ample amounts of sparkling snow glistening in the sunshine. Harry graciously came by with his snowplow and made a path to the main road for Beverly to travel home, when she was ready. The town received fourteen inches of snow last night and people slowly started moving about after uncovering themselves from the thick blanket of snow and some heavy duty snow shoveling.

The main roads were plowed and sanded and Beverly had no problem driving home, except that she was sad to leave Ernie's side. But she did need to go work that afternoon at the hospital, so she had to leave. She would see Ernie at the Children's Christmas party tomorrow evening anyway, and that would be a fun night for her to meet new friends and see the happy children. Beverly was anxious to share the good news of her new beau with her daughter and would call as soon as she arrived home.

Ernie helped some other volunteers, including Mark and Mike, bring the toys from the service station and Harry's Barber Shop to St. Cecilia's School for the party tomorrow evening. Ernie was amazed at the load of toys that needed to be driven over. Piles of brightly wrapped boxes, shiny bikes, wagons, and doll buggies. Each man had to make two trips with a pickup truck just to gather it all.

In the school kitchen, women bustled about, preparing cookies and sweet bread, sloppy joe sandwiches, and salads. They tried to do as much as they could ahead of time so they could concentrate on attending church tomorrow morning, decorating the school in the afternoon, and warming up the food just before the guests arrived. Before going home, Harry plowed the school parking lot and made sure drivers could pass in and out of it. Mark and Mike would be leading the children's choir at Saturday evening mass tonight. And Ernie had other plans.

Following dinner, Ernie got in his pickup truck and traveled twenty miles away for a visit. He pulled into the parking lot of the Torch Lake Police Department, gathered the bag that was on his seat, and walked up the narrow stairs into the building. He registered at the front desk, showed his identification, and was searched from head to toe. An armed policeman led him slowly down the corridor to a cell. The jail radiated a miserable smell of disinfectant and body odor. The cement floors and walls were a dismal gray and lacked any feeling of welcome. It was dark, except for a few overhead lights, and the only sunlight was on the outside of the building. Ernie would not let what he saw or felt distract him from his mission.

Ernie stood at the cell and peered through the silver bars at a young man who lay on his back looking up at the ceiling. The blonde man wore a yellow jumpsuit and black wool socks. The policeman announced, "You have a visitor, Atkins."

The inmate sat up, his blue eyes poised on the policeman and his face had no reaction until he noticed Ernie. He nervously stood up, looking ashamed at first, and then slowly walked over to the bars. A smile crept on his lips. Ernie sat in the folding chair that was against the corridor wall, and Greg sat on the cold cell floor. Ernie extended his hand through the bars, and Greg reached to gently shake his hand. The guarded policeman stood near.

"Mr. Price, thank you for coming to see me. You are only my second visitor outside of my mom, who visited me two weeks ago," Greg said.

"You have been on my mind, and I just wanted you to know that in person," Ernie said.

"You look great, Mr. Price. How are you doing?" he asked.

"I am almost one-hundred percent, stronger every day, thank you," Ernie said.

"I have had a lot of time to think while in jail, and I have been doing lots of praying, too. I am sad that my life went so haywire and I hurt so many people," Greg paused and cupped his face in his hands. "I am sorry for hurting you."

"I know you are sorry, son."

"I just wish you came into my life before I ever lost control and went on a rampage. The way that you reached out to me in the bank, I will never forget. You really saved my life. I know I don't have much of a life stuck inside a jail cell, but I will make the most of the time here and pay my debt to society."

"Unfortunately, you will need to right your wrongs by going to court and serving time, but I want you to know that your soul is already free in Jesus Christ," Ernie said.

"I know that is true. And it is that freedom in Him that gives me hope. Thanks to you, Ernie."

"I am called by God to respond in love, as well, and I cannot see love greatly expressed in any better way than through sharing God's word," Ernie said, reaching into the brown paper sack that he had entered the jail with. A police officer had thoroughly searched it, prior to their visit. Ernie pulled out a new Bible bound in burgundy leather and pushed it between the bars to Greg's waiting hands. Greg looked at the cover and paged through the Book and its beautiful gold-edged pages. He sniffled it, cleared his throat, and looked up at Ernie in thankful disbelief.

"Please turn to the bookmarked page, Psalm 119: 169-176 and read it," Ernie directed.

Greg fingered through the familiar pages of a book he knew long ago. He admired the antique handmade cross bookmark, a family heirloom, no doubt, then his eyes scanned the page until he found the scripture, and began to read:

May my cry come before you, O Lord; give me understanding according to your word.

May my supplication come before you; deliver me according to your promise.

May my lips overflow with praise, for you teach me your decrees.

May my tongue sing of your word, for all your commands are righteous.

May your head be ready to help me, for I have chosen your precepts.

I long for your salvation, O Lord, and your law is my delight.

Let me live that I may praise you, and may your laws sustain me.

I have strayed like a lost sheep. Seek your servant, for I have not forgotten your commands.

Ernie's hand reached into his shirt pocket. He pulled out a light blue handkerchief and handed it to Greg. Greg took the handkerchief and blotted his cheeks, stained with tears.

"There is a song I would like to share with you, too. I brought my guitar with me and though I play well, my singing voice is not up to par. So please bear with me. This song is called 'Turn Your Eyes Upon Jesus.'"

And Ernie sang.

O soul, are you weary and troubled?
No light in the darkness you see?
There's light for a look at the Savior,

And life more abundant and free.

Turn your eyes upon Jesus
Look full in His wonderful face,
And the things of Earth will grow strangely dim,
In the light of his glory and grace.

Through death into life everlasting
He passed, and we follow Him there;
O'er us sin no more hath dominion
For more than conqu'rors we are!

His Word shall not fail you, He promised;
Believe Him and all will be well;
Then go to a world that is dying,
His perfect salvation to tell!

Turn your eyes upon Jesus
Look full in His wonderful face,
And the things of Earth will grow strangely dim,
In the light of his glory and grace.

"Thanks for sharing that song, Ernie. I remember my mom singing that song in church." Greg paused for a moment, as the lyrics traveled inside of his head. He continued, "Ernie, I want to thank you for everything, especially helping me find my way back to Jesus. Though I am likely to be judged by man and sentenced to many years in prison, it is God who will be the utmost judge. I may have made a mess on Earth, but I pray that God can accept me into an eternal future with him."

Ernie almost erupted from his chair.

"It is never too late! Don't be thinking like that. You have made the first step already, Greg, and I am confident that you will continue to grow closer to Him. And I will do anything I can to see that you continue this journey."

"I have a long way to go. I hope that I don't let you down."

Ernie leaned forward. "Greg, don't spend your time worrying about me or what anyone else thinks. Your relationship with God is between you and Him," Ernie insisted. "This Bible is a gift from me, as Jesus was a gift to us all. Please keep it, read it, and learn from it. Allow His word to change your life and maybe you can change another person's life, even someone here in jail. You can do God's work anywhere," Ernie whispered.

The policeman interrupted, "You have two minutes."

Greg let out a sigh, sad that his visit was near an end.

"I will never understand why you haven't turned your back on me, but I am glad that you haven't. Can you come and see me again?" Greg asked.

"I will be back next week on Christmas Day," Ernie said.

"Yeah, I will be here. They will move me after the first of the year to the prison where I will await my sentencing. I will probably be sent to the Marquette Correctional Facility. Since I am pleading guilty, it won't take too long."

"Whether you are here or there, I will come visit you. The prison is two hours away, but still a short drive to help a friend in need."

The policeman announced that their visitation time was up, and Ernie stood to leave. He folded the chair and gave it to the policeman. Ernie walked toward the iron bars that separated him from Greg. Ernie reached both of his hands through the bars to touch Greg's strong hands. Greg squeezed his hands back and placed the tear-soaked handkerchief in one of Ernie's.

"Goodbye, Ernie," Greg mumbled.

"May the good Lord bless and keep you, until we meet again," Ernie smiled and turned down the long, dark corridor, feeling sure that this young man was starting his journey back into God's loving arms.

When Ernie was out of sight, Greg took the Bible and opened it. He stretched onto his back in his modest bed. He opened the gold-trimmed pages to see handwriting in the corner of the first page.

You were lost but now you are found. Always remember that you are His and he loves you with an undying love. Your Friend, Ernie.

Greg blinked back tears and turned the pages again. Genesis 1. And he read, "In the beginning, God created the heavens and the earth…"

⸺◦《◉》◦⸺

Scott and Darren received assistance from their mother on how to put on their green tights. Yes, that's right, green tights. The boys were getting in costume for their big holiday role as Santa's elves at the Christmas party. The boys moaned and groaned about how the tights itched and how they were supposed to be for girls. Their mother only laughed and finished the final touches of the costumes; tying their sashes and donning their hats. They wore a long red tunic shirt with a gold sash belt, green tights, black pointed shoes, and a red and green oversized hat with a white yarn pom-pom ball on it.

Now for another part that the boys were sure to dislike. She took them upstairs to her bathroom and brushed their little faces with rouge to make their cheeks rosy red. She dabbed a little color on their lips, as well, and kissed them both on their foreheads.

"You boys are simply adorable. I am so proud of you for volunteering to be elves at the Christmas party again. Now do you remember the order of how the party will run tonight?"

"Yes, Mom, we went over it with Ernie, Mark, and Mike," said Scott.

"Well, then you won't mind telling me again, will you?"

He groaned a bit and then he began.

"First everyone will be asked to go and eat. Next, Ernie will welcome the crowd. Then, they will sing Christmas songs," Scott said.

Darren piped in, "Then a Bible verse will be read and they will talk about gift giving."

"Then Santa and us come in and everyone claps and goes c-r-a-z-y," said Scott.

They all laughed and then their mother said, "Yep, that is how it is all supposed to happen."

"Then, why did you *ask*, Mom?" said little Darren in a huff. She laughed and knocked his hat off his head onto the floor.

"When do we get our presents, Mom?" Scott asked.

"Remember, you get your presents after the party. You need to do your part as elves first and then in private Santa will give you your gifts, okay?" she whispered so Kimmy would not hear.

"Ohhhhhh. It is soooooo hard tooooo wait," Darren whined and stomped away.

"C'mon boys, it is time to go. Let's get your sister Kimmy. Your other sisters are already gone and practicing with the choir before the party."

<hr>

Mark and Mike had already set up the musical equipment at the school hall and were busy herding the choir kids to remain in one room, while Ernie and Beverly welcomed the guests and invited them to partake in the meal and then mingle with friends. Kids arrived with all kinds of emotions. Some were super excited and running around, and others clung close to Mom and Dad, not sure what was going on. There was joy and anticipation in the air and smiling faces everywhere. Ernie looked around the room and was in awe of the number of people who were in attendance. Twenty-four families and ninety-two children were at the party, anxious to receive gifts.

Ernie walked to the microphone and tapped it gently to get everyone's attention. People began taking their seats and the lights dimmed. Backstage, the children in the choir lined up, ready to walk on the stage before the big accordion curtain. Ernie walked back to the microphone and made his opening speech.

"Welcome, one and all, to the twenty-fourth annual St. Cecilia's Catholic Church Children's Christmas Party! I would like to start us off with a prayer, so could you please bow your heads?"

He paused.

"Dear God, thank you for the celebration of Christmas and the birth of your son, Jesus Christ. He is the true meaning to the holiday Christmas and he was the perfect gift to us all. As we receive gifts tonight, let us be mindful that it is through Jesus' love that we receive and are blessed by others. History states that Saint Nicholas, or Santa Claus, was the patron saint of children and was the giver of gifts, often helping poor and orphaned children. He was a Christian who was sent by Jesus with the intention of spreading Jesus' love. So let us not forget that Jesus is the reason we celebrate Christmas. Amen."

Ernie, Mike, and Mark took their seats and began strumming an instrumental song of "Go Tell It On the Mountain." Then "Santa Claus is Coming to Town," and the curtains slowly drew open. Two large Christmas trees sparkled on the dimly lit stage with silver and gold garland strung from one side of the stage to the other. Lisa and Renee, in their red floor length gowns, stepped forward on cue to their microphones and started singing.

The kids in the audience began clapping and singing along, while the parents snapped pictures. Other secular songs were sung and enjoyed but the highlight of the evening came with the Christian hymns. "The First Noel" started, a beautiful reverence of their dear Lord and Savior, and the audience members rose to their feet. Some people in the audience who didn't know Jesus felt an awakening inside themselves, a curiosity to know Jesus more.

"The first Noel, the angel did say,
Was to certain poor shepherds in fields as they lay;
In fields where they lay keeping their sheep,
On a cold winter's night that was so deep.
Noel, Noel, Noel, Noel,
Born is the King of Israel…"

The last song was "Away in a Manger." Again, everyone rose to their feet, in adoration and worship. The littlest children in the choir took solos on this song and brought everyone to tears. Little Kimmy sang her heart out, even though she forgot the words.

She sang, "The cattle are snoring, the poor baby wakes." The crowd chuckled and nudged each other, knowing she was supposed to sing about the cows "lowing." Sometimes it's the innocent mistakes that are the most memorable and sweet.

Suddenly, the sound of bells echoed from the kitchen, growing closer. Through the kitchen doors walked Santa Claus and his two elves. The kids screamed with delight. They could hardly contain their joy. The two elves passed out candy canes, waved to the crowd, and shook hands with the overzealous kids. Santa took his seat on the comfy chair wheeled onstage and his elves stood at his side.

Santa welcomed the crowd with a hearty, "Ho, ho, ho. Hello there good little girls and boys!"

The kids squealed with excitement, because each one felt like Santa was talking directly to him or her. Santa began to call the last name of families on his list. "Ho-ho-ho. The Beaudoin family. Please come up and see Santa."

The four children and their parents went on stage. Santa's elves brought up their gifts and called out each child's individual name. Each family also got one large gift that was not wrapped, so the children could see it. This larger gift was usually a bike, pogo stick, skateboard, baby carriage, or a sled. The children took the smaller gifts home to unwrap on Christmas Day. Imagine the Beaudoin boys' surprise when Santa and the elves helped push out an air hockey table. The little Beaudoin girls received shiny pink bikes and a baby doll. The children danced with glee and the parents wondered how they were going to move the air hockey table home. Santa put their fears to rest and mentioned that a truck would safely deliver their toys and the table since his sleigh was full. The parents sighed with relief and smiled.

When Santa called up the Muljo-Manninen family, Lisa, Linda, and Kimmy stepped forward. Little Scott and Darren, who were also a part of this family, continued acting as elves and would receive their gifts later. This was the hardest part for little Scott and Darren. Kimmy ran onstage, excited to pull on Santa's long white beard and to receive her much-awaited present -- first, before her sisters.

The elves wheeled up a light blue baby carriage, and Kimmy covered her mouth to contain her scream of happiness. Her little feet danced with joy. She looked inside the baby carriage and found a little doll resting under a blanket. She tenderly lifted up the doll and saw that it was a Cabbage Patch Doll. Her doll had blonde hair and blue eyes just like Mommy. She looked at the tag but could not read its name because she was too young to read. Santa announced that the baby doll's name was Jerome Fitz. Lisa was delighted that she received new ice skates and wanted to try them on immediately to see if they fit but her mom warned her not to since she might rip her gown. Linda received a Chrissy doll and immediately started brushing the doll's beautiful auburn hair.

Kimmy grabbed her doll and gave him a big hug and said, "Hello Jerome Fitz. I am your mommy, Kimmy."

The crowd let out an audible sigh at the cuteness that they just witnessed. They all hugged their own children tighter. The night was filled with many other memorable and moving moments like this. Everyone walked away feeling touched by Jesus and the Christmas spirit.

After Santa had passed out the last Christmas gift and waved goodbye, Ernie made his final announcement.

"Every good and perfect gift is from heaven above. May the joy you feel today warm your hearts on Christmas Day and every day."

Just then, Greta hurried to the stage, carrying a large manilla envelope. She handed it to Ernie, who excused the interruption, reached into the envelope and retrieved a note. He read the words on the paper. As his eyes saw the words, he felt his body shake with emotion and his knees wobble a little. He regained his composure and stepped to the microphone.

He paused and announced, "Can I have your attention, please? We have an unexpected gift given by an anonymous donor. This person has used $430 of his own money to arrange gift certificates for each family to receive a free ham from Lewis' Market. So I will have the certificates available at the door when you leave. Greta, can you help me with that?"

"Sure thing Ernie," Greta replied and hurried to retrieve the envelope with the certificates from Ernie.

"God bless you all and goodnight!"

The crowd began cheering and clapping, moved by the beautiful party and now thrilled about the free Christmas hams. As they filled out of the auditorium, people asked around, trying to figure out who the anonymous could be. Was it from the church? Several suspected it had been a gift from Enie, but then they remembered how surprised he had been after he read the note. He couldn't have acted that out. Was the gift from Greta or Harry? That would be too obvious. Ernie's new friend Beverly? Perhaps a child saved money for the offering? While the town speculated who "anonymous" was, Ernie knew the truth.

As the room emptied, Ernie's heart filled. He smiled and held the paper close to his heart. The anonymous donor, Ernie knew, was sitting in a cold, dark cell, but had the light of Jesus' love again in his heart.

THE END

Epilogue

A Note from the Author

Hubbell, Michigan, is a real town, I should know, because I lived there. I have great memories of the people and places that have enriched my life.

I have wanted to tell this story for a long time. The main character, Ernie Price, is based on a childhood friend and mentor who had the same generous heart and was loved by many. He instilled in me my appreciation for music and singing and kept me in church each week, through Sunday evening choir practice and Saturday evening mass. My real-life friend and mentor, Ernie Poisson, did own a service station, was a children's music director for church, loved country and folk music, and threw a yearly Christmas party for the unfortunate in town (my family being a benefactor of this yearly event).

However, this story takes Ernie Price through many turns and trials that were not lived out by my friend, Ernie Poisson. Other people mentioned in this book are based on some friends and real faces in the town with fictional stories to tell. I do not intend to represent or disrespect actual people, living or otherwise.

This story is meant to be a feel-good tear-jerker that reminds you to appreciate a simpler life, helps you to learn and question your own faith, and encourages you to find opportunities to witness to others the love of our Lord, Jesus Christ -- be it extending mercy, grace, and forgiveness, or trusting in God through the dark times in your life.

I hope you find His immeasurable love and joyfully share it with others.

Bibliography

These references are made to support the written story. All efforts were made to attribute correctly the proper source of reference, whether it be, a bible verse, song, movie, website or historical information.

Acknowledgements

NanoWriMo (National November Writing Month): This organization provides challenges to spark creativity in writing. Each November 1st, you are given the opportunity to write a 50,000 word novel in thirty days. Other challenges are offered in different months. For more information, contact: www.nanowrimo.org

Prologue

Psalm 37:37 (NLT); New Living Translation Bible, Tyndale House Foundation. Tyndale House Publishers Inc., Carol Stream, Illinois 60188, www.BibleStudyTools.com.

Chapter 1

Joke: Nairaland Forum, www.nairaland.com

Catholic Prayer: "The Lord's my Shepherd," www.marypages.com/
Shepherd.htm

Song: "All That I Am" (Catholic hymn)- ©; Copyright 1967 OCP
Publications 5536 NE Hassalo, Portland, Oregon 97213, USA.

Chapter 2

Psalm 100:1-2 (NIV); New International Version Bible, The Holy
Bible, New International Version, copyright 1973, 1978, 1984,
2011 by Biblica, Inc., www.BibleGateway.com

Song: "Holy God We Praise Thy Name," words attributed to Ignaz
Franz, Vienna 1774 ("Grosser Gott, wir loben Dich.") Translated
from German to English by Clarence A. Walworth, 1858, www.
cyberhymnal.org

Chapter 3

Matthew 25:21 (NIV), New International Version Bible, copyright
1973, 1978, 1984, 2011 by Biblica, Inc., Bible Hub by Bilios,
www.biblehub.com

Song: "That's Amore'," composed by Harry Warren, lyricist Jack Brooks,
signature song sung by Dean Martin in 1953, www.wikipedia.com

Chapter 4

Psalm 82:3-4 (NKJV), New King James Version Bible, commissioned
in 1975 by Thomas Nelson Publishers, www.biblegateway.com

Luke 10: 25-37 (NIV), New International Version Bible, copyright
1973, 1978, 1984, 2011 by Biblica, Inc., www.BibleGateway.com

Psalm 91: 16 (NIV), New International Version Bible, copyright 1973, 1978, 1984, 2011 by Biblica, Inc., www.BibleGateway.com

Chapter 5

Psalm 23 (ESV), The Holy Bible, English Standard Version (ESV) is adapted from the Revised Standard Version of the Bible, copyright Division of Christian Education of the National Council of the Churches of Christ in the USA, 1952 and 1971, www.BibleStudyTools.com

Romans 8:38 (NLT), New Living Translation Bible, copyright 1973, 1978, 1984, 2011 by Biblica, Inc., www.biblestudytools.com

Chapter 6

2 Corinthians 4: 16-18 (NLT), New Living Translation Bible. Scripture quotations marked (NLT) are taken from the Holy Bible, New Living Translation, copyright 1996, 2004, 2007 by Tyndale House Foundation, Tyndale House Publishers, Inc., Carol Stream, Illinois 60188. www.BibleGateway.com

Chapter 7

Philippians 4: 4-9 (NIV), New International Version Bible, copyright 1973, 1978, 1984, 2011 by Biblica, Inc., Bible Hub by Bilios, www.biblehub.com

Song: "How Far is Heaven?," words and music by Jimmy Davis and Tillman Franks, performed by artist Kitty Wells, Copyright 1955 by Peer International Corporation, 1619 Broadway, New York 19, N.Y., International Copyright Secured. All rights reserved including the Right of Public Performance for Profit.

Song: "May the Good Lord Bless and Keep You," originally published in 1950 and sung by Kate Smith, again sung by Eddy Arnold and The Tennessee Plough Boys and his Guitar in 1950, and Jim Reeves in the album, Songs to Warm Your Heart released in 1959. www.wikipedia.org/wiki/wikipediaReusing_wikipedia_content

Chapter 8

Matthew 5:44 (King James) Authorized Version, Cambridge Edition, translated in 1604 and completed in 1611, www.wikipedia.com.

1 Peter 5:7-11 (NRSV) New Revised Standard Version Bible, published in 1989, www.BibleStudyTools.com

Song words from: 'The Love Song of J. Alfred Prufrock," written by T.S. Eliot, 1910

Chapter 10

James 1: 2-4 (NIV), New International Version Bible, copyright 1973, 1978, 1984, 2011 by Biblica, Inc., www.BibleStudyTools.com

Matthew 6:14 (NIV), New International Version Bible, copyright 1973, 1978, 1984, 2011 by Biblica, Inc., Bible Hub by Bilios, www.biblehub.com

Song: "Just a Closer Walk With Thee," author unknown, credit given to Elijah Cluke as the writer, second half of the 19th century

Chapter 11

Song: "An Old Christmas Card," words and music performed by Vaughn Horton, song sung by various artists, including Jim

Reeves in 1963 on his album titled Twelves Songs of Christmas. Copyright 1947 by Southern Music Publishing Co., 1619 Broadway, New York 19, N.Y., International Copyright Secured. All rights reserved including the Right of Public Performance for Profit.

Song: "Take My Life and Let it Be," words by Frances R. Havengal, 1874; music: "Messiah," by Lewis J. H'erold in 1930; arranged by George Kingsley 1838, public domain use.

Movie: "It's A Wonderful Life" (1946); based on the short story "The Greatest Gift," written by Philip Van Doren Stern in 1939 and published in 1945.

Chapter 12

Psalm 119: 169-176 (NIV), New International Version Bible, copyright 1973, 1978, 1984, 2011 by Biblica, Inc., www. BibleStudyTools.com

Song: "Turn Your Eyes Upon Jesus," words and music: Helen H. Lemmel, 1922. "Glad Songs" published by the British National Sunday School Union. Lyrics inspired by the Gospel track, "Focused," by Lilias Trotter; www.cyberhymnal.com

Song: "Go Tell It On The Mountain," is an African-American spiritual song, compiled by John Wesley Work, Jr., dating back to at least 1865, that has been sung and recorded by many gospel and secular performers, www.wikipedia.com

Song: "Santa Claus is Coming to Town," (sometimes with "Coming" changed to "Comin'") is a Christmas song. It was written by John Frederick Coots and Haven Gillespie and was first sung on Eddie Cantor's radio show in November 1934. It became an instant hit with orders for 100,000 copies of sheet music the next day and more than 400,000 copies sold by Christmas. For more information about this song, see www.wikipedia.com

Song: "The First Noel," classical English carol likely from the 18th century. First published in "Carols Ancient and Modern" (1823) and "Gilbert and Sandys Carols" (1833), both edited by William Sandys and arranged, edited and extra lyrics written by Davies Gilbert for "Carols of the God." Today, it is performed in a four-part hymn arrangement by the English composer John Strainer, first published in "Carols, New and Old" in 1871. Public doman use, www.wikipedia.com

CPSIA information can be obtained at www.ICGtesting.com
Printed in the USA
BVOW04s0311200215

388507BV00006B/87/P